Advance Praise

"Capturing the befuddlement of sustained imprisonment, the dystopian novel *Redshift, Blueshift* focuses on a man who's alone in a cell, and who becomes a prism through which to explore multiple interpretations of reality."
　　—Susan Waggoner, *Foreword* Reviews, 4 Starred Review

"The loquacious narrator at the center of *Redshift, Blueshift* is a prisoner to memory and obsession. He is a prisoner both literally and figuratively, confined behind broken memories and behind actual cold walls, and as his history unfolds in epistolary form, the reader is asked to struggle alongside him with memories untrustworthy and scattered. The novel is wonderfully paced and Jordan Silversmith expertly reveals how this narrator has come to be surrounded by thick cold concrete and gaolers and befriended only by the birds flitting in the sky; his only relationships invented by his limited access to a past that is exposed and raw and filled with his own jealous neediness and sins. Redshift, Blueshift is a philosophical and metaphysical delight, a mystery that both the narrator and the reader must unpack, tension and momentum rising by degrees, the lyrical language from Silversmith paving the way over cobbled streets and iron overpasses and even into the torture chamber where so much is revealed. This book is a gem, and it will last, and if all is right in the world, Silversmith will soon be a familiar name to readers everywhere."
　　—Seth Brady Tucker, contest judge and author of *We Deserve the Gods We Ask For*

"If you love reading fiction, it is a special pleasure to come across a new and memorable voice. Jordan Silversmith's writing brings back memories of Kafka, and Orwell, the Golding of Pincher Martin and the infernal world of Ivan Denisovitch, but *Redshift, Blueshift* is no homage but the real thing, a novel to rejoice in and be changed by."
　　—Richard Cohen, author of the forthcoming *Making History*

"A piercingly eerie, if sometimes-blurry, account of a prison sentence."
—Kirkus Reviews

"Jordan Silversmith creates a new voice of his own by resurrecting a Beckett-like monologue in which all imaginable experience is compressed into writing, into narrating itself. Piercingly witty reflections on absurdities of the human condition, yet with uncanny coherence, rich in apt allusions to literature and culture, connect with the commonest and most abject in everyday life. This text rivets attention and stirs uncomfortable emotion by its evocations of extreme experiences—such as being a prisoner in solitary confinement humiliated by sadistic guards or being a Robinson Crusoe alone without even a surrounding world. All is filtered through and fuses with the extreme experience of being conscious in a body. The 'entries' offer an anatomy, an archeology, an analytic of existing as a self. Yet the monologue is sustained by and suspended on simply the compulsion to write—or to read. This is a read that seizes and does not let one go."
—William Franke, Professor of Comparative Literature, Vanderbilt University

REDSHIFT,
BLUESHIFT

by Jordan Silversmith

Arlington, Virginia

Published by Gival Press, an imprint of Gival Press, LLC.

For information please write: Gival Press, LLC P. O. Box 3812 Arlington, VA 22203 www.givalpress.com

First edition

ISBN: 978-1-940724-31-7
eISBN: 978-1-940724-32-4
Library of Congress Control Number: 2021941992

Cover art: © Galyna Andreushko | Dreamstime.com

Design by Ken Schellenberg.

"Who am I? Why am I here?"

Admiral James Stockdale,
1992 Vice-Presidential Debate

Entry No. 1

I saw a bird this morning when they let me outside to go circling round the yard. I don't go outside much anymore, I stay inside most of the time, so the faint light in the sky burdened my eyes until they adjusted and then I saw the bird there, in the yard, the bird. A nice bird, which I will miss seeing, fine plumage, bright burnished red all over, a mess of blood at its liberty. Then the bird, seeing me peering, averted its eyes, waddled away, and began to fly. And as the bird flew, I watched it wobble in the wind; and it wobbled and wobbled in the wind and then it was a freckle on the sky and was gone, gone over the walls and beyond the trees, gone far away for its own sake, I hope. Perhaps he will be back. He can decide. I will go on envying the bird, which I cannot help doing, the seeping envy, because of his wings. I have no wings, and if I had them, I do not remember having them. Perhaps I wrote about having wings in what I wrote before, perhaps not. But no matter. I saw a bird in the yard and then it was gone. I don't go out much anymore, haven't been elsewhere, for some time. I stay inside, where it is safe. Inside I am fine, for the most part. Away from the squalid world, outdoors. I do miss the bird, but today he is gone. That is common around here, being gone. I want to be, too, to be gone, from here, like the bird.

Gone, gone, gone: everything is gone again. I came back to my cell after my walk round the yard, and my journal of memories was gone. Everything I wrote before, everything I remembered, gone. I don't go outside much anymore: these are the risks: that everything will be gone. The anguish I felt and expressed in various noises with fine supplication made the guards come back quick. They explained to me that my journal of memories had been taken away for my own good. To remember so much, as I was in the habit of doing, would bring me so much pain, they reminded me, and, most importantly, such writing is prohibited here, and I am fortunate that this dispossession is the extent of my punishment, and remember what happened last time. It would be better, they feel, if I do not remember anymore and stopped trying. I do not believe them. They are afraid of what I would find if I proceeded through the past, as I had been doing. At the end of my memories, when I get to that final point after which there is nothing else to remember, the clearest memory as it is shaded up against by nothing at all, the last grasp of something, it is there, surely, that the memory at the end of the mind will show me why I am here, where I am, and how to get out from here, inside, where it is safe, for the most part. The fact is, these are times of fear. Fear and awareness. Wretched times, wrenching times. These are times of fear when you are outside. Everything is all about you, out there. Things can envelope you, draw you in, render you, and so I don't go out anymore. You do not know, and you know you can never know when it will happen. I don't know. I don't know enough. I know, that I don't know. It doesn't bother me too much anymore, truthfully. Things changed, for the better, I like to think. But then things change again, as they did. The sheer mutability of the thing, small impermanent thing. A task beyond all chasing. The hope that shares its light with the sun. The sheer mutability of the thing: I can't take it, so I don't go outside much anymore. I don't see much, I hear some but don't see much, I have an idea that things are going on, but I have nothing to go on, in making that estimation. Pure gut, a hunch: why *wouldn't* they? Be going on? Of course, they are: they've always been, they always are. What else are they to do? Nothing, nothing at all. And yet, why do things feel they are coming to an end? Why do I feel things are coming to an end? A rest, an ending? Something has approached me and seen me and known me and in that moment of equanimity passes me by, and I am changed. I don't know, I don't go out anymore, I have an idea of things, but I cannot confirm, I don't know, the fact stands, that everything I had written down of what I remembered is gone, my journal of memories is gone, I would go and find it if I could, but they won't let me, there must be a reason, I don't know, I don't go out much anymore.

Now I wonder if I can start over again, inside here. Start over and remember again, remember my life and that world and some things in it, some people, faces and limbs and eyes, what I saw, what I felt, what I smelled and what happened to me and what I made happen in the life I am certain that I lived, my life. Pressing back against the past, pressing myself against the past, moving memories closer to me so I may see them clear and find the path through them into a place in the present beyond these walls, a new place, that is safe for living again, outside, beyond the walls. And beyond the walls, the sea.

I have been going through the books they supplied me, it was long ago that these books were brought here, squalid things from outside:

- Four chapters from *Robinson Crusoe*, wherein, among other goings-on, the island is visited by people who fancy other people for their meals;
- The third volume of the diaries of Samuel Pepys in Lingala — I cannot read Lingala;
- §§201-389 of Ephron Chrystostom's Syriac lexicon;
- A self-help guide for dentists; and
- A history of the umbrella.

I read back through the lexicon sections but could not hack it, all Greek to me; *Crusoe* made me hungry; didn't bother with the Pepys because, again, I cannot read Lingala; skipped the dentist book because the teeth I have left all hurt and I would prefer not to spend time thinking about that; skimmed through the history of the umbrella and something stirred in me somewhere, something was radiant but only for a moment and then it was gone, all dark again. May have to look through that one again, or perhaps if I do, then I shall expect to see the radiant thing be radiant long enough that I can comprehend it, and it will not be so, and I shall be despondent again as I usually am. Forget it. No more with the books. I don't know. I don't go out much anymore. I cannot remember what I wrote before, so I remember nothing but what I saw today. That bird. Outside, in the yard, where things change, our home in the world. The sheer mutability of the thing.

I write now, to restore the lost time and make up for time that will be lost. And so, this entry is both the first of what will be many and one of many already written, one point in a long grey line, or maybe it is the only visible point of an ancient burial mound that a dam has otherwise submerged below the visible world. Everything that came before is as though it never was; or maybe everything that came before is a ghost, present somewhere but invisible the way the distant future is here in every one of our sighs, to be heard only by angels; or everything that came before is as the memories of past lives we live in the womb. I don't know, I don't remember, it's all mere speculation, I don't go outside much anymore.

I can try to recover my memories by writing down what I remember from the entries I wrote before, they who were taken from me, now in exile or sheer corporal destitution. And yet, that kind of writing would seem to make no progress at all, no, because that kind of writing invents a story that only turns back on itself, turns on itself, always going down a new path before returning to a beginning again no matter how far it advances, diverging and changing before retracing its path back to a source that is gone, ancient light arcing back on a long-dead star, returning, returning, and always returning like a river running round a bend from the short sea back to its source and it is too late already, it is always too late in the beginning, much time has passed and more time remains but not enough time and never enough time, even when it was early it was already too late, it is always too late, again. No matter: now I cannot even remember what I wrote down before. To try to recover those memories is a futile task like most of them, coming to naught. One must embrace futility, to go on. It is the only way: march forward toward nothing. Take pleasure in one's encounters along the way.

I am sure I can remember again. That faculty does not desert a person so quickly. I must remember again, and I must make myself remember. But even if I recover the memories I have forgotten, no memory will come back the same, after having wandering outside in the world, squalid place. The memory will be amended, refracted, fractured, transfigured; the memory will return but it returns with new words, new stories, a new glimmer in the eye, different voices, in a new guise or avatar; the returning memory cannot be anything. But another memory slighted by remembrance so that it has become something new in the past, and the past must then be amended. I must remember the memories of life that I lived and not the memories that time has transmuted into new memories not my own. I must exhume new memories that, revived, will capture, and return to me the fugitive ones that are where I do not go.

There is no hope, but to see again — a new way.

An inventory of my surroundings may help. Cramped quarters here and not much to go on, in any respect. Not much is in front of me. I look ahead and I see this stack of someone's stationary, this pen, a puddle of something near the door. A few tears I shed earlier in shame. Nor when I look around do I see much: more wetness, more dust, more dark, some wooden beams, more dark, walls, walls, walls. But I make do; I'm still here. I don't get around to reading much literature here except for the *Crusoe*, let alone what passes for contemporary literature these days — nothing contemporary here where everything is beyond the consideration of time — these days, ashes all these days. But I will write and write and write, or I will write and write, and by writing I will impel myself to remember. I hope.

Hope. Hope, what a thing, for the having. I hope much, with my writing. I don't go outside much anymore, so I write, in here, where I am safe from the squalid world outside, and hope. Unfounded hope, stupid, blighted hope, hope that shares its light with the sun; it is what I have, what I hold onto, what remains with me, inside. Hope that in writing I will continue to exist, that in writing I'll be attested to, that in writing I will remember myself and will be remembered. Hope that, in writing, I will sustain myself through the longueurs of this dismal play, be it the second act or Lord willing the last, please let this be a play and let the curtains come up and let me take a bow to the sound of their applause, please. No, it is not a play, this is life, this is the world, a world rather, say there is another world, I doubt it yet. No, this is the world, but I will hope and be homesick for another world. I hope that in writing my mind will not become as feeble as my body's become, that my mind will remain whole, my thoughts lucid, my memory memorious. I write and disinter myself. I should be freed to live a life of experience and not a life of memory. I don't know, what is out there. I don't go outside much anymore. But I hope, for the world. Maybe I will put together some kind of testament for the world, and the votaries of some distant and yet-unfounded faith in the far-off future will find these entries here and use them for their breviary and look at them each day. Maybe these entries of remembrance will wind up in a dry ditch and will survive through the despondencies of history and will be stumbled upon by some goatherd, and what I've written will be held in reverence with hopeful hands. Maybe it'll end up in the same ditch and be digested by worms. Who knows? I don't know. Either way would be some kind of art.

Art, beautiful art. Beauty: aptness with purpose. Beauty: hope manifested. Beauty: art by other means. Art: for the birds.

Consider the worth of art and ask the canonical question: less than, equal to or greater than? Equal to and greater than are granted a spot of time in memory, less than is set outside of time and dilapidated by the wind, forgotten anon.

The severe judgment of time resolves much debate about the worth of art. Time is the final judge. We will not be here to attest to her judgment. Believe that it will come. In time.

I will transfigure what I remember of my life into a new life, and in that transfiguration I will live again. Somehow. I don't know. That is art enough: to live again.

Entry No. 2

Awake: all nightly wakefulness waiting for the dawn to break. The long grey blue clear dawn, with its rising wisps of rosy-red exhausted butterflies, light on their wings as rising from the exposed bony tendrils of tree roots come so many vain sounds that mean nothing and soon lapse into the busy-bodied day, day busy with bodies rising so as to better waste away come night again. The many little sounds of day a refuge from compunction, all meaning nothing, explaining nothing, proposing nothing, demanding nothing, receiving nothing, and giving nothing but the brief assurance that necessary night has gone away, and a blue sky will steal into all the secret crannies that the earth keeps hidden, simple secret places where nobody goes because nobody knows, all in thrall to light whether willingly or not, whether coming to something or mere nothing at all. This dawn will not come, at least in here, inside, where it is safe. The light will stay where it is light. Let there be light enough no matter.

Back to the matter. Make memory move again.

Upon inspection of my quarters, everything is the same and nothing is changing, but the absence of my journal of memories. Other than that: the same. I am familiar with the premises, inside. A dim bit of sunlight filters through a little window at the far end of the room, never enough to know what time of day it is, never enough to know more than that it may be daytime. The light is not bright enough to see anything. Say I think that I see something; it's probably a play of light and shadow, and so it is probably nothing, nothing at all, even if I swear, I saw something, it's only a trick of the light, a falsehood. Faint light, false light.

Sight won't help me much, then. Touch is best in here, a better sense than sight. I can tell some things about my room by touching or not touching. The room is narrow, such that when I stand in the middle and face the door, extending my arms, I touch the walls. If I recall correctly, I am not large: my arms do not extend so far. The room therefore must be quite narrow. Yes, it must be so.

The room's narrowness is redeemed somewhat by its depth. When I lie on my pallet, I can stretch my legs straight out and do not touch a thing. There's even room enough that, if I feel the urge, I can wiggle my toes. I have tried this earlier and can verify, it is true.

I just jumped with my arms straight up to touch the ceiling and did not touch it. I feel anxious when I imagine what is up above me in the dark, a ceiling or no ceiling, a firmament, or no firmament, I don't know, I haven't been up there, perhaps some automated scythes would cut off my hands if I reached up high enough, perhaps silent man-eating spiders beyond a firmament or no firmament, in any case nothing's up there I can reach.

Floor: the same old familiar thing. Grubby, dusty, and cold. Days like today the floor is damp and slippery, and I assume that's on account of rain. I don't know, I don't know if it rains, I assume it still rains, though I cannot verify. I don't go out much anymore, nor, when I do, for long, at least long enough to get a bead on the weather. I have not seen rainfall in the lager. At least, I do not remember rain. Perhaps a bird could verify that it rains, but even so that would be pointless, since I cannot understand birds, and they fly away if you stop to talk with them. There are no birds, in here, inside, these days. Days like these, dust clumps and makes walking without slipping hard. That isn't to say I walk much unless they make me to walk, that I remember, and then they make me walk until I forget that I ever was not walking. I do not walk much otherwise. Not much room. But still I walk, a few paces here and there, enough to keep things loose. Stretch of the legs. But for the most part when I am in this place, I hunch over, and I scuttle. The smaller you are, or make yourself to seem, the less you risk the danger of being noticed, and its subsequent punishment. No, I do not walk upright, I hunch, and I scuttle. Sometimes I think I am a crab, a very fast one at that. I saw a fiddler crab once, I remember that. Maybe more than once. A ghost crab too. But that must have been long ago. Here if there are crabs, then I am king of the crabs. Festoon me in my laurels and hail to the king of kings and crab of crabs, brackish-born, first of his shell, breaker of claws. No, I disavow that, I take that back. To be king of the crabs would invite attention, and attention brings mischief. Anyone would notice a large crab milling about in this place. They could step on me or boil me even. Let me forget I ever was a crab or saw one either. Let me go back:

for the most part I hunch over and I scuttle. Otherwise, I hardly walk at all, nor scuttle much either, as far as I remember.

Doors: the same. I remember seeing the entrance to my new home and its two doors, one outside the other when they first brought me here unshackled and unhooded. The inside door is of some kind of wood, lumpy, and I have touched it; the outside door I presume to be made of some kind of fortified metal. I have never been permitted to touch it so I cannot confirm that, but I presume it is fortified metal because of the clangful reverberation when it is slammed. I say it is fortified metal, but I don't know if it is in fact fortified. I don't know what it would even mean for metal to be fortified. *Fortified* makes it sound more impenetrable. Even if it is not fortified, it is all the same impenetrable, no light slips through below the door, and it is clear from the reverberation when they slam it, that it is not the kind of door that I am free to open. And since I am not free to open, I cannot leave. And since I cannot leave, I stay here and, if I feel the urge, go down on my pallet, and wiggle my toes, touching nothing, clean and free. There isn't much else to do. This is where I live. I don't know. I don't go outside much anymore.

My inventory did not help me remember anything worthwhile. I remember what is around me and above me, doors, walls, floors, walls, firmaments. Remembering the present will not help me to remember my life and the world where I lived it. I should begin writing to remember what I have lost. I'm tired, though, and my teeth are itching again. I can poke them with the pen, but I fear that would cause some kind of infection no one here would care to cure, or else tattoo my gums with the ink, something I would resent myself for having done. Would I had tattooed my body with the prior entries; then remembering would not be so hard unless they peeled my skin off.

I will write and writing will call the memories to me. My body will remember. If not, at least my hand will move and letters will beget words that beget sentences that become thoughts, pleasant ones, I hope. That way perhaps I'd feel some sort of liveliness again. I will begin. Sometime I will begin. Or rather, I will continue. May I have a world enough and time.

Entry No. 3

When they let me out for my constitutional around the yard today, as I circled the worn foot path cincturing the rest of the yard, I veered closer than usual toward these long flat edifices that stood stark out of the ground on the eastern end of the camp, outside. I was walking close to them when the wind whipped up and carried a fetid scent to my nostrils; and smelling that great raw acridity, I remembered something. My old cell. The one they put me in before some event I cannot yet remember, it may have been important, no matter. My old cell. They put me in it while I awaited something, one thing or another. I stayed there for a long while, I believe, longer than I remember. But I remember my old cell. My old cell had a hole. I hid nothing in the hole. I miss the hole. I could defecate and piss in it. In my present cell I must plead with the gaoler on duty to take me to the duncan, as we call the outhouse. Why do they call it the duncan? No one has explained that to me. I have no idea. Perhaps once upon a time there was a prisoner here named Duncan and he was a very good boy and loved and admired by all and so in his honor they named the outhouse, where the parts of us we no longer need are given their freedom, after him. I don't know. I can't be certain. In any event, the procedure by which they lead me to the duncan is, in my opinion, unnecessarily complicated, inefficient, and not economical at all. They could do better, but I don't think they care. If there was a camper named Duncan, then they dishonor him every day. The gaoler must open the first and second door of my cell, yes, the two doors, then he must guide me to the door that sections off my ward, then he must announce to the gaoler on the other side of the door that the door to the ward is about to be opened, then he blindfolds me, the door opens and I am guided to the duncan; then, once I have finished my business or the gaoler decides I have finished, I am guided back, still blindfolded, down the hall, at which point the gaoler announces to the gaoler on the other side that the door is to be opened; then the door opens and I am guided through, my blindfold removed and I am pushed back into my cell and the doors are closed. Depending on the temperament of the gaoler on duncan duty, he may amuse himself and tell me I am in the duncan when I am not so they can watch me piss and then they laugh, or he guides me with a gentle loving hand so that I stumble into it and I am besmeared with excrement. Sometimes they grow bored with this game and cease responding to my requests to be allowed to urinate outside my cell. When that happens, I feel around for a corner that is far enough from my pallet and where I usually sit so that I may vacate my premises, or, when that corner smells like it will overflow, I defecate on myself. It stinks. I do not rejoice. When the stench grows so strong that it passes through the doors and begins to irritate my gaoler, I must then receive a special dispensation to have my clothing washed. I then wait naked in the cell until my clothing is returned to me; I stand naked and aim to cover myself with my arms because I am cold, but my arms are not so long that I can wrap them around my body and warmly embrace myself. Sometime later my garments are returned to me. I cherish my clothing at those times as though it were a suit I have just retrieved from the tailor, and as though it were a suit, I fear any small speck of soil that may defile my clothing. But I know that sometime soon I will have to dirty myself again, subject to my gaoler's inclinations as a newborn in a crib save that newborns are treated with tenderness and care because they do not yet have the motor functions to move themselves to an area established for the purposes of defecation and urination whereas I do, or did, or thought I did, perhaps I don't. All the same I wish I had the choice, the power. This is why I miss my old cell: I had power over the hole. And before my old cell, the barracks, yes, there were barracks, full of arms and men and legs and even more men, so many I cannot recall, all of us there against our will when we were still able to be willful. Although things were bad then, things were nicer then than now. I would take my constitutional after I worked and then I would return to the sound of other people around me. They were not pleasant sounds, but they were sounds, human sounds, more lively than the silence that malingers in my present residence. One must find the good parts to remember and be grateful for, even the companionship of a fetid hole.

The dismal dumps of recollecting happy times in doldrum days. Oh, it aches, it throbs. Like a stone in your shoe when you've been marching all night. And it never ends well, remembrance — other voices come, and other voices go, inundating voices that recede and, in their wake, leave a whole lot of scattered torsos and a rage too flooded with regret for these wilder beasts. A fitting end that always comes again. Exeunt omnes, profugi fato.

That's a memory, not one I cherish but a memory of my life all the same, a memory I have just now written down. Perhaps more will come. It will take some time to get to some good ones, but they'll come around I hope, and Lord willing whatever scent urges the next memory forward will be more pleasant.

They are singing in the hall outside my room. I do not understand. They will not stop.

Entry No. 4

Either the sun has gone out of this world or it does not care to shine, has given up. Even when I go into the yard I can't tell if the sun is around. Who knows; who cares; we go on.

Was given the usual rations today: the bad soup before dawn and again in the evening, a chunk of the grey bread — good for three days, the bread, five if you really stretch it. The soup — the unhurried tawny liquid arrives with the overwhelming taste of thatch cooled after a summer afternoon rainstorm and leaves on your tongue the combative earthiness of dusty rutabaga stalks. Before I was placed in my present abode and still lived in the barracks with other men, I would drink the stuff and wonder what it was. Most likely it was locally sourced. The chefs never told us how they made the soup and we never asked: we were too preoccupied with getting as much of the hot stuff as we could in the time we were given before the earth began to lighten and labor began, all of us going out into the factories, offices and fields to work, that strange and uncanny taste of the earth below us staying with us in our mouths, the taste of being at rest and readying oneself for the work of day. I could not ask the chefs even if I wanted to. I never saw the chefs. No one did. We waited in the yard in the dark before dawn for our rations to be brought to us by the gaolers. They might have made the soup. I don't know. Labor began at dawn. We worked through the afternoon when we were given a brief siesta but no food. When I held onto enough bread, I would take three or four bites, chewing plenty for lack of water, before swallowing and going to rest. The bread was without the leisurely sweetness of the bread I ate as a child, which, because I ate it as a child who had never tasted any other kind, was the archetype of what I thought bread should be. Sometimes a memory of eating the bread my mother put out before dinner would come to me as I drowsed and fell into a soft light sleep. When the bell rang out, we woke, and we worked again until darkness engulfed us, and we puttered through the dark back to the barracks where we rested before the performance began. Sometimes they still take me out of my cell for the performance. When we perform, I play the tuba. I do not know how to play the tuba. I am consigned to play the tuba all the same. I will play the tuba until they take away my mouth, which may be sooner than I'd hope. They will never take away the tuba.

That routine is gone. I have no one to break bread with anymore. Since I have been moved to my current domicile I merely eat, write, do other things, sometimes when allowed in the yard for a spell I go there. But not today. No visitors to my cell today, not even the gaolers. No faces, voices, eyes today. All quiet. Well, not quiet — one hears certain sounds — quotidian rather, no, what's the word. Unremarkable. Yes: today was unremarkable. And here I am, remarking. Would I would shut up.

The absence of visitors today does not surprise me: while I have come to expect occasional visits from my gaolers so they may hit me, mock me, and laugh at me when I scratch at the doors as they close them, visitors from else-where are strictly verboten here because this place is not to be known to exist outside of the walls where that wobbly bird flew. How can you visit someone who dwells in a place you don't know exists? I wouldn't believe I existed if you told me I did; if you told me I existed, I would be rather dubious of the notion and wonder if you were touched in the head. Still: some acknowledge I live. The gaolers and this one sow in the farm out back whom I will sincerely mourn over when she is slaughtered. Other than them, I have myself. All I can do to acknowledge myself is to try to write from time to time. A line here, a curve there: these symbols don't birth themselves; someone must have created them, it must have been me, I must have existed once upon a time and what a time it was. But no one can confirm that: there is no second opinion.

Today I write. Yesterday, too, and the day before and the day before that one, as well. I wrote some days before that, I must have, otherwise I would never have been able to fill up my journal of memories, my sweet journal that was so wrongly taken from me like a chick that a lingering ferret plucks from a nest. Since I have been in this room, I occupy the time that I have to myself with writing, transcription, and such. I never used to write, hardly at all, when I was outside. Why now? Why here? Where did it come from? I have some sus-picions.

I had spent months I believe, months and months doing nothing but ensur-ing the dimensions of my room are constant and mathematically sound from day to day and taking a muted pleasure in my constitutionals out in the yard. Before that — I don't remember right now. I'm sure I saw things out there then during my walks, but I don't remember what they were. I don't know. Others? Other people? Possible. Plausible, even. Other prisoners, gaolers, guards, ghosts. A chimney, a roof, smoke, and ashes. A tree over yond perhaps, walls much closer than the trees. Maybe a possum. But I never wrote.

It was some months after they brought me into this cell something happened to me, or in me. I do not consider myself susceptible to influences, yet an alien impulse, a lonely impulse in what I am confident was nighttime, overtook me that night. And the impulse said: perhaps I could write. Perhaps. I believe it was an impulse speaking to me. It may very well have been a gaoler outside my cell or some being beside my window who whispered it to me and only to me. More likely, though, the alien impulse arose from somewhere inside me rather than from elsewhere, and it was an impulse to write.

Of course, many people may write: a letter here, a letter there, a space and a full stop and before you know it, a sentence of your own making, congratulations, you really did it this time. No, I don't mean forming letters, words and sentences, punctuation marks and paragraphs, thematically coherent paragraphs of at least three sentences, &c. I have surely been literate for some time now. When someone says, "Hello, I am a writer" — that is a thing certain people say — when someone says that he does not mean he is a writer of recipes. I intend no disrespect to the worshipful company of recipe-writers, but when someone says, "Hello, I'm a writer and I am writing," he means writing in the same way I mean writing: to *write* — I say it like that, my voice rising dreamily as the vowel rises in intonation — to *write*. In a word: creation. In another word: imagination. In yet another two: power and control. No more words: I understand what I mean: I felt an impulse to *write*. *That* I remember.

Kind of them to give me paper, a pen too, though not so kind that they can take it all away whenever they fancy. I will make do with what I have while I can, inside.

Writing: a new way of ordering the world.

The pale rage to order: it is always flaring up in us.

Writing, for its primacy in recorded history — which, since all that is recorded is history, may simply be called *history*, while all the unrecorded stuff that only the earth remembers is called *prehistory* — cannot exist on its own.

What — who can? *No man is an island*, &c. Writing may not beget itself. Autophagous? No, that's not the word. Autogenous. Yes, autogenous — writing is not that, is not autogenous. No, it's not as though I think of writing and my body commences to write, how marvelous is the human form. No, the human form is not marvelous, the human form is serviceable. No, none of this. This isn't happening.

Writing is contingent on so much more than an impulse, lust, or desire to write. Writing depends on there being a world or space amenable, conducive even, to writing that exists before the word is written. You must have the necessary conditions. You must have the necessary accoutrements. Writing implements, for one. Or rather, because I am talking about writing the way I mentioned before — to *write*! create! immanentize! — I will call implements, *instruments*. Yes: writing cannot exist without writing instruments. And I have one, a fine one at that, ink, and all. That's one thing writing depends on, writing instruments, paper as well. I had the desire to write, I had a pen and I had paper. You also need something to write about: a subject. Without a subject, you risk digression and abiding wandering. Even having a subject, you may find yourself lost in a moraine of your own making. But having a subject at least lessens the chances of losing oneself where no one can find you. So, I went in search of a subject.

I did not discriminate in my search. My subject could take any form, real or unreal, no matter. Long ago somewhere around here I lost the ability to tell what is real, and I don't really care that I did. It doesn't bother me much anymore, truthfully. I can, at least, *imagine* reality. Birds that are bards and an empty pallet: both can be real. I have imagined that people live, prosper, and freely die somewhere outside the camp, but now I know that there is no proof that the rest of the world is not like my world in here, inside. Perhaps the entire world is composed of these camps and everyone in the world is now kept in them. I don't know. I don't go outside much anymore. I have no idea. I cannot imagine the world anymore. I did, though, or at least I imagined enough to make my own world positively creeping and crawling with potential subjects, some always visible, some only visible in darkness, some never seen, only known by what they leave behind.

I hit on the idea of writing a biography, a biography that would not only untangle the skein of some illustrious individual's life, but almost illuminate his world and milieu, both of which a biography shows can emanate from a single person existing in time. Biographies are always good because biographies write themselves. The life has been lived, the facts have been fashioned, all that must be done by the biographer is attestation, that he say, Lo, this life was lived! And what a life it was — a lived life! The danger in writing a life, however, is that the chosen life will slip out from under the nib of the author's pen and escape into a world beyond the author's purview. Everything heads for the margins; everything flees from the collapsing center. Lives are no different. One must always be mindful around a life: a life can flee in the time it takes a breath to fall out of your lungs. And so, with great tact, attention, and delicacy, I started writing a life of a man. A real man I imagined, a real man of imagined reality. Dyfrdwy, I'd call him, or Dee for short. He was real enough to me. A flesh-bound thing with eyes and a beard, and that is what he really was.

Yes, that would be what he really was even if he were not here. My subject would be drawn into a world similar to ours but for being a fictive one, one invented by me, an imperfect creator, and imbued with certain similar material and governed by certain similarly imperfect laws. Gravity, for one. Society, for another. Yet I had to ensure that, despite perhaps having the most aesthetically respectable view of an imagined world, I did not conflate it with the world I remembered, out there, squalid place. The sheer mutability of the thing. Both emerge not from my body's sensory machinations but from elsewhere in me: the imagined and remembered world emerge from the mind, where they have lain long enough like coal deep under the earth to be sorted out from other vagrant particles and pulled from the depths as diamonds. And then, once discovered in their new form, they refract the mind outward, imbuing the way you live in your world with their own unique radiance, retracing in reverse the path of experience, light traveling long distances that alone confirms the existence of some original radiant source, light finding a way out of what can never give in, carrying you back to a single source where what is imagined and what is remembered are one. The light they refract is beguiling, so much so that only the most perspicacious can tell the difference between the light of imagination and the light of remembrance, and by then it may be too late already: what you see as a memory is invention, and invention remembrance. The twain ought not meet, but, as with most parties proscribed from mingling, they do. It is at that point you must look past the light and, with all due candor, ensure the necessary boundary between the world you have invented and the world you remember remains impermeable. You cannot risk a man born of a capable imagination crossing over into the world of remembrance and staying there, waiting, biding his time, waiting, and growing unseen underground until, like a scourge of locusts, he emerges from the earth, obscures the sky and its light, and blitzes your world, razing it, ingesting every living thing, leaving your remembered world barren, empty and bleak. I had to be careful.

Now I had my instrument, some paper, a subject and a fair mind about me: I had the facts, I had his life, I had his world and the means of creating it. Having those, I began to write the life of Dyfrdwy.

Ah, Dyfrdwy. He taught geometry. A sterling professor, a beautiful mind, Dee, as they called him. Every day Dee would kiss his wife goodbye and tousle his children's hair and tell them to be good before he went off to the stony halls of his university to teach his students geometry. When the lesson concluded, the students would say, "Gee, Dee, you really do know your geometry." And Dee would say, "Yes, I know geometry." And the deans and the vicars would hear tell of Dee's aptitude and, gobsmacked, would say, "Dee certainly knows geometry, how else could he teach it so well." And everyone regarded Dee as not only someone who taught geometry, but also someone who knew geometry, which is unusual in that those who know don't often teach and those who teach don't often know. That Dee was regarded as someone who both knew geometry and taught geometry pleased everyone from the deans and the vicars and the students to the warlords who bided their time in the mountains counting constellations. And because everyone was pleased that Dee both knew geometry and taught geometry, everyone was happy. They were happy: because of Dee. Some people even thanked him when they saw him, saying, "You have taught us geometry and now we understand the movements of the spheres, thank you Dee." Or else they would visit him in his library, which was small and had character, and say, "Because of you I can now properly measure the circumference of my yurt, thank you Dee." Or else they would say, "You speak of geometry, tell us about the circle, does it begin or end, tell us about the circle, tell us." But Dee would not speak of circles because he was a sober and a pious man who would not speak of things that do not end, and Dee would smile but Dee would say nothing. And even though his piety prevailed on him not to speak of the circles, all the same Dee remained pleasing in other people's eyes if they had them. If they had no eyes, he remained pleasing in their hearts. If they had no hearts, he was without recourse: hearts are necessary things.

But Dee was also, depending on what you think about hocus-pocus, either a lunatic or a prophet, either moonstruck or capable of seeing through reality. And after having been thanked many times and having been found pleasing if not on as many occasions as he was thanked then at least for longer periods of time, Dee had a thought. He had thoughts before, surely, many of them, but this thought differed. He did not write it down, so neither historians nor I can attest to what that thought was. Possibly it had to do with circles. But let no one say that because this thought was not recorded that it did not exist. The thought existed; perhaps it still does. It may be one of those other things, the things that are not remembered, I don't think thoughts expire, they just go elsewhere.

And this thought changed Dee. Although he was a fine teacher of geometry and many thanked him and found him pleasing, such earthly considerations and pleasures no longer satisfied Dee. Because of this thought, this one single thought that kindled an impulse in Dee. An impulse for more. More knowledge. More life. Now Dee needed greater pleasures. Now Dee wanted to transcend the earth. Now Dee looked up and saw birds. Dee wanted to be like them, the birds. If only he could fly. Perhaps he could learn the rudiments of flying from them. Dee was a teacher of geometry, but now it was time for the teacher to be taught.

It came as a shock when Dee decided to leave his teaching post and life as he knew it behind. The deans warned him not to leave and his students felt betrayed. He said goodbye to his wife, who was teary-eyed, and he adjusted the wigs of his children, who looked on sheepishly as a moment whose significance they could not yet comprehend was in the offing, and to everyone who had gathered there the morning he was set to leave. They said, "Thank you, Dee, we shall miss you dearly;" or they said, "You will live long enough to regret this, Dee, but not long enough to repair the circle you have broken;" or they said, "Dee, you have pleased us so, do not forget us, come back in the end, don't forget us while you're gone, you must return here to complete the story of your life, that is how stories must go, they must end by returning to where they began." Much like there is no ending for circles, there was no ending for Dee, only endless beginning canceled by awesome catastrophe followed by endless beginning. This similarity between circles and Dee's peregrinations is what makes me think that thought of his was about circles, but that is speculation. We will never know what he thought. Other humans are unknowable. So are we.

And so, Dee left his teaching post. He sought the birds. A few sentences ago I wrote that *now it was time for the teacher to be taught*, but it was a two-way street Dee and the birds travelled on. The birds would teach Dee their knowledge of flight and how to obtain the hollow bones requisite to fly, and Dee in turn would teach the birds about geometry and how the sphericity of the earth could be gleaned from the sky. And Dee would pass from forest to forest, field to field, crag to crag, nest to nest, dispensing and learning. Dee had become a travelling scholar, dedicated to the disinterested pursuit of wisdom for wisdom's sake; or else he became a nomad or a vegan, no, vagrant, yes, or else he became a nomad or a vagrant, a rudderless madman, a miscreant, a hermit, a batty old professor: I still have not decided what we should think of him, whether he was to be admired and revered or to be used as an allegorical figure to caution other people with anti-social and deviant tendencies from going off on their own to wander to and fro upon the earth. Regardless of what we are to have thought of him, Dee pressed on. He was not aware of what we may have thought, a task difficult enough for us, nor was he aware of us, for I invented him.

Dee pressed on. Oh, did he press. Let us assume Dee assumed this: birds are part of our world, but because they can fly away, they are somewhat not part of our world, thereby being both familiar and alien, beyond our world but of it, swinging low from time to time much like angels do but without the swinging, swinging low does not seem an angelic movement, I should think angels *descend*. Perhaps Dee remembered that angels were seen and told of, and in these tales the angels looked like humans. But they are not human, of course — they are angels. Angels take on the form of a human because that is better than taking the form of a bush or a cow. If you received the Lord's instructions from a fiery cow who was mooing in alarm, you would not heed the message so much as the messenger: prophetic flaming cows are terrifying. Some angels excepted themselves from the human form, sometimes manifesting as a smoky hand or a lightning bolt or a vision of a kind. But for the most part, logic prevails on the angels: appear human so not to frighten humans.

Even if angels appear human, however, real human beings may sense something is off. I cannot attest to this — or, rather, I may be able to attest to this, and I will tell you why later, if later comes, why I think I can attest to this. But not now — this isn't about me, nor is it about angels, it's about Dee, and Dee wondered about the birds.

Dee wandered through the continent and partook in *spiritual parliament* with flocks of wailing birds. He learned much during *spiritual parliament*. There he learned that some angels take the form of birds, and during *spiritual parliament* he transcribed the visions and the dispensations of the fiery angels who spoke their speaking through the squawks of birds in a language of his own making, still undecipherable to modern archeologists, cryptologists, and linguists. He thought his world was expanding, or he thought that he realized that his world was one in a larger world embracing other worlds around it, or he thought the birds were very good interpreters of the angels' lessons. He recorded everything the angels told him through the birds, but this would prove to be an inadequate means of transmitting information to others through time because historians would be unable to decipher the code that he used. Nonetheless, scholars would be certain that what Dee wrote down was what he heard from the birds. And Dee was satisfied. He had a great and marvelous time and learned much. Dee pleased Dee.

But there still was more for Dee. More that Dee desired. That he desired to know.

Things changed. For reasons I never explained, Dee returned home.

Going home was a mistake. It is always ill-advised. One should never go home. If you have the opportunity then get rid of your home as soon as you can, to return is to die, every circle is fatal; and Dee got home, and his home and the endless library — Dee's quaint library full of character had become endless for reasons I never really figured out — were plundered and despoiled. No one said, "Thank you, Dee." No one said, "Dee, you please us, here, have a shovel and some beans." No one asked Dee to teach of the circles; no one asked anything more of Dee than that he go sit in a room and quietly wait.

I am not sure what happened next. I am not sure that what I just wrote happened. I did not write it down and I forget what I would have written. There are possible endings, possible continuations of Dee's life that never occurred.

Perhaps the deans took pity on Dee. Perhaps they gave him a hovel near the building where he taught those years before his excision from society, before his life was englobed within other lives, the distant lives of angels, unperceivable lives he had invented or had claimed to have seen, we can't know. And then for good effect, perhaps he dies. Alas, poor Dyfrdwy! I never knew him, a fine man misunderstood, now dead. But he would have been buried in just about the finest coffin you'd see in your life. And so, it ended, an inglorious and foreshortened end to Dyfrdwy's unfinished life, which I admit was all my fault because I never wrote it, the poor sap.

Or perhaps Dee never died. Perhaps the deans of the university told Dee the only way he could be returned to his past life would be to record everything he learned from his peregrinations among the birds and share it with the community, and Dee did so, and Dee completed his written testament of the teachings of the birds, and everyone in the town learned how to fly although some could never succeed in getting off the ground for more than a flap or two. I cannot be sure because I put Dee's life aside and left it behind me. I was unsatisfied. I could make a much better life, out of this one or of whole cloth. I set it apart from my world. Unlike a circle, Dee's story ended, but not the way stories are supposed to end. Dee's story was left unfinished, abandoned. To have one's life only told in part before it is forgotten is not an end, it is a cosmic ellipsis. None of this rubbish about birds, angels, circles, or geometry, no more thanking or pleasing, no more life, thank you very much. No more of Dee. Small, imagined lives endure somewhere but it isn't here that they endure. Dee may still be engaged in his bird-talk, but not on my watch. On life, on Dee — reader, pass by!

Yet Dyfrdwy's life is still present in my life, his life is still here in one way. The paper I wrote it on is in the corner, and if there were more light, I could see it and know the half-life of Dyfrdwy is with me in this room, another life is around me, o joy. Although Dee's life endures here in some fashion, the story is incomplete, and no one cares about it or will ever read about it anyway. I certainly don't give a hoot about it. As far as I am concerned, I have dispensed with it and doing so have dispensed with Dee. Let him wander, let him live his life as he would have it lived. Let him flee, let him live or die, let him fly away and go a-squawking, let him go in search of lost knowledge. No matter what Dee does or does not do with his life, I will put his discarded and incomplete life to good use. I will line the floor with it or fashion some kind of wrapping for my feet with it. I will tell his story as a cautionary tale to anyone I encounter who is thinking about birds. Pure tragedy: Dee's life is unfinished, and it is over.

And that is my fault. If Dee could ever have the emotions, we fleshy humans feel, I imagine he would feel anger towards me, or sadness, would desire vengeance maybe even. Who wouldn't? I left him behind. No one likes to be left behind. Especially to be left behind by one whom you trust. Dee trusted me. Or if he existed, I believe he would have trusted me and have been let down. Because I betrayed his trust by leaving his life unfinished, unfulfilled, incomplete. A foreshortened and elided life.

Perhaps Dee is out wandering in a world somewhere, wandering in a possible world, looking for something to do, or at least looking for a way to fulfill himself and complete his life. That is beyond my control. Dee was always looking for something. If he were alive now, he would be looking for something. Something to bring his life to a close. Someone to bring his life to close. Someone. Someone like me. Perhaps Dee would be looking for me. But he would not find me here in my cell. I don't know where I am. No one can find me. I can't even find myself. But I would welcome him all the same. It would be nice to see my creation face-to-face, to at least ensure that I did not make something malformed.

Perhaps Dee has no face. I did not spend enough time describing his appearance, it was cursory at best, I mostly imagined how he looked as I wrote. Perhaps he has my face. I'm not sure. I put Dee aside, I put Dee's life aside and wiped his face from all remembrance, and doing so I left him incomplete, unfulfilled, inhuman. And for that I am sorry. If I met Dee, I would apologize. And I hope he would understand. If I were in his clogs, I would understand. And perhaps he would: I authored him after all, and I wrote his life out of my own life and all my sentiments and thoughts. Dee comes from me. Came from me. And I did not give him enough of himself to let him go out on his own. He is still with me. Somewhere.

Perhaps his life will find fulfillment someday, the circle will be completed, and Dee will return to his world. But Dee's life is over for now, poor Dee, because I brought it to an end. Or if not an end then a break, a halt, a suspension. Dee lives a suspended life. What a life to live — a life in suspension, a life put aside, a life adjourned. Poor Dee. I can commiserate with him. My life is the same. I don't live right now. My life has been suspended. My life was adjourned. I have been elided from the world.

May my life one day resume. Perhaps then Dee's will too.

O Dee. May the road rise to meet you, wherever you are. And if no road, the sky.

Entry No. 5

Trying to remember and trying to forget: the insoluble dialectic.

Stage 1: I will remember.

Stage 2: I will forget.

Stage 3: I will remember what it is to forget.

To not remember: sometimes it has its purpose. It's just that that purpose is not clear at the moment of, or passage towards, oblivion.

Entry No. 6

And after Dee?

After all that I still wanted, still needed to write. The impulse that had wended into me that one night would not leave. When I was writing Dee's life and could catch myself in the act of writing it and observe myself for a moment, I noticed this strange, subtle vigor filled my body: I was strong enough to press on through life in this world. When I abandoned Dee's life that vigor abandoned me. I wanted it back. I wanted to feel that I could endure. I could not go back to Dee's life to find that feeling; I felt too much guilt for abandoning him. A few times I tried to go back and wind-up Dee's life. I could not. When I would set out to write more of his story, I would see his shadow and I would look away in shame; if he turned and looked at me, he would look at me with the recognition of a predator whose hard and determined glare picks out the weak and soft parts of his prey. I could not bear to look back on Dee's life and find staring back at me from the darkness a pair of eyes more my own than my own. I could not look back at Dee because he was sequestered in a world that has passed by or had been passed by. If I continued looking back at Dee I could never look forward, and I wanted to find something to look forward to each day, something other than the bad soup and the bread and my occasional pilgrimage round the yard. I didn't want to look back at Dee, a man who never existed and whose story was never told. I wanted to look forward to another life, yes, another life in my life. Dee's would not do. I wanted to have another life that would not become a poltergeist that would follow me around and punish me for failing to complete it and leave it at some fitting final resting place. If I were to avoid the reoccurrence of that fate, then I needed a subject to be unimpeachably real: with a fictitious subject, the onus would be on me, the creator, to make the subject's life cogent and authentic enough to be accepted by the rational imagination, but with a real subject, I have no responsibilities and can merely sit, observe and watch a life go by in one direction or another, forward or back, noting what happens as it happens.

I tried to think of life, what it resembled, whether it had some physical shape I could imagine. But that did not work. Life, too fragmented and too disparate, is fleeing and moving at incredible speeds through rapidly flickering light of alternating brilliance and absence like shadows on the lawn of leaves departing branches in a sudden gust of wind in the vibrant late light of fall. Life always goes elsewhere and gathers, heaps, mounds, and accumulates there, somewhere you don't expect because you have not lived enough of that life for the experience of it to be incorporated into your being through the transmutation of experience into memory and then from memory to who you are. I could not imagine life as a whole, stable thing, rather as something that proceeds or through which we proceed. I began to think of where my life could go: the future. I needed a subject with prospects, a future. To have a future, something must have existed and must still exist. And to exist there must be in the beginning a world or a potential world. But when I thought of a world that exists in which a subject with a future could itself exist, I could only think of memories.

For so long I tried not to remember. Memory was the enemy: to remember life invited anguish, resentment, depression, guilt, anger, shame. If I were to survive here, I reasoned, I needed to protect myself from remembering too much, too much. To remember that I had been a person, a freer one at that, that I too had been free in my way to roam the wide world or spend some time in a still place upon it, alone or with the ones I love and tolerate, debilitated me. My life so far in the camp had taught me what Dee would have learned from the birds and angels had I allowed him to exist long enough, namely that around every life you live in this world may grow a second life lived in a second world. Not everyone will see it, let alone know that such a second life can be brought into the world; it is rare knowledge that waits for the desultory ones, the ones who are dispossessed of life on the earth and forced to live within themselves in blank destitution. Your first life in your first world, of course, is what you live: experience. But then as time passes those experiences are passed through a sieve, and what remains of experience are the elements of that second world whose constituent parts, its fundamental elements, are memories. Everyone who seeks to may thus live twice: an experienced life and a remembered life. The first nourishes the second, which in turns renews and invigorates a world for the first life to be lived.

I wanted this double life as soon as I realized it was possible. One's lived life needs protection from the effect of these gales from the past, to be safe and dry beneath some canopy when the torrents pour. Yet since my experienced life is limited to this cell, this place, this world, my remembered life is so massive in comparison that it overwhelms all experience and reverses the way one's double life should be lived: rather than experience percolating into memory which in turn nourishes experience, the first step is omitted and rudderless memory transmutes into experience, but not normal lived experience; rather, here memory is at the center of the world, where it creates the experience of re-membering, which is something apart and different from living life, a sensory experience that, because so many of our hours are committed to preparation, routine and reflection, amounts to only a few small, intense hours of feeling. Those hours are massive, heavy with experience. They set the world on fire. They enrich and deepen the rest of life as you live it from their location just beyond the horizon where the eye cannot perceive anything but the boundless possibility of tomorrow. I wanted this richness of experience, this depthless arcing of life forward through time. I wanted to disrobe myself of this phantas-magorical greatcoat and to reclaim my experienced life — living — meager as it is — from memory's whelm. To do that? Write down all the memories. Write them all down. Experience writing them down, experience putting them into the lived world. That way you concentrate the stuff of remembrance into the small presence of some words on some paper and you see it for what it really is: a presence in the life you live, a stolid presence in experience that you keep around and dip into from time to time as you please. And then you go on past the horizon where the world is new. That's what you do: you go on.

That's what I wanted to do. I began to make common cause with memory, writing down whatever it brought back to me and finding life in the experience of writing down these experiences that, once material, are no realer than what they are imagined to be when recollected in tranquility. I wrote them down and collected them. And then they were taken from me — and then they were gone. Now I write them again knowing they may be gone again someday. But, for these heavy good moments of life, this second life, they are here with me, protecting me, sheltering me.

Entry No. 7

I dreamed I was awake and woke to find myself dreaming again: it was nighttime. The first thought I had was that my house was on fire. My eyes adjusted to the dark and I remembered where I was. My house, in flames or not, was far away. I would not see it and I would not know if it burned. We had fires down behind the house when I was a kid, and then I started thinking of remembering my childhood then thought better of it: couldn't think of any good reason to remember the good and innocent times now that I am here since remembering them would only defeat me and my goal of living a life beyond mere memories again. Sat around instead and wiggled the toes, noticed the chthonic throbbing of my teeth again, how could such pain avoid notice. Again, thought of a house on fire, pushed it aside, thought about rain. Went for my constitutional in the yard, fell as soon as I was outdoors, the muscles have atrophied so. Guards laughed, one slapped my bottom, another came up and kicked me in the thigh just for show. I lay there awhile and observed the dirt. It smelled of our soup. Arose betimes, came back in, the foul odor of this place immediately perceptible after having drawn breaths elsewhere.

I shall take up my task again. I shall endeavor to remember some things, childish things I've put away, withdraw for inspection and attestation some memories of being a child, rather of having been a child.

There was a load of cows that got loose that one time and then the slaughter of my kinfolk: aside from that, my childhood was uneventful. My father was not a member of the Party, I swear this on his memory, may his memory always be a blessing. My mother was good; I speak no ill of her nor think it either. Family: an anonymous family, one of the many in the valley, seeking neither fame nor glory, just subsistence and time enough. Not political animals of any sort, we were not agitators. We lived in the valley and tended to our cattle, selling their milk at the market every week, and renting out grazing space to the cows of others for a small sum. Nothing of interest. Nothing anyone would remember because nothing of interest. A common tragedy.

Except — except there was a small library one could walk to, yes, there was such a quaint edifice, one could walk to this library from our hovel in under an hour if one walked with purpose and avoided the highwaymen. One would walk past emerging haystacks and a distant bell tower, and the bell tower's shadow would have grown so long by the time one reached the library. When I was not helping my family move vats of milk to the market, my parents allowed me, as a reward, to take an afternoon to myself. I have many such afternoons to myself now, but back then it was a reward, not punishment. Me and the afternoon: what fair light. Those afternoons I went to the library and read in the library. The world seemed more immense in there, more immense than what I could live of it, a little larger than the universe. And in that immense place which, like other places and institutions we remember from childhood, is likely much smaller than I remember it, one could read. The collection was not massive: there were more books on engineering and mathematics — practical, functional things — than *belles lettres*, but there was a smattering of magazines wherein one read stories and poems. I don't remember the library in fact, its rooms and such, librarians &c, but I remember reading those stories and poems there and the pleasant feelings of elevation and dislocation reading them gave me. Their content has escaped me. But they were stories and poems, literary artifacts of a kind, of this we may be sure, at least of this. Yes, once upon a time there were stories and poems and they satisfied a while, moving one elsewhere to a new and exciting place that is not the place where one read them. Aside from one little calf named Looloo whom I loved dearly until she too perished from the rinderpest, after which I never let myself grow close to a bovine again, those stories and poems became my best friends. And like many friends, I could not remove them from where they were kept, that library, I could not risk being seen in their presence or rather with their presence upon me, they had to stay where they were, quarantined from without. Even as a dull and stupid little boy I knew the danger of the presence of certain books in one's library record. Yet I was and am grateful to those little friends of mine for permitting me those assignations. They taught me to find recourse in my imagination to confront the troubles I was sure to encounter in life as well as those I had already encountered, such as the loss of my beloved Looloo and the memory of my kinfolk's decimation. Those stories and poems showed me a way to live. And I believe that I have lived. Belief: I have no proof, but I believe that I lived, and I believe that those little stories and poems showed me a way to live. But that is all. Let it end there.

But wait.

I remember a book from the library that I read. I did what I ought not to have done: I took it home. My life of social deviancy, it seems, began early. I remember the book, but I cannot remember what it was about. I remember looking at the gilded spine of the book on the shelf, the book with its golden arabesques around a title and name I cannot recall, and a feeling swelled inside my heart: an impulse to take it and possess it. And that is what I did. I looked to my left and my right, leaned closer to the shelf, slid my hooked index finger over the top of book until I could grasp it with my left hand and slip it into my rucksack. I walked out of the library into the lengthening afternoon shadows and walked home. By the time I reached our front door, daylight had gone out of the world and a candid moon had settled in the sky. I went down the hallway to my room and opened the book.

My mother and father were out behind the house that evening, which they only had time to do one day of the week, so it must have been a Sunday evening, and music floated into our house from the valley, sweet sounds, no tubas, just rhythms and voices, and my parents stood outside in the dark, listening. I had secluded myself somewhere reading and I heard the music, the voices choiring and drums pushing the voices forward into our home, and I remember that I read a book that night, my parents outside in the darkness and the music from the valley but the book, ah the book, I can't remember.

I remember the way that I read. I was a very disrespectful boy. No, I take that back: I was a very good boy, I was not as deviant as I say, rare were the occasions I received a clout on my bottom, rarer at least than the smacks I receive here in the camp, but as it went for reading, I was very disrespectful of the author's intent, dare I say I was rebellious. I did not respect the author's desire that the pages be read one-two-three &c, no, books were a game to me, and I hopscotched through chapters. And I felt vertigo from passing through chapters in that way. But the vertigo was not unpleasant, rather it was revelatory, it revealed a different way to see, where time's power was not so readily and fearfully respected. An example: a child would be playing in his backyard and then a man would be bitten by a viper on a very distant island, and then the man would be introduced into the story as the prodigal uncle of the child, returning to make him the king of his ancestral home, and the man would be returning home on a boat in the bay and his father saw the ship glimmering in the light on the bay and knew yes, yes this is him, my son is returned at long last O I never thought I'd see the day nor my son again alive in this world that is passing strange, and the father ran out to meet his son, but he was dying from the bite of the viper, dying slowly, and his father would reach him and hold him in his arms, and then the story began and once upon a time there was a time. Reading that way, the game of a child, was the only way I wanted to read, a way of making the world ignore time and its oppressive logic. Now that I remember reading that way, hopscotching through chapters and turning a story that someone else wrote into a story of my own, I realize it brought to me the sense of the way I imagined death approaches someone and shows him his life, or the way that someone approaching his death sees his life flickering before him in episodic filigrees, however it is that death comes or one comes to death, to the end, yes, that does not matter, in the end a man must see his life flickering before him in episodic filigrees, the law ordering the images unknown, oh it was too mortifying, every image too intense for someone my age. I became a traditional reader for a time, beginning at the first page, come what may.

And now the book that I read is returning to me, fragments shored against time. The book began with the man and the man was not like most men in books; he was a passive man, a man remembering his nights as a boy. *Sometimes I would be in my bed as the late light of twilight fled, a book in my hand, and find myself drowsing,* it began. *And I would drift off into a most pleasant sleep, the sound of my parents and their guests in conversation downstairs pacifying me as my breathing began to take on the mechanical patter of a clock, keeping time but not aware of it.* Perhaps that's how it began. A strange beginning that did not mark the start of any kind of discernable tale, more like a book that dipped into the stream of someone's conversation with himself and pulled up what it found and, having no choice, began to construct a story from what it found in that moment.

Perhaps it continued: *But I was not a child,* perhaps it continued, *I was myself, now, a man. Somehow the crackle of burning logs in the fireplace and the power of sleep removed me from my present state and sent me back to a different time, a time when I cared for less, worried for less, felt at home in myself* and at home in the world. *I was a child again, free.* If that is how the story went on, then it seems I was reading a history of a life I had yet to live. And if that was the case — let us say it was the case once upon a time — to see how I would live, how I could live, I read on.

I remember a story my father told me about my grandfather, a botanist who would permit my father to accompany him on his sojourns. They had gone to a small atoll off the coast of the largest island near the mainland, so small that it will not appear on any map. The strangeness of the reports coming from this atoll was inversely proportional to its size; that is to say, its strangeness was enormous. The rumor was that there existed on the atoll a certain herb that the natives would consume in copious but measured amounts. While some might consider the herb a traditional psychotropic drug, its effects were far more potent. When ingested en masse, *as was the tradition among the inhabitants, they would fall silent for several moments betimes until the most beautiful, most profound thing would come to pass: they would break out in song, together, choiring. And these songs were not rehearsed or even previously in existence; they were songs that were never written. They sang new songs they had invented as a collective, which they would sing all day into nightfall, at which point they would end their song and never sing it again. It was believed that, upon the ending of their song, they entirely forgot the song they had sung.*

This herb's effect of catalyzing creativity while proffering amnesia was of very great interest to the government of my father's homeland, in particular to the national artistic secretariat: if you could create art without the creator remembering its creation, there was no limit to the profit you could reap. Such a heady profit going directly into the government's coffers without the complications that arise from taxing income of a petulant citizenry could fund any number of things: roads, palaces, new and beautiful wars. And so, my grandfather, in the service of his king, began his journey to this fabled atoll to research the prospects of harvesting this herb, my father in tow.

When they arrived, they were shocked. But for ragged palms and low shrubbery, the atoll was barren. The natives were gone and, with them, the herb. What remained were gaggles of giant hares rhythmically chortling in groups, sunbathing tortoises, darting sloths, and the birds in the trees. What had happened? Where were the natives? Where was the herb? My father and his father timidly explored the atoll together, finding nothing worth remembering before they left.

Why this fractured memory comes to mind, I do not know. Thoughts have their own adherence to the tide, and some memories rush in and inundate the tawdry shores of consciousness before receding whence they came. In this instance, I reckon it came about as a consequence of my contemplation on the very nature of memory, how these moving images are, as a function of routine, created and forgotten. When one goes to seek out the source, one falls upon a meaningless coterie of disconnected objects, shored against complete and utter ruin, be they giant hares or otherwise.

What kind of book was I reading? What was my life? *Nothing, perhaps, my life resembled nothing, because this isn't life, this is memory; and yet, as I write, it does become, in its own way, life, does it not? The brightness of the sun, the light glinting off the cornice of my desk in the afternoon, the shadows distending with the day's occurrences, the closed bedroom door, the hushed flicker of the fire, the sudden onset of drowsiness at night; these fragments gathering themselves together as a part of some ancient routine; is all of this not life?* No, I think now, that is not life, that is remembrance. You drag up a memory or a memory drags itself up, nothing to do about it, remembrance isn't life, life follows a progression, time has its laws that remembrance does not obey. To remember is to defile time. A book that remembers makes its reader wander, the slight divagations from the route wending their way further and further off into an undiscovered land, eyes pass over the same words the author wrote but the mind drifts off, establishing its own colony in the book that the eyes surveille. And when the book ends? You leave, you do not return, the colony is razed by life's rioting. But no one will dispute that that colony existed once upon a time, the briefest possibility of a new way of ordering the world in the night alone upstairs in between the covers of a book, my republic of night. And the book will endure.

And if it does not? Ah well. There are other books to burn, other republics to raze.

What could have happened after I was reading? Perhaps nothing; perhaps I never read a book like this; perhaps everything I have written above was never written by the author of that book, perhaps that book never existed, perhaps the author never existed, perhaps this memory remembers nothing that happened, and I have invented it now. As a kind of consolation. A tender one at that, even if fictive, contrived.

If this book existed and my memory of having read it is a true memory, then while I drowsed in my bed that evening someone took the book from me and threw it into a fireplace, covered it with logs and lit everything on fire just like they did before. By the time I could remember that the book was missing there would have been nothing but cold ash, the music from the valley would have been stilled, and I would have begun to forget what it was I had read that night so long ago.

Let us forget this book if this book ever was a book, if this book ever existed. Let us put an end to books. They have put an end to books for the benefit of the commonweal but let us do it of our own volition this time. Let us move on.

Perhaps I remember other things from my childhood. When the men bought their motorcycles, they stopped praying.

No, something else.

Birds, perhaps.

Yes, birds.

I wonder what birds would think if they knew what we thought of them. Do you think birds would act differently if they knew how much they pop up in our conversations, how we watch them do their birdy things, how we catalogue them? How we turn them into emblems of freedom, that you can feel *free as a bird*, that we look to them flying through the sky and wish we could be like that too, going wherever we want at very great heights far from the mute and baleful earth? Would they become self-conscious, jaded, cynical? What would birds do if they knew that we watch them circle out over the ocean, cawing at some mackerel before turning back towards the shore to glide onto a dune, or circling high in the sky for what seems to be all day until descending faster than lightning onto a rodent no one could see skittering across a field, or skating through the gusts of wind near a mountain-top with a short thrust of the wing, and wonder what it would be like if our days too could be passed in like pleasures rather than days passed in regret for what we did and remorse for what we did not? A bird flies on or does not fly. A bird does not think of how it would fly if only everything were in its place in the world, if only it had no obligations that need tending to to dissipate its anxiety and permit it to fly freely and single-mindedly unencumbered by the impingement of the quotidian to-do, no, the birds do not worry over all this, they just fly.

I remember a hummingbird. Let me consider the hummingbird.

How excited we grew when a hummingbird approached one of our flowers out on the porch — what glee it was we felt. It's summertime, the flowers are in bloom, the sun has yet to rise but there is light in the sky, a lax golden hint of the day that will come. And you, sitting at the kitchen table waiting for the coffee to cool so that you can take a sip, thinking about going out to the cows, the cows and their mooing and they have so many stomachs, or thinking about whether they will bring enough accordions and tubas for the musicians to play, will the market have enough eggs, how is this life, what is this life. And you are wondering how the rest of this day, unique like every other day, will distinguish itself when a swift shadow passes across the veranda: a hummingbird! And the hummingbird is approaching the thatch of trumpet creepers, zinnias and hyacinths, the columbine, the bottlebrush, and the sage, the trumpetbush, fool's bane and fuchsia. You planted all these flowers hoping that a hummingbird would come by some day and drink their nectar; and here is that day. The hummingbird seems to dart out of nothing, a bird born in and borne by shadow. It is propelled by those rapidly fluttering wings whose flapping you hear as a nervous, vital hum. And you're staring at it, excited and entranced, because it seems to defy the laws of nature, it seems to be bucking science, it looks as though it has decided to ignore gravity and levitate, to drink nectar from the bells of the flowers, the trumpet creepers, zinnias and all the others, but in particular the eternal hyacinth. The bird will stay here for only a few moments, and in those few moments, a peace beyond words overtakes you. You do not worry about going to work soon, nor the traffic on the roads, nor the cows or the eggs or the accordions or tubas or the vagrants or that malevolent van that comes to the valley to collect your kinfolk and neighbors seemingly at random, but perhaps it is all by some dark design, you don't think about those things right now. You feel joy. You feel joy, and you know the joy is evanescing because the hummingbird will be gone soon, off to explore other plants in other places, and with that hummingbird will go your joy — your momentary stay against waking life — that moments before seemed beyond the reach of time. And what's more, you know that in a few months the bells on these plants will wither and die; the hummingbird will not be back for whole seasons when in the winter months she follows the flyway south and follows the paths diverging across the islands in the southern sea.

You remember the bee hummingbird, which weighs less than a penny. You've dreamed of seeing one one day. These tiny birds are the smallest of every bird you could ever hope to see, but you will never see a bee hummingbird. They are endemic to one area on earth, the archipelago in which your valley rests, and particularly to the region of the big, flat-sided residual hills that rise like hasty mistakes in geology surrounded by long, flat alluvial plains. Your grandmother saw a bee hummingbird perhaps, and perhaps on seeing the bird outside the window of her uncle's hovel on the plain where the donkeys were lowing outside, she felt the same rush of excitement, the same rapture you feel now, and her mind flew to a metaphor, thinking about how free she could be if she were that small and could fly. Maybe she would fly back in time if she could. Fly back to when her father would bring her out to the field where he tended to his potatoes. He would have her check the shoots for certain kinds of bugs that even the goldfinch wouldn't eat. Sometimes in the afternoon he would fry potatoes and perhaps she would eat them with a gulp of cold water from his canteen, and he would ask her to hold her hands together under the donkey's mouth so he could pour water into them for the donkey to lap up with his tongue tickling her palms. And then her father would say, Look, Look, there's the thrush, can you hear how it sings? And he would start whistling the thrush's song, and the thrush would respond in kind; then he would whistle again, only slightly differently this time, and the thrush would respond differently, again corresponding to her father's whistle. If you are good at whistling and you listen, he would say, you can talk to the birds and they will talk back to you. Then he would begin to whistle again and wait for the response, but a sudden rustle in the forest would flush all the birds out of the trees and make them flee hither and yon. Her father looked down at the ground, the color gone out of his face, and that's what she remembered, the face of her father that day, because they took him that night and the next morning he was gone, and her mother made her go live at her uncle's house in the *mogotes*, where she'd see the bee hummingbird stop by her window and she'd wonder if it had spoken to her father. But this bird wouldn't sing, only flap its wings, which made a small quiet hum as it drank from the *flor de Jericó*. Perhaps the bee hummingbird, even though it didn't sing, had passed by a bird that talked to her father once and they communicated in their own special bird way, and the finch told the bee hummingbird that her father was okay, and he would be back soon. She wished she could be as small as the bee hummingbird and fly away. Then she could evade anyone, being that small and able to fly she could go anywhere. She could be free. Maybe the birds began talking to each other more after her father was taken, talking about the different humans coming into the forest, how they spoke with different accents and laughed different laughs and even when they tried to whistle at the birds they whistled with accents, they whistled as though they were from another place and grew up talking to different birds from a different land. And maybe those people knew something about her father and the birds could hear them talking about him and how wonderful he was doing and that he'd be back soon because he loved her and maybe the birds sang to each other and a nightingale would fly to her window and sit there singing to her of her father while the bee hummingbird hovered nearby, small and in night's trenchant dark nearly obscure. She was small, it's true, but not as small as the bee hummingbird, nobody was. What's more, she couldn't even fly, so she was stuck in that land until one day she wasn't, and then she could never go back, could never again see the bee hummingbird, which she now began to call a new name in her new tongue so that her new compatriots would understand what she was talking about when she talked about the bee hummingbird. She would miss her father, the *flor de Jericó* alongside her window, the *mogotes* that she came to recognize as her home only after she'd gone, the donkey lowing in the vespertine heat by her window outside, the call of the thrush and the nightingale; but most of all she missed her father again and all the little things he did that she couldn't forget, how he'd wipe the sweat from his forehead and adjust his hat by its brim or suck on his upper lip when he focused on something, or how he'd fry up potatoes for her and for the donkey before talking to birds. She would wonder if he had always talked to birds, if the birds of the island knew about her father and still remembered him, the man who is almost one of us, or at least talks with us sometimes, and although he mostly says nonsense, we humor him because he tries, and it is a generous, loving nonsense he speaks. Perhaps she would think of the bee hummingbird when she saw how small her children looked crawling around the begonias in the yard. Perhaps she would think of her father when she saw her son focused on fixing his motorcycle in the garage, sucking his lip the same way her father did, and she would almost ask her son if he ever thought of talking to birds. Perhaps she thought about telling her grandchildren about the bee hummingbird when they asked what birds she saw when she was a little girl in the place she was from, and she thought about telling them but realized she couldn't tell them, it would be no use, perhaps they were too young or too late to understand the way the *mogotes* rose up from the core of the earth and the *sitieras* and the plains, how the hairs on the donkey's nape stuck up when he drank water from her hands, most of all how could they ever understand what the bee hummingbird meant to her, how could they ever understand when I myself can't understand? How do I justify a memory I don't even possess?

Maybe someday you will see a bee hummingbird and you will call it by its true name, but not today. Today you have to be satisfied with the ruby-throated hummingbird at your veranda sniffing the columbine. Today you will have to be satisfied only with your love of the bee hummingbird, the bird that does not consider itself distinct if it considers itself at all, ignorant of the joy it always brought you because it never did anything it could recognize as special or unusual, just doing what it always did for generation after generation, even back to a time when the god of war was depicted as a hummingbird because the bird's sharp beak mimicked the instruments of violence, an icon the hummingbird never knew because the hummingbird only followed its intrinsic desire to drink sweet nectar from flowers, never adjusting its behavior because of the weight of a man's gaze, never stopping to consider what a girl is thinking about when she is looking closely at that bird sipping nectar from a bloom.

But then consider, my love, if birds do that already. And we are the ignorant ones, the observed.

And the valley was on fire.

These memories won't suffice. They are not even memories. They are frescoes drawn to prettify the blankness of immuring walls. Let us remember other things.

Entry No. 8

Today something from the past began to come to my mind but then it de-murred and receded and took the path to oblivion. Aside from the sense of a memory's presence, nothing remembered today.

Entry No. 9

In the yard this morning for my constitutional. Unusual light outside. Glad to be outside for a bit even if only to confirm my suspicions that daylight still comes around from time to time. I had grown unsure whether the old diurnal rhythm still abided. Good to find out it does or did the while I was out there. Cannot confirm if daylight is singular or quotidian. Must investigate further, my captors permitting.

Wondrous things to behold out there in daylight. In the yard. Our yard, our field to roam. The other campers in the yard, lounging at ease, all waiting for something whose nature they will not know until it has come and gone; only then will they know what they'd waited for, and only then shall they begin waiting for confirmation that what they'd waited for was indeed what they'd thought it was and not something other than what they are again waiting for now. Fellow campers waiting, some eventually going to the foundries and factories and some bound elsewhere; some urns I saw, shards of them right near a trough; bands rehearsing, possibly a performance this evening. I will not attend.

But foremost in my memory of what I experienced on my little ramble is another bird that I saw. And not so much the bird but its eyes. My constitutional concluding, my gaolers guided me back to my block. And as the entrancing stultification of the process of remitting me to my quarters began, I felt something looking at me, the weight of a heavy gaze. I looked up to where I felt this pressure emanating from and saw that bird. Plumes shifting between violet and dark brown, iridescent. But those eyes: they were the eyes of another thing no less a stranger to the sky and air yet no more than a bird is human. No, I can't place it — those eyes, I felt the sultry breeze of recognition — mutual recognition. Perhaps we'd seen each other before and birds are much more memorious than we prideful apes account them to be, I don't know, there was a definite and palpable something there. The bird seemed wary of me considering too much, because as these feelings of familiarity crested in me, she glanced off and flew pleasantly past the chimneys. And that bird was gone.

Something about the eyes, some dark entrancing brown color flecked with some iridescence, not unlike the plumage. Must be a name for the color. My knowledge thereof is feeble. I don't know — shiny brown? Wolfsbane? Tumbleweed? No idea. Who would know, I don't know, women seem to know colors much better than men. My wife could see colors, she always helped me in that regard, my wife knew colors and the reason for colors. She knew about birds too, colors, birds, light, she'd never tell me, she knew the secrets of the breeze. Knows? Knew? Knows.

Now I am remembering. Now I am remembering. Now I remember meeting my wife, oh, I do yes, I do.

Yes, I remember meeting my wife. Who would not? Surely you remember the moment you encounter certain people and that moment often marks the start of an enduring presence in your life, a presence as obdurate as the present which, just as the present is, is always passing on from experience to memory; it seems my wife is one of those passed-on presences that now endures only in my memories, one of many though first among equals, that woman, she who was or is my wife. I was on a train heading north, on leave from the service. I had been conscripted into the forces as were all boys back then; I was conscripted and I served, with distinction or not I don't remember. I was lucky to be on that train. The trains never run on time and are always delayed for one reason or another or no reason at all but still I just barely made it on before the train departed. I note here, to clarify for my own purposes, that I am not the most punctual person. Not the most punctual, no; I am not punctual at all, in any way, shape or form. Timeliness, despite the regimented behavior we were instructed in at the academy, was never a talent or skill I acquired. Mathematics, biology, chemistry, history, martial arts, the janitorial sciences — these subjects I mastered. But I was always late for the lessons. My tardiness caused copious demerits and even more clouts on my exposed bottom in front of the class. I have forgotten the instructors who smacked me, and I am glad of that. May others remember them. As for me, I was otherwise an excellent student and a fine marksman. But I was never punctual. I was always late, too late, and now I am far too late.

My belated arrival ensured few seats remained on the train. I consequently had no choice — choice, one hardly ever comes across one of those, a choice — I had no choice but to choose one among a row of empty seats adjacent to the bathroom, which discharged a hideous odor. It truly was foul. Fouler even than the duncan down the hallway from my quarters in the camp. It was that bad. Truly odoriferous. In any event, I sat there quietly and anonymously, bothering no one and inviting no mischief, surely thinking about the time I would have to myself when I returned home and what I would do on my leave when, several stations later and many gaps minded, a young woman walked onto the train. I looked up at her and I saw her.

I swear that she was the most beautiful, resplendent, glorious person who has ever walked, crawled, or stumbled to and fro upon this world. I swear to this although I cannot remember many other people or their appearance and whether that appearance was pleasing or disgusting. But I trust my word. Yes, my word is what I have, better than my vision. My eyesight has never been very good, I can't always trust what I see. And yet I can declare with utmost certainty that she was peerless. Hair of black iridescence rested gently in gentler waves on her shoulders and framed a face whose color was dark olive illuminated by a subtle honeyed hue that seemed to pulsate outwards with radiance; she would always shine brightest in the early morning. Her hair faintly flickered in the stiff air of the cabin as she moved down the aisle, and she had the slightest of widow's peaks. She was not tall at all, no, much shorter than I am and I am not tall at all, and her figure was slight, taking up no more space on earth than needed. Nothing wasted, nothing superfluous or redundant, everything about her with its purpose in its place. Yes, I remember these features of her appearance, perhaps I will remember more later.

I hoped she would walk by me just so I could look at her longer and closer and gather more of her effulgence into me, just so she would bless me momentarily with her presence, just so I could tell myself later at times like these that I had been a witness to her, perhaps she was even wearing a fine perfume that would momentarily cover up the bathroom's stench. But she did not walk by. Forgoing another seat further on in the cabin if any seats remained, she deftly lifted her luggage and stood on tiptoes to place her luggage in the overhead compartment before she sat down. And when she sat down, she sat down next to me. Having seated herself, she smiled at me as strangers will smile to strangers in greeting under public transportation's typical conditions of compulsory proximity. Then she looked down and pulled a book to her face and began to read it. I presumed she was literate, and the years to come proved me right. Back then I did not know if she could read or only held a book up to her face so others would think she could read to engage in the self-torture that is respectability. It did not matter. I sat next to her transfigured and enraptured. She had deracinated me already.

The train moved along, she read or feigned literacy while I fidgeted and adjusted my posture with concerning frequency. Naturally, I looked at her as well, that too with concerning frequency, maybe twelve times in twenty minutes, perhaps more in less time, I wasn't counting, I should have counted, specifics are requisite for accurate recollection, now I can only remember that I looked at her repeatedly. I aimed for discretion and hit upon what I supposed was the ingenious tactic of hiding every momentary but intense glance at her in a sweeping visual observation of my environs: I would gaze at her before moving my eyes slowly from her along the room, sometimes turning my head as well to increase the appearance of nonchalance, as though my happening to look at her was inherent in any man's disinterested examination of his world. Yet I suspect she gathered at approximately observation #7 that it was a rather piddling ruse on my part to hide my infatuation with her from her, that I could not keep myself from looking at her: no one need observe a train's interior as often as I did. It would make sense that she surmised this. I have no proof she surmised this nor did she ever admit as much, but I believe it to be so, and for this memory belief will suffice.

All those brilliantly hidden glances were not enough for me. I had to choose: luxuriate in her presence however long she remained before she left my world forever or invite her to acknowledge me. It had to be a good form of acknowledgment, she had to see me in a fair light, not something wretched such as tripping and falling or a paroxysm of some kind or eating chocolate cake from my trouser pockets. No, I had to impress upon her that I was impressive and desirable, an intriguing fellow. Confident, even. And so, I began to thump my left foot up and down — I remember now I was always inclined to rhythm, often stealing into the music hall at the academy at night to play the timpani — in the hope she would notice me. She did not notice me. The occasion called for something more decisive, more drastic. Something like talking to her.

"I see you're reading a book," I said. I couldn't confirm that she could read but I had to wager she could.

She looked up at me and — and she smiled a smile I have never been able to forget however much I have tried to forget everything. Perhaps it was not so much the smile itself as the way her smile spread through her face and shifted her plump cheeks upward before radiating whatever light the smile shot off into her large, bright, shining oval eyes looking directly at me and into me that seemed to make the world a more luminous, more worthy place. I was transfixed and must have looked shocked if not also clearly in love. And I was.

She chuckled three or four sweet soft chuckles. "I am," she said as she placed a bookmark between some pages of the book with a languid movement of her long dexterous fingers and sat the book on her lap; she rested her hands, the right hand draped over the left, on top of the book, and she looked at me with what was now a faint smile shadowed with blooming affection, her head cocked just slightly to the right — the cock of curiosity.

The cock of curiosity — no, that won't do. Stupid, stupid man and your stupid, stupid proclivity for consonance. Leave the words alone, let them come as they will, anything you do with them will never really get to the gist of what it is you're trying to get across. Words do not suffice. Acknowledge that: words do not suffice. But they must. There is nothing else. Only words. Nothing else. Words and silence and nothing else.

Back to the matter.

And so, it was she looked at me with her head cocked just slightly to the right in a look of something or other. We began to talk; not even the overpowering, eminently disgusting stench of the lavatory could impinge on us.

Were we kids? From this vantage we were. Perhaps we were not — I had been trained to fire a gun to kill a man dead and she was already a woman. Perhaps we had put childish things away and saw the world as it was. Kids or not, it was love that we felt. True love. Some may consider it gauche to speak of true love, but I speak of it anyway because this world is beyond all consideration: it was true love. And true love calls for courage. Although I served in the forces, the most courage I ever had to muster was when I dared to speak to that woman, particularly in the onslaught of the repugnant fetor emanating from the toilet. Yes, courage: I had it once. And love: I had it once. I had fallen in love, and I believe she had too. We had the courage to love and to continue to love: we have been together ever since. Or were together: I do not know if she knows I am alive, or if I was declared dead and she has since moved on and remarried, or something else — yes, there must be something else, some other awareness she has of me, there must be, perhaps I will find it as I go through these memories. But I move on from this thought to another: to be able to sit next to her was a blessing that makes my interment here worthwhile. No. I remember the beatings and the claptrap they call food around here and the deprivations and the ceaseless boredom and I resolve to amend my prior statement: to sit next to her was a blessing that almost makes my interment here worthwhile. Almost.

We continued to talk while we sat on the train, whispering and smiling as though thick as thieves, and a corpulent old harridan shushed us for conversing so inconsiderately when she was dealing with the most indefatigable headache and our flirty back-and-forth was no help at all — so we smiled and looked at each other and I tried to hide my smile because one ought not feel such joy on first meeting someone, or at least one ought not show it, no, prudence calls for patience. But I couldn't wait, nor could she, no. I do not remember what we talked about, I only remember the world we made out of the words we spoke to each other — the forest and not the trees as it were — and that our conversation seemed to last no more than the sun in wintertime before we disembarked from the train at our various points, but not before we exchanged whatever information we needed to reach each other. Address, phone, clan. We were not so far apart. It could work, I thought — no, I thought, it must work, this is the only way, this way, or no way. We had to be together. And we were.

It took time. Of course, it did. Good things come to those who wait, &c. Everything takes time, and nothing gives time back.

I had to complete my service in the forces. I did not do much at all. I waited. I never saw the field, the theatre of war. I don't remember. There were noises there but nothing that signaled imminent conflict. I thought of her then, I wrote of her, wrote to her, wrote long letters, no response, letters have trouble passing through a front, letters have their own little fates among the stars. Many letters sent and none received. No matter. Service concluded shortly thereafter, my hand was shaken, and my lapel pinned, and I returned to the valley, not many were left there, my parents surely were, ah how they beamed. I lounged there for a bit, helping out with the cows, my father's spine having grown twisted and his hands gnarled, I think he might have become a linden tree. He hobbled along for a while until he did not. Club foot perhaps, as well. What became of mother. What became of mother. What of mother? Perhaps another time. Another time I will remember the fate of my mother. The cows are all gone now, and the farm is decrepit now if it still stands. While it stood and while I was there, I applied for, was accepted by, and entered the school of law while the girl from the train studied mathematics, endeavoring as she did to find some internal coherence to the universe beyond what we readily order according to our own understanding of it. Between her second and third year of schooling and after my first year at the school of law, and after receiving from her family their blessing and giving in return a small but respectable dowry, we wed in a lavish but tasteful ceremony in the country, down in the valley, where my people had been. My family was small, but her extended family was large, and they readily accepted our scant clique into their tribe. Sitting at the wedding table at the reception, I heard the loons calling for each other as the waves lapped and the sun gently set over the lake, meagerly making its rays rake across the land so that the land appeared aflame, below the table her hand discretely clasping mine. I have often returned to that time and that place in my time here in the camp, if only in memory. Yet it grows fainter and farther away and the loons' calls grow weaker and smaller such that I begin to wonder if that world is not a fable that I invented both to console myself with the knowledge that my life was once resplendent and radiant and to afflict myself with the remembrance of such a resplendent and radiant time of life in this doleful time I inhabit now. My time in the camp is almost longer than my time as a free man wedded to her. Almost.

Nor am I obliged to explain what I mean by the word *love*. Love: like an aardvark, you know it when you see it; or, like a breeze or shame, you know it when you feel it regardless of its origin, within or without you. Peerless philosophers and poets have expended unquantifiable quantities of words explaining love and have got no nearer to showing what it is than a night-gazer has the dark side of the moon. We know it's there, but getting there with the rudiments of our beastly state is the labor of a fool, and I'm no fool. But even if I were a fool, even the most idiotic of the feeble-minded can feel love, its envelopment, its warmth, the feeling of coming back home. And I felt I'd gone home; I felt love.

I relive her now. Her hand runs over me, a hand of water, surprising, soothing, gone. Like more water, in time it dissolves everything or else many things. I feel myself dissolving, the rough elements of myself made discrete. Part of me is there with her then. Hidden in a secluded grotto, perhaps.

What I see of myself is bound to what I remember. I cannot help remembering her, or better said, parts of her. Those coruscating filaments of bright dark light that were her deep black hair in autumn wind, that humble fleeting look when she looks into your eyes and then looks away and down and she smiles that gladdened smile, the way she would prepare hot meals of porridge, sausage and gravy for refugees who begged for bread near our home. I remember meeting her and loving her.

And now I remember certain other scenes as well. I cannot help it. One remembers what memory impels one to remember. And I remember these sadder scenes, these images that heap upon me until my eyes well. To remember them reminds me of my failures and my weaknesses, failures that for all their faults prove that I was real and so were we. Because the marriage was real it was not spotless. It had its faults. We each had our faults. Hers are with her and mine with me, my faults, so many of them that, when examined, reveal that they are only extrapolations from one primal, original, true, and cardinal fault. My jealousy.

Ah. Why this now?

Examples. Stories. Anecdotes. Apercus. An illustration.

It must have been six months after the wedding. I say six months because that timespan seems to place this event in its proper timeframe: we had been together long enough that my naïveté had been tested but not yet broken. But I can't be sure. But let's say six months. Six months, then.

She had a conference coming up, she told me. A conference that her professors wanted her to attend, she was their favorite, a real star pupil. She would be travelling to a conference in the week to come and they would pay for her to go to the conference and learn about geodesics and in particular Riemannian manifolds, which I could never understand no matter how many times I nodded slowly with distant eyes to feign understanding when she would explain the concept to me. She would not be travelling alone; she would be travelling with another person, one she knew well, this fellow student in her department, a man. That is all it was: a trip and a man. That's all.

She told me this nonchalantly but not flippantly when we were in the kitchen. I was retrieving something from the icebox, and she told me she would be attending a conference that week with a member of her department. She told me and I accepted it. I accepted it outwardly. I must have forced a convincing smile and uttered good words of assent. I was otherwise consumed by roiling jealousy.

It was not the trip itself that roused my jealousy. I don't recall ever being so possessive that my wife's attending a conference would threaten my manhood or whatever threat it is that jealousy tries to neuter. No. It was that my impression of this trip was layered with memories of prior instances that each provoked a flicker of that feeling: the trip was the final coat of paint, itself composed of various extant elements, applied to a freshly laid lime plaster wall. Every occasion that triggered my jealousy alone would never be enough to make it endure, only enough to cause a transient anxiety that would invariably fade. But every instance gathered with every other instance created a sense of interplay, allusion, almost etymology: if you study the roots of words in our language, their origins, they gather several meanings distinct from their mere utility in a sentence such that the words catch fire, or become variegated, multifaceted, prismatic. The comment about the infeasibility of friendship with men because they inevitably grew to love her; that man from her class who continued pursuing her when we were together while she did nothing to dissuade him, inviting it, encouraged it rather; the spontaneous escapades that always left me fearing the next episode of impulsivity brought on by alcohol; that date she went on after we had met; everything. Each moment was its own volume of illuminated words, each volume belonging to a canon of jealousy, commenting on each other, offering exegesis, explanation, provocation, elucidation.

I have mixed my metaphors: books, painting, chemicals, words. I am not a storyteller, more of a storywatcher. I watch what comes out and transcribe it as it appears, including metaphors so mixed. I am too far along to remedy the situation and start over. They will have to stay. Perhaps that they are mixed means something. A layering. Enrichment. I don't know. I will let the images accumulate and entwine with each other. I will tear them apart shortly.

And so, she told me of this trip. I listened, smiled. I carried on. The possibility of transgression would not leave me. The trip was colored by those other memories.

An illustration.

Once we were discussing school friends we no longer knew, friends who were dear to us, who seemed to have secured a permanent place in our affections and our lives but had somehow been untethered and, like the sailor who wakes to find his skiff huddling on some foreign shore and only then remembers that he never set the anchor down, had drifted off elsewhere. "I've never been able to keep most of my guy friends," she said. "It's so hard for me to be friends with men; they're always attracted to me." Nothing alarming in itself, I don't think, that sentence. It was just one sentence, one sentence I remember, perhaps one of many in a conversation, a throwaway line. One sentence among many I'm sure, and those other sentences perhaps providing forgiving content, maybe the heart of our conversation was in those other sentences, she could have had something very important to say in those sentences that I now overlook, perhaps an explanation for the arrow of time or a unified field theory or the way that low-dimensional objects embedded in higher-dimensional objects inherit the characteristics of that higher-dimension object, who knows, then again perhaps the crook is part of the arrow's design and she explained it all, the fate of those other sentences we won't know, they with every other forgotten breath have joined the choir invisible, only that one sentence still lives, only that sentence do I remember; it was that sentence alone among the rest that survived, that prevailed, that remains, that lingers, that endures. She knew, or should have known, the effect that sentence would have on me. She knows, or knew, that every time she was alone with a man, I was wracked by the rack of worriment: for all her brilliance, she possessed an awesome gullibility that invariably guided her into distressing situations, or at least situations that distressed me enough to make me curl into a ball and wish for the wallpaper to bury me. There was the time at the university when a medical student she knew said to her, "Follow me into this room, I want to show you this new way to take your blood pressure," and like a child told to come hither to receive a gift, she obliged and followed; he closed the door, placed his fingers on her neck and kissed her, or tried to, I'm not sure, one does not try to kiss — consensually or not, one kisses or does not, there is no try unless you happen to be attuned to the threat and capable of an artful dodge. And she told me about this medical consultation when we were together in bed. It seemed an odd position to tell your lover that kind of story. Perhaps she told me so that I wouldn't worry about her hiding things from me, perhaps she wanted to allay my misery with radical candor, in any case she had no intention to make me break down in snot and hot tears, but every action beats back beyond intent. I told myself and tell myself that she told me so that I wouldn't worry, but she knew, or should have known, what it would make me do. It made me question her, her candor, her dedication, her love. But then we kissed, and I held her close and felt her skin on mine and smelled its scent and what a wonderful scent it was, sweet but not saccharine, the soft sweet smell of home, ah sweet it was, and my jealousy dissipated.

Another illustration.

One man had pursued her throughout her schooling, was onto her scent. Even after she and I met, even after we began a relationship, even when he learned we were together — I don't know how he learned but he did, at least he must have learned, otherwise things would not have become as they did, he knew, yes, he must have, even though he didn't know me nor I him but somehow, he knew — even then he continued his hunt, what a relentless pursuit, the envious hunter. And she had allowed herself to be caught before, to be snared. I knew this and tamped down the flame, but it smouldered and continued to, no, some fires will not be put out.

"I'm going to a party," she said one night. "Who with," I asked, "Some friends from school," she said, "friends from the department, you know," and I told her that sounded good and that I would miss her, sitting as I was at home, at my desk, doing something or other or nothing at all, perhaps tracing circles on a pad of paper. She went to the party, I had horrific jealous dreams and then the next morning she told me he'd been there, that man, and he lived close by, so they chose to walk home together, and of course reaching the terminus of their trek they turn to each other to say goodbye and he tries to kiss her. She told me she turned away. "Why even put yourself in a situation where you'd need to turn away," I said to her, she knew what his intentions were, he was no good, "you wouldn't have needed to turn away if you hadn't walked home with him," she looked at me and smiled and held my hand, no answer forthcoming, jealousy pursuing me.

I should mention, at the risk of betraying her confidence, that she is sweet and she's small and she's slight. People of such constitutions do not tend to take to their alcohol too well.

An illustration.

She does, or did, spontaneous and irresponsible things when drunk; she said this to me. She herself drew the illustration. She had taken a trip before she met me, and the illustration is brief: she met a man there who gave her a ride on his motorcycle. Fine enough: the kindness of strangers. And then she told me something else later, something that amended and changed the story: that not only had he given her a ride, but they had *gone back together*, which I understood to mean they had made love. "That is reckless," I said, "I was so young then," she said, "How old were you," "I'm not going to tell you, you'd judge me," "It couldn't be so long ago," "It was, over four years ago now," "you're twenty-six now, so you were twenty-two," "I don't want to talk about this, I'm not going to tell you, you'll judge me," "you were twenty-two, that was how old we were when we…we," "I'm not going to tell you," and so on until she held my hand and smiled at me, and I was consoled.

And when she told me later, she had gone on a date with another man after I had thought we had already started to date, my jealousy of her past stirred, I don't know, as does a hippo from the shallows: for nourishment or to attack. "Did he kiss you," I asked, "Why are you asking," she said, "I'm just wondering," "Why," "I'm interested to know," "I'm not going to tell you, I liked him though," "Why would you say that and why won't you tell me," "Because you don't need to know," "Why don't I need to know," "Just because," "That's not a justification," "It's good enough," "I don't think so, I think you owe me a little more," "You're not going to get it," "Please, if you love me," "No," "Okay, then what happened," "Then you said we were dating," "And that's what put an end to it," "Yes pretty much."

That she chose me over him would have the charitable, optimistic view, but I had long lost the trait of charity. She must still have had feelings for him — what a phrase, *have feelings* — or still does have feelings, and she only stopped seeing him because I fortified the status of our relationship, putting up a stockade between her and him; I barricaded her in our love. As I am barricaded here in the camp and my feelings for her have not ceased, perhaps being cloistered in my love had not brought an end to her feelings for him.

Sometimes I do not want to write. This is a time I do not want to write. Sometimes remembering is too much, makes hot tears spurt. This is a time when remembering is too much and my tears tumble. Those are the times that I remember that if these pages are taken away again, I may forget everything for good. These are the times writing about my memories batter me until I cry. These are the times I want to get rid of my pen and sand the wart deep down in my right thumb's cuticle by sliding it back and forth against the wall until it is less than it was.

When I am writing about the world that does not cincture me but rather the other things, everything absent, elsewhere, pausing in their passage to nothingness for a moment to linger in memory, I sense I am not alone. I sense I'm not alone here, that I speak with others, someone else listening with care and understanding, charity and grace. And when I write about the felt consequences of having lived those memories and the results, I invariably find myself circling around one and one always and alone, and I write and feel alone; I write, and my writing fails. Fails again, fails worse, keeps failing. Fail. Fail to be worth reading even by me, someone present who is listening and has nothing else to do but to gaze at walls, to hear wails, to fear that I will be pulled from my cell again and made to play the tuba again for the man in the house who whistles the tune and taps his umbrella as he commands us to strike up the dance. When I scrape my wart to and fro against the sharp wall, it bleeds, and I see a result from my actions, a consequence, and seeing the blood fills me with a lame and neutered hope that even if I have failed and fail and will continue to fail, at least when I sand down my wart it will bleed, and I was the one who created that result through the triumph of my will. I can accomplish something.

But then sharks can smell blood from a hundred miles away so maybe I've accomplished what I should have known was the result. I sabotage myself.

I dreamed my daughter was a fish.

But for now, I write.

This is what jealousy does to the mind in conversation whether with oneself or an idea or another person: it is manic, frantic and everywhere at once, molding itself into suspicious conversation, interpreting, re-interpreting, overinterpreting, turning and turning over every word looking for evidence of a crime, denying, affirming, connoting, hinting, lying, accusing, deceiving, marauding our emotions: when jealousy takes possession, everything uttered becomes a tablet in an almost-decipherable language capable of ten-thousand familial but distinct meanings. Just as someone on a sunny day who, looking and seeing a peerless blue sky, reminds himself that there is always a cloud somewhere, jealousy finds the impenetrable dark object that will interrupt your bathing in the rays of light love radiates: it seeks out lapses, omissions, inconsistencies, reticence, and shame, and finds totems of betrayal, criminality, offense, disregard and hatred; be they done ignorantly or knowingly, innocently or cruelly, the jealous daemon passes over every frontier and through every wall and perceives them all.

Jealousy thus replaces love: pleasure in the presence of the beloved yields to the succedaneum of the anguished, torturous need of the beloved one, the beloved idealized, moulded as the lover made her, an agonizing need to possess her alone, a nonpareil whose complete possession is impossible. It is a mad perversity of jealousy that one finds a painful pleasure in those discoveries of betrayal and insubordination. Every one of the beloved's acts of infidelity, real or imagined into reality, pains the jealous lover with the realization that, in his sagacity and sound instincts, he was justified, right in his sense that some mischief had been done him: nothing comforts like confirmation, even confirmation painted with pain.

These little instances that sparked my jealousy accumulated: they diverted me from the experience of living with the real woman and to poring over memories looking for the clue, to wild speculation about the truth — her feelings for me, the concealed desires animating her daily life, the secrets of her heart and all its intermittencies; and instead of loving her, I would love a collection of traits that, because I would never see or know them, kept me in perpetual thrall to her so that a day of revelation would arrive and I would see reality clear and plain. But I know I did not want that day to come. If the mystery were resolved I'd no longer need to love her.

My jealousy was born from my fears. Fear of abandonment, fear of loss, fear of lonesomeness, fear of being alone, fear of the vessel I had poured all my love into being taken from me and then being without it and mourning its departure, fear of having entirely misunderstood the nature of our relationship and consequently having mislived my life, living a convincing fiction that no one perceptive enough would mistake for a real life. But this sense of fear was not innate. I never felt it before I met her because I never had a reason to be afraid like this: I had lost so much of my family but that was before I could remember and so it made nothing leap or sink in me, and I had time enough to get older and get over losing them; I had not yet lost her and I saw that if I did lose her I would not have enough time in the world to get over having lost her; I would be consigned to remember having lost her, to remember her having once been had and then being gone, to remember the presence of nothing more. Our world was immense when we were together, and when we were together a distant unseen star shone through me and all I saw of myself was fear. And fear will make you do things you once knew were strange that you now see are merited, right and just.

An illustration.

She told me her itinerary for the trip. She would be there for a week. She'd meet her colleague at a tram stop near a bridge that we often walk across when we go out for our twilight constitutionals. They would take the tram to the bus depot and they would get on a bus that would drive several hours until arriving at its destination where she would meet other colleagues and participate in the conference.

I did not want to follow her all the way to the conference, no. That would be lunatic, and I am, or was not, a lunatic. And the thought of being caught there or seen by one of her confreres who I would not know but who would know me was enough to make me fear what I could not confront, the discovery of my faithlessness in her and my faithlessness in myself. No. To see her go to the tram stop near our bridge with this man would either confirm or rebuke my suspicions. Confirmation: that was what I needed. Confirmation painted with pain: what the jealous lover seeks.

The morning of her departure came out of a night of constancy. She was looking over a grant proposal while I was preparing to go to work and perhaps never see her again, I always worried about that possibility, endings sometimes come to a life before the matter's settled. "I'll miss you my love, have a safe trip," I said. "Let me know if you need anything or you just want to talk. I'll be available." "Thank you dear," she said, "I imagine the schedule will be rather packed, but if I find some time I'll be in touch." "I love you." "I love you too." "Love, it's going to rain, maybe you should be taking an umbrella." "I think I'll be fine," "Do you have one already," "No, but I'll be fine, don't worry," "If you say so," "Mmm," "Safe travels my love," "Thank you dear, have a good week."

That afternoon I told my secretary I had to leave the office; I had a family emergency that I had to attend to, I said, though I didn't have much of a family to speak of and that was a well-known fact, but when you say you have a family emergency to tend to, no one will enquire; and since no one enquired, I didn't have to tell anyone I would go to the bridge near the tram stop my wife would be going to. I had taken an evening earlier that week to perform reconnaissance on this route and had found a pub where I could sit and wait for her to pass, myself unseen, unconsidered. I ordered their brown ale and sat down with a book, I don't remember what book, nor does that matter because I didn't read it, no, it was only to hide my face, yes, I was literate but feigning my reading, merely using a book to obscure myself; and I held the book up to my face with my left hand, peeking over from time to time to look out of the pub's front windows to see if I'd see her, no, not yet, and from time to time I'd take a sip of the brown ale, and I couldn't help think of an atrocious beer-related joke: why did the bar-maiden complain at the railroad station? Because the stout porter bitter. Terrible joke, terrible, terrible.

Soon enough a weird man came over to my table. Courtesy called for me to put my book down. "Have you seen the sky this afternoon," I remember him saying, "it looks like there might be a storm brewing. How do I know, you may be asking yourself. Well, I'm in the perfect position to answer you. I'm retired now, a very recent affair, against my will my retirement came about, I've only been a "VIP" — you know what they say down there, a "VIP" of course is a very important person in our language, and they know that and make a pun of it because the way they say "I'm retiring" is *vado in pensione*, so when two older folks approaching retirement are talking to one another and the subject comes up, one might say, Eh, I'm a VIP, and of course they both understand the pun and they may laugh, it's very clever polylingual stuff, but what else would you expect from them — as I was saying, I'm only recently retired, but before that I spent most of my career on the road, I worked for the state, a surveyor, forty-eight years working for the state before things changed as they recently have as I'm sure you're well aware, yes, there's so much of our country that still needs to be mapped out and understood, the terrain is so strange, you see, and the weather's unpredictable, you really have to learn to read the sky well enough, read it like a book almost, and you also want to pay attention to the birds and what they do, you can learn a lot from them, and let me tell you I learned so much, you wouldn't believe the things I learned out there underneath the wide sky and the things I saw..."

The retired surveyor's disquisition had interrupted me from reading or pretending to read, he had at least presented an unanticipated complication in my plan, and as I smiled at him and nodded at him, I saw over his shoulder and through the establishment's windows outside a woman with lustrous black hair walking by. It was her. And she was walking with someone.

I recognized him.

It was him.

The hunter.

I didn't know him, but I had done enough research to figure out who he was and what he looked like. A fortunate son, he was not of my stock, rather high-born, from the capital, ancient lineage his patrimony, noble in blood but ignoble in deed.

This was the man who she would travel with and perhaps more.

Had she been able to put him off her scent?

Or was she still enjoying the hunt?

Was it a hunt? Or a game?

I did not know. I do not know. They walked past the bar, I stood up from my table to leave the babbling retired surveyor and pay for my ale and left the bar so I could observe them. I went outside; the door groaned as it shut behind me.

They walked slowly and I walked slower. I stood by the bridge. I heard the water rush past.

Rain came falling. I had no umbrella. No, I had an umbrella, but it was broken, helpless against the rain. I threw it down.

They had an umbrella. Or rather, he had an umbrella and he shared it with her, he kept her safe from the elements, they were close to each other beneath the umbrella, dry. I walked onto the bridge and watched them from there as they walked. I felt the old stones of the bridge uneven beneath my feet and remembered how the dirt pathways around settlement in the valley would be changed after the spring torrents: while they were still dirt pathways, what had been smooth and low-lying areas had mounded into unsurpassable heaps and the groaning mounds of dirt that had gathered had deliquesced into the river, where their nutrients were carried downstream to fan out in the delta some thousand miles downriver. I stood there on the bridge and I heard the water rush past, those ancient arches below, how many grey dawns had the water rushed through them bound for the sea. I heard the water rush past.

They walked further away, and I did not follow, they began to fade from my sight, they would soon be lost. But before I lost them, I saw them together, and her posture showed she was at ease, comfortable, pleased perhaps, and then. Then.

Then he moves the umbrella to his left hand. He moves his left arm around her. Arms and a man. The umbrella is now to her left, covering them both, she is embraced by his left flank. And she leans into his shoulder and seems happy.

I shake my broken umbrella at the sky and threw it off the bridge into the water below. I heard the water rush past. I heard my heart pounding and plunging. I saw my umbrella bob in the water as it floated away, bobbing, and nodding and tumbling before it dove under the water and settled in the sediment with the rest of the stuff that finds its ways into the silence of the river's depths.

The rain came down. I walked past the pub and saw the retired surveyor inside, watching me with his mouth open. I walked past. I went back home.

The next day came, and then the one after, and then many more days came and went, have come and gone.

Why him? Perhaps it meant nothing, the way they were walking, perhaps it did, perhaps it meant something else, I don't know, and I couldn't know.

Why him? Perhaps she thought, why *not* him? There is nothing between us, she would say, the past is long past, I love you and that is what matters, never mind the past. We tell ourselves to never mind the past but the past always minds us. That man emanated from her past; he was not gone, he was not past, a mere memory, no, he was present right there with his arm around her.

It must have been her beauty. It made a fool of me; I knew it would. I knew it when I saw her on the train. Everyone else who sees her knows it. Beauty is a problem. Beauty is the most immediately cognizable aspect of a person. You may meet a person and not have been able to get at the way of her heart for months, years even, you may never know what she cherishes, what she disdains, her quirks, her weaknesses, her strengths; but beauty speaks to you on first sight: beauty is the common tongue we never need to learn but which we always seek because it is always disappearing. And it is her beauty that makes her a fugitive from me, always seen by someone new and thereafter always threatening a final leave-taking from my lived life. I was always circling back around the time I saw her first: we were in transit on a train to disparate points and I made a stay against her flight into memory by speaking to her, inviting her and her light to linger in my life, to be an essential element of every experience I would live. I spoke to her so she would stay. Our life together after that was only the constant recapitulation of that moment and the fear that it created, the fear that she would be gone forever if I did not supplicate myself to keep her there a while longer.

The fear a lover's beauty provokes, however justified, will always entice you to recriminate yourself and find reasons why you deserve jealousy's asphyxiation, its pressure, its pain. The pain of jealousy seemed to me to emerge as retribution for having allowed my family to be forgotten, for leaving the valley behind and living in the capital, for allowing my relatives to be slaughtered before I was born, for leaving what was left of my family and cleaving to her. The guilt endures. But why guilt? Guilt breaks in half the arrow of time, dispensing with time's logic so that one may be guilty for sinful acts or omissions done or not done before one was born for which one may never logically be found culpable. This punishment rises from deep in the ocean of the past as the cresting wave of jealousy, a wave that grows and grows but never crashes down, hanging over the sunny shore of consciousness sempiternally, threatening to come down and wash it all away although it never does; and its never doing so does not abate the fear that someday the flood will come and drown you.

This must be why I am writing about my jealousy. It was jealousy that catalyzed my love for her, jealousy that kept me in thrall, jealousy the upland source where my love for her began to flow; and it is only jealousy, the intense rage to know and in knowing hurt myself enough so I could never understand why I'd want such scathing wisdom, jealousy alone that causes me to remember her so lucidly alive. Who I remember is who I love. I remember but I do not experience. My lives diverge: the remembered life holds what the experienced life gave up. And what it holds are the transmuted elements of that experience, the stuff that endures at least a while. Who I remember is who I love. As for how she truly was or is today I do not know. Jealousy: I could not have her then and I cannot have her now, so I remember her.

And still, I would go back to those days with her. Take me back. Take me back to the loons calling, take me back to my jealousy, take me back to the train, take me back to her everlasting arms that last no more, take me back, take me back.

Too much — perhaps it is too much: too much to remember happy days while dwelling in these dumps. I remember and I feel bliss and then a moan recalls me: I'm no longer there, no longer with her and enveloped in her love, I am here, and I am alone — she may keep me in her heart, but since so many years lie between now and when we saw each other last, it's likely that she thinks of me less and less if at all. Perhaps from time to time she will hear or see a thing and recall a man from the valley across the mountain range that they call distant past, a man who loved her fully, a man who lost himself in the wilderness of his love for her. But more than not being with her, what makes me more despondent is to consider that she doesn't remember me often if at all. Even if you love someone, if that person is not part of the life that you live rather than the life you remember, parts of them fade: a face perhaps remains, a hand, a thing he said, clothing even, but the smell of him disperses first and then the voice's echo stops, and then his body turns to ash and smoke and if a face remains the face remains a formless shape around two vacant eyes which stare but do not see and don't react, don't give off the iridescence of recognition. My image slowly pulls apart in her memory like strands of water in an emerald. What am I to her? A thing that resided in her life for a time. That time is gone. I can remember it, she can remember it, but it is gone out of life. She will go on. I will go on. We both go on and we go on separately. And yet — yet I hope it is true what I thought long ago: that my wife and I, our separate lives were bound clandestinely together — no, not bound, were truly one and one alone, one little ball of light careering toward our disparate ends but still entangled with each other, twinned. It would be then that what you knew I knew, my love, what rain that I endured foisted an umbrella on you in your sunnier clime, and the strangers who greeted you on the train were greeting me as well. It's not to say that the darkness was foregone, no, rather that each good thing in it grew step-by-step more luminous, not enough to make the stars shine brighter than their wont but sufficient yet to make our images pellucid as the sapphires deliquescing in our dreams. Ask not, I tell myself, why such happiness no longer will exist — but still I ask: why won't such happiness endure, why did it so soon come to seem that solitude and dejection were where the compass rose had guided me — ask why the clocks slow down little by little these forlorn days, why a minute of my life takes an hour to remember and aphasia's everywhere. It seems my compass was much brighter when it had more water in it. How do I go about repairing time when the arrow's crook is part of its design?

Never mind this all. Remembering has exhausted me. These memories return to me on feebler wings like fruit flies in every autumn further from the sun. I hoped that in remembrance I would find renewal. Instead, I've retrieved jealousy. Jealousy does no good in here. Let it rest.

The evening star the morning star: halves of a clue dissolved in an alembic and scattered in the inmost darkest blue, their mobile and immobile flickering recrystallizing now in a different form, manifold, refracting something else that's passed yet present in its own strange way.

I have dark days and darker dawns to absorb before my story ends. A life behind me, daybreak in my eyes. It will be sleep tonight. Let it come down.

Entry No. 10

I have remembered too much. I remembered too much of her, my wife, so much that I felt her here, her presence, I relived her, felt her dwelling in me, felt the jealousy possess me again. I felt her, sensed her, saw her walk away without me. She is not here. She is far away. There is nothing here. Nothing but darkness and me. Nothing more. She is shining somewhere far away.

To remember her so fully as I did is too much to live with. I remember now why memory for so long has been the enemy. I have allied with memory because I believed that, rather than fighting off its incursions and sallies into the present, inviting it to occupy and find quarter here instead would allay its onslaught and reinvigorate a life of experience. Memory is better prepared, more powerful, and ever eager to strike wherever, whatever and whenever it may, which is everywhere, everything and always. Its resources seem inexhaustible, its lust to conquer insatiable. It cannot be defeated nor controlled or contained and its forces are legion. They swarm. And I, memory's sclerotic co-belligerent, am overwhelmed by the swiftness of its ascent to total domination and usurpation of the little republic of my mind. I did not expect so much to rush forth. To remember so much only debilitates me. I would feel justified desisting, justified in surrendering, justified in letting myself be absorbed into memory's infantry to disappear into the anonymity of the theatre, slaughtered, waylaid. Memory has overwhelmed the experience of writing, pressing back upon it, compressing it, nigh obliterating life. I could desist from remembering anymore.

That would be ill thought-out. Impulsive. Unwise. Without this inundation I will never find out why and how I arrived here. Nor find a way out, Lord willing there be a way out, nor an end, Lord willing there be an end. Nor would desisting from remembrance prevent my experienced life from invariably being overwhelmed at some future date by a massive and unanticipated memory come floating in. It would drag me down to Hades. Another hell. This is hell nor am I out of it yet. I would like to get out of one of two hells. Either one will do the job. I cannot get beyond these walls, I cannot fly away, cannot leave this one. I can free myself from the assaultive memories, however. I can no longer submit myself, volunteer myself to my memories. Let them no longer impress me into service and ferry me far away across quiet dark water to fight their own wars of conquest, let them no longer hunt me, let me hunt them. I need memories' force to reclaim my lived life from memory. This I can only do if I raise the experience of writing my memories to its own unique aesthetic level. I must take control over my memories. I must pursue these memories, catch them, and defang them, domesticate them, make them my own. I must be the supreme commander of my memory.

To stop remembering, to consign memories to paper, have them secured somewhere other than my mind: it is necessary. My mind does not have the room to store them all; it is preoccupied with surviving every day here. Endeavoring to maintain an inventory of memories in my mind wastes energy better spent maintaining an inventory of practical skills to help me survive this place. Preservation has its costs. And moving memories from my mind to these pages lets me revisit them in an orderly way that may yet lead me to an epiphany. Thus, my stolen journal of remembrance, thus this one *in media res*.

I am all the more convinced that if I continue on in my task, I will not only find out why I am here, but I will also find an answer to a question I have not yet asked. I must not only find the answer but the question too. Whichever one that finds me first will help me find the other. There is something missing in my understanding of the world and to ask this question and provide it its answer will aid me in my continued attempt to exist free of memory's whelm, in control of the past. They will come in time, the memories. I must be patient. They will come. For now, I buffet them unseen, waiting for them to yield to me. I am the storm of memory.

But I must change tacks to accomplish my task. Mere exhibition of memory to assure myself I can remember a life of experiences will get nothing out of nothing. The true work starts in forgetting and then recovering your very self to transform your memories of reality so that, transfigured, to remember them and recover who you are is nothing less than the experience of living again, experience renewing and reinvigorating the present, the foreign but familiar majesty of a sleeping king returning from far away to rule over you again as is his ancient right. Pull apart, rearrange, reconstitute, relive.

I will start the true work. I will endeavor to write only what need be written for my task and to use only the words that need be used, nothing more.

I will remember only memories that will lead me forward to a higher form.

I will be a being of will.

Entry No. 11

To remember someone sets her in amber: one who is remembered is suspended in memory as she is remembered and only that way. She does not grow old, she does not change, she does not feel new feelings or think new thoughts, have new experiences, she does not grow old, she does not die. Remembered, one is eternal. Eternal as long as there is someone to remember one. Entirely dependent, a babe who must be fed and rocked to sleep. If one is only remembered one does not live. One is lived by someone else.

This is no good.

May I be more than memory. May I live again one day.

Entry No. 12

Was let outside for a constitutional around the yard this morning. Fewer campers abounding in the yard, numbers seem to be thinning. A wind came round and almost heaved a rake into me; I managed to step aside and let it pass me by and go on to scuttle across the yard, almost hovering over the ground but dragging against it all the same, making that annoying scuttling sound. It continued drifting across the yard until it was beyond where any camper is permitted to go to retrieve it. Now it will serve no use. One may see it outside, huddled in isolation in a distant corner, useless, without purpose, a waste. What was employed to make the earth presentable now huddles where the wind blows over it and makes it rattle. The rake's progress.

I was brought back in after my tour around the yard and settled into the dark again as they closed the doors. I heard muffled laughs fading.

I crawled around the floor looking for my stationary and my pen and wondered, do I continue writing? Should I? Do I dare? I have set myself a task and I have no idea what its completion may look like. What is the face of fulfillment and how will I recognize it? It would be nice for it to visit me one day and say, "Hello, I am what you are trying to accomplish, and I am perfected. Marvel, if you will." But it won't.

I have nothing better to do nor anything more enjoyable to do than writing all this, which isn't to say this is enjoyable, because it's not. I just don't know what else to do. Nor will I know the point of what I am doing until it is done. Then I can look back and see what it was I was trying to do this whole time. But not till then. Until then I will write, will think no more of it than I must to write. Nothing more. Writing and nothing more.

Entry No. 13

A camper here made a chain of leaves and placed it around his neck and said, "I'm afraid I will lose myself here, so I made this so that I will know myself by it." One night as he slept, the leaves, frailer than ever, disintegrated, and when he woke up, he said to me, "O friend, I lost track of myself as I slept; you may be me, so who am I?" After that day I never saw him again and I don't know what happened to him.

Entry No. 14

They would like me to remember my life as they would have had me live it, a ghost of contractual pity. No past to remember having lived, only a guilty shadow cast across the lawn by dying cypresses. But I cannot do this. I cannot invent. I cannot. I lived as I live. And I will remember that. I will remember how I lived and how the way I lived changed when they arrived. Pursue the past and flush it out.

When the revolution came my life did not change materially. Some small changes around it but life itself did not change. A different flag to honor, a different anthem to sing, relationships with different nations emphasized or minimized. A change of dress for the state in its next performance. I continued to work in the capital, and my wife and I continued to live there. Together. I was still an arbiter, a barrister, an attorney at law, esquire, what have you. That is to say, I interpreted the law or played with it. And my work did not change. Laws governing those injuries and courts interpreting those laws continued to exist, human inventions like guns, drugs and combine harvesters still harmed people, people got hurt and people must pay.

Did I put someone in a place like this?

When the rule of law falters, who do you trust, who do you count on? When the rule of law falters, what rises to rule in its place? Nothing does, and nothing is ineffable and therefore unnegotiable. No, the rule of law can never falter, must never be allowed to fall into desuetude. One party must give laws and another enforce them. The process may be circuitous, beginning in a lonely impulse in the minds of many and ending in the grip of a guillotine's stocks, but there is always a giving and enforcing. If this place were paradise — no laws written because all laws understood, all externalities internalized, all ambiguities resolved amicably, every transaction and interaction efficient, everything and everyone rational, self-interested, cooperative, civil, socially contracted, bound together like a bundle of sticks, *homo economicus* or *homo reciprocans* — were this place paradise, no laws would need to be given and so no laws would need be enforced. But our world was not paradise and our world is not paradise, at least the world as I remember it, fine as it was, better than this, no, even beyond what I can remember it never was paradise, even the first man was tasked with naming every single thing, labor like ours in that it has no end and is lonesome. No. The rule of law must rule supreme: contractual obligations must be enforced, statutes codified, reparations made, punishments meted, rights secured, freedoms protected, the weak protected from the strong, the strong protected from the evil, the evil protected from the zealous, the zealous protected from the languid, the languid protected from themselves, everything frangible in balance with everything imperishable. And that's what I did. I enforced. I arbitrated. I weighed and balanced. Equitable. Were it not for me and others like me, society would have deliquesced. But it had not — had not yet. Things changed but, *mutatis mutandis*, things stayed the same.

And yet I should have known that things would change because they were already changing. The capital city was repurposed into a library of mortality, its passages and historical centers overflowing with volumes of all different subject, size and condition: revolutionaries, rebels, shell-shocked brigadiers, ecstatic privateers, mountain people, swamp folk, landless gentry, disaffected squires, coffee-drinkers and -offerers, arrivistes, metics, parvenus, mercers, ostlers, coopers, crofters, kulaks, bednyaks, burghers, proles, plebes, daytalers, yurt-dwellers, lightmongers, cordwainers, cutlers, chandlers, wallahs, hut people, scampering children with wide hungry eyes, all of them daily living, sleeping, waking, striving, loafing, loving, hating, fighting, hoping, dying. The convergence of blood in the heart when too much flows in faster than too little can flow out is a symptom warning that the constitution is in danger. But who will see such a change in the constitution, invisible and aery as every other constitution, unobservable to anyone but the most crack-pot prophet glimpsing auguries in the entrails of the wind? No one. And who takes a prophet seriously? No one. That is to say: no one but someone who is no one to anyone. That is to say: someone outside society. And that is someone we cannot imagine. I imagine no one is me. Because that is me now: no one. The one writing these words: no one. The one who remembers: no one. The one who has lived: no one at all.

If I were no one then I would have seen what was happening and what was coming and could have saved us from the metastases in our body politic. But I was someone then. I saw nothing and so did nothing.

In the beginning the revolution was a welcome change. Change is welcome for its novelty and not necessarily for its result. The status quo bores because we are beings who grow bored. We cannot sit still in a room and so we grow bored. We sleep with the same spouse night after night and so we grow bored. We share wisdom and are revered and so of reverence we grow bored. We live the same life day after day and so we grow bored. Curse us and our inability to endure boredom. Curse us and our inability to endure boredom and our consequent restlessness. Perhaps that restlessness is the reason the revolution came. They came to power not through violence, social unrest, or mobilization of clandestine cells. They just arrived and then they were there, fresh and new. They said they were mere stewards of our nation's heritage, stewards with one task: make it new. They woke the beast from its slumber, the beast that lay sleeping in its autumn umber. And we all awoke to a new reality, their reality, a reality different from ours. You'd expect something called reality to be reality or at least reflect reality, to have some discernable relationship with the world as it objectively exists according to several as-yet uncontroverted laws of nature, to be founded on empirical facts, meticulous research, moderation in pursuit of justice: the truth. You expect reality to be the truth. The wind blows warm and southerly; reality dictates that the wind is *in fact* blowing warm and southerly, carrying other voices to other places. But to them, our new rulers, whichever wind blowing warm and southerly could be blowing cool and northerly or east and mildly if you say so, a sirocco could be a zephyr, a mistral, a tramontana, a levanter, leveche, llevantades, gregale, a fohn, khamsin, maestro. The wind blows where they say it blows. *That* is the truth. And because the truth begets legitimacy, reality for them constituted at its core intolerance for anything contravening what they held to be the truth. Say the wind blows west and the wind blows west, say the wind blows the voices of the past to the ears of the living and the wind blows as such. Say it and it is so. Anything that challenged their legitimacy was inherently false. Let the damn wind blow where it may or let the wind blow where they say it blows. Reality became whatever they believed to be the appropriate means to ensure they themselves would not be swept away.

The wind is blowing, and the graves are shuddering.

One noticed minor changes, the hot air and cold passions of a new government going through its adolescent flower, moving from the idealization of proper rule in thought to the actuality of ruling in deed. We were patient, though. I was. I welcomed them even. Before them was an unbroken thousand-year reign, ancient and inured and ragged and bored. No one liked them anymore, we all cursed them. Under our breaths. Whispers to ourselves. No one will hear you except someone who hears everything. And that someone who hears everything came to us with the face of revolution. And I saw that face one afternoon at work.

I had been reading at my desk, I seem to recall, reading a book as one does if one is literate. Which book it was I won't even try to remember but let us assume it engrossed me, that I was not paying attention to any work that needed to be done, any contract, complaint, brief, memorandum, motion, notice, nothing. And if I was as engrossed as I assume I was, I would have been shaken to my heart to have heard a booming voice calling me down to the human development office. I hadn't been there before, the development office. Their work was administrative and only tangentially related to mine in that they ensured lawyerly work like mine could be done smoothly and well. A lubricant in a way, much like mayonnaise on a sandwich ensures that the content between the bread is delivered in a savory and well-disposed fashion. They were the mayonnaise of legal work.

And so, if, as I imagine, I heard the voice that shook me from my reverie, I would have known I had to proceed to the human development office for one thing or another, whatever it was they did and whatever it was they needed me for. And I would have gotten up from my desk, adjusted my cravat if I was wearing one, and proceeded thereto. I know I got lost in the stairwell, momentarily locked out or locked in. A janitor who was passing through the door opened it and let me glide in behind him. A nice man he was, a shock of white hair, a good guy. One of the last to let me go through a door. Doors otherwise have become as good as walls: beyond them is everything, but you never pass through, and so there is nothing. You need a good janitor type in those cases, or better yet an angel, or a bulldozer, or whoever may come to me at the appointed hour here in this world. But that is now; I am describing then. Yes, the janitor let me glide in behind him. What was his fate among the stars? I thanked him and he nodded, never looking away from me. I entered the human development office where I waited until my name was called again — by whom? I don't know, voices sometimes escape their possessors and speak for themselves — and I was called again and invited to another smaller office within that office. I went in and sat down.

Behind the desk sat a smudgy-spectacled, sweaty cherub I never saw before. I assume he was always there before. I don't know. He was sweaty, quite sweaty, and greasy, which must have accounted for the bare translucence of his spectacles, which even before any words were exchanged between us he had removed twice to clean and degrease by tugging out enough fabric from his lapel to use in degreasing his spectacles; and every time he summoned vapor from his throat in the way one does when seeking to clean mirrors or any such radiant surface before rubbing his spectacles with the fabric from his lapel, he would peer at them, stare at them even and, seeing that the greasy residue could not be removed, he would frown, sigh and resign himself to never seeing clearly, to always seeing through a glass smudgily, imperfectly, to always seeing the world through grease-tinted glass, to seeing the world the way he was required to see it, grubbily, grimily, foully. "Good day," I said, then he blinked at me twice. He removed his spectacles again and began the cleaning process again, which he should have known by that point in his life would not have the desired result, a process one nevertheless repeats over and over with the faint hope that something will change, that the dam will finally break, that by repetition the constraint will give way at last and the accomplishment achieved. He peered at his spectacles and replaced them again, and I could hardly see his eyes except to see that they were peering at me from behind those translucent foul halos and blinking. Not one for small talk or niceties, that man. He was a blinker.

Perhaps he was saying something to me with all that cleaning and blinking — I had not considered that until now.

Had he been trying to tell me something?

Had he been trying to tell me something that I missed? Something that would have saved me from all this?

Was he warning me?

Why couldn't I see?

Never mind. He cleaned his glasses and he peered, and he blinked and said nothing, he did not talk much if at all. Then again why ever talk. Sit silent. Be silent. Become silent. No mischief comes to the silent. He was the wise one. He directed his eyes toward his desk, and I looked down.

On the desk were a pen and a letter. The pen was fine, somewhat nicer than what we used in the office, certainly nicer than the instrument that I use here now, it had a nice nib I believe, I would have liked to use it to poke at my gums. Ah, my gums, my teeth are sore, I am parched. I believe it was a nice pen but I'm not sure. And other than the pen, the letter. Even less sure about that. My memory is good but not exemplary, no, I've learned this much, sometimes I question why strange people and things appear in my memories when they've no business being there, sometimes I question whether someone else has remembered my memories before I got around to it and what I recall are second-hand memories, the past twice-removed, once by time, again by an interloper. Or perhaps I am not letting myself remember. But I remember that I recognized it was a pledge, an oath. To them. To the law. Their law. Their law that was now our law: our freedoms, our constraints, our boundaries, our society. Bound to it. That we were bound. Upon pain forte et dure. That we had to sign. That by signing we abjured any memory for good or for ill of the previous regime. And by signing become a party member. Dues due biannually, send to the following address, remember it's tax deductible.

I thought nothing of it, nothing at all. I signed without a second thought or even a first thought come to think of it. No thought at all. As I've said I was not a political man nor am I now. I was never involved, never agitated for systemic change in the relationship between the state and the individual. True. My earthly concerns were my family, my work, my reading. Food, too. Loyalty, no, I didn't consider that; fidelity didn't concern me. And so, swearing to the new regime was no great shakes. Nor was there choice. Or perhaps there was a choice, but a false choice at that. Not signing would bring certain death to me and ruination to my family and signing would occasion no hardship. And since the new regime did not seem a transient thing, to pledge allegiance seemed the wiser path to travel down than following principles, my principles, when any principles I could muster would have to have been created on the spot.

I signed the pledge and he removed his spectacles again to clean them, which I took to be his way of thanking me, and then he made two blinks, which

I took to be his way of asking me to leave, perhaps he was not dismissing me or thanking me but asking me to help him in some way, perhaps by sending a message to someone or secreting him out of that office in my topcoat or buying him a new pair of spectacles or just some fair to middling cleaning solution, I don't know. I got up to leave and the sigh I heard coming from him ringed as a faint kind of valediction as I left to go back to my office and I never saw him again, it could be he's still there repeating that ancient futile custom of cleaning his spectacles, out damned smudge out, he thinks, it is time to do it, out I say, ah it is murky, ah nothing will come of this, nothing to be done but nothing must be done all the same, who would have thought the man would have had so much grease in him, perhaps he is thinking that and perhaps he is still there although I doubt it, no one stays for long, and in any case I never saw him again nor thought of him nor what I did in there for a long, long time.

Now I do. Now I think again of that moment and those words, or rather those words that belong to that moment, those words, so many of them so many, so many and none of them my own, even the name I signed below them hardly my own since no one speaks it anymore and I have not heard my name in so long, three words that belonged to me, those three alone and now they are gone on their own with the rest of the words, I should not have thought I could have been undone by so many, I precipitated all this word-borne destitution, I precipitated their tumbling down on me, I signed my name and set them off and they did not go where I hoped they would go, no, words will have their own little fate far, far apart from our own. My name signed below indicates the words are my own, the inquisitor even evinced this at trial, saying, Look, he pledged allegiance in his very own words, he violated his own oath, how could you trust a man who writes one thing one moment and then something quite different at another, no, this is a man who cannot be trusted, you cannot trust a thing he says or writes, to believe him would call for you to engage in the willing suspension of disbelief and this is neither the time nor place to do so, nor the world to do so either, no, a man whose word and words cannot be trusted cannot himself be trusted, if your word is no good you cannot be trusted with a farthing, if your word is no good you cannot be a member of society and ought for the good of the rest be cast out, don't believe him, don't believe a thing he says, his words are empty ephemeral promises by which not even a ghost could stand.

But lo: those words were not mine. These words were theirs. I only signed and in signing was made to possess them, made to appear to possess them, but that is no kind of possession at all, it is an illusion, a mirage, a play of light on the eyes, a fatamorgana out at sea on the horizon, it is legerdemain, pure sleight of hand, a trick of perspective, a trick and only a trick because if you look closely you see nothing was there, nothing to possess, no one to possess anything, no me, nothing, nothing at all.

If I could go back to the moment in that office when I signed that pledge, I'd show a bout of choler and grow red in the face, shake a bit so that my rightful anger was palpable or at least discernable to that man with the smudgy spectacles if he could ever see me, ah at least my anger would be discernable to myself, yes I'd show a bout of choler and spit on that document and say, Fie on this, a pox upon your page; and then all the same I'd sign it again. I'd sign it again because I had to. Because it was necessary. Because I had no choice.

Choice. What choice did I have? Choice: that seductive and beguiling word. Choice: that word so whispered tells you you are free, that your life and its decisions are not already spoken for, that you need not watch your own life being lived out from afar, that the project of having lived a life is yours alone and not a supernal cast-about's, that you are a being whose will is pure and true, that you may fashion the world or at least your life as you like it, that all will end well if you will it so, that you can live your life as you would love it lived. No: don't be a fool. No choice abides, not then or now or ever. Small choices, yes, meager, and paltry ones, hardly choices at all, barely deserving of the epithet in fact, because the real choices, the great decisions, the only choices, the supreme *dilemmas*, they are not ours to choose, no, others will decide them for us. To make a choice one must be one's own master. To make a choice one must not have become someone else's. To make a choice one must possess oneself.

I could have chosen not to sign my name, others may think, I could have chosen not to have signed my name and in doing so I erred. Stupid man, they would think, he signed his own letter of marque. I admit that I have surely erred and do so daily — an errant human, a human erring, I understand myself to be something of a human yet — but in this instance, just for once, in this instance I would not have been in the wrong, no, I did not err. If I had chosen not to write my name, what would have become of me sooner rather than later? If I had chosen not to write my name, do you think I would have gone home again that evening? If I had chosen not to write my name, do you think I would have had even that one more night, precious as all fantasies of life, to see my family again? If I had chosen not to write my name, do you think I would not have been forced to feel such searing pain from something pressed to my chest that same day and be impelled to sign it all the same? If I had chosen not to write my name, do you think I would be writing right now? If I had chosen not to write my name, do you think I'd be, for lack of better words, alive?

And here I am.

See: no choice. Signing or not, here I am. Others chose for me. My choice was spoken for so that in effect no choice ever was. A choice must have consequences. Each choice must beget a singular consequence; if one choice yields the same result as any other choice then it is no choice at all, only the mirage of a choice, sleight of hand, a fatamorgana on the horizon out at sea, it is no choice, no, it's a trick, only a trick, there's nothing there to choose from, there's nothing, nothing at all. I had as much chance to choose my lot as I can now choose whether to piss on myself more so on my left flank or my right. What a choice: either way I am soiled. What a choice: either way yields the same result. What a choice: crapping here, pissing there, moaning everywhere. Choice: a stupid sound. Choice: anthills annihilated by the rain. Choice: the kingdom of a child. Choice: a turgid concatenation of a word.

Sign then or sign later in pain: that was the choice: a choice between deferral and immediacy: a temporal determination: a moment sooner or that same moment later. Whatever I begot by signing my name would have made me come a cropper one way or another. I sign then and then fate comes quickly. I do not sign and then fate comes belatedly. No difference and therefore no choice. The consequence of that moment. That same moment lived again later but more fatally. A moment that will not end; a choice that yields no fresh road to hoe; no road at all, no ending, no choice at all, nothing, nothing at all, my life was spoken for, it always was, it was not my life it was no life at all.

Wasted words, lost time. I am angry and I need to console myself. I get nowhere. I chose to remember only those memories that will lead me where I need to go, to write only the words that need be used, to be a being of will. I have got nowhere. This memory has led me to a digression, bringing me back here to my cell. I have no control. I don't know what I am doing. Whatever will I possess is feebler than my body. I am powerless. I am aimless. I need consolation. I will go wiggle my toes for a spell and look up and see what I can see, firmament or no firmament. I may quietly go hum a song, but I am not allowed to hum, I am only allowed or rather forced to play the tuba at certain times of their choosing, and I still have not learned how to play the tuba so I do not know how to play the tuba and I shall never learn to play it right but still I'll play the tuba when they choose to strike up the band, and so I will hum, and I will hum but not loud enough that the gaolers will hear me and flog me. And then after I have hummed for a good while perhaps, I will look around and see if I can tell if it is day or night. That will take some time, the rest of the day even, or the rest of the night, whichever it is, but perhaps they are the same now and there is no difference, do they still have day and night out there? Yes, I will stand at the wall and aim to look out the window for a little patch of light or lack of light and work my way towards determining whether it is night or day or neither one. That will take my mind off things.

For now, I will not write. I have chosen not to write. I will not write for now, but I will return to writing later on. Writing has been postponed, of my own accord. And look: I have chosen! And it is not much of a choice. I can make a choice not to write, a choice of the smallest things — the unimportant things, the evanescent, inconsequential and ephemeral things — I may choose to put off writing for a spell, I may choose not to write a journal that will not be seen, a journal written by one who does not live if he ever lived, a journal whose words have no consequence or sound, whose words yield nothing, give nothing, do nothing and make nothing, inconsequential markings, useless, words hardly words. I can do no more than that. The choice is not mine to make. Let the river swerve and course where it may, let the mountain shiver and the avalanche come tumbling down, let the road fork and beat a path among the other trees, I have no say. It is all beyond me now. I have made my choice. It makes no difference. I have made no choice. It makes no difference. This way or no way what will come will come. This way or no way my life is not my life. This way or no way I am gone. I feel nothing. I do nothing. I have made my choice. I choose nothing. Nothing will come of nothing. Let nothing envelop me; let nothing embrace me; let nothing choose me; let nothing become everything, my everything, let nothing be my master and I nothing's apprentice, let nothing teach me, let nothing turn me into nothing; and since nothing cannot be destroyed, in that way I will be free. Let me be free: let me be nothing.

And there I go.

Entry No. 15

O what a small fire we spend our lives dowsing.

Entry No. 16

I do not want but for writing, and I write only what I remember of myself before the camp. It is troublesome to remember, hard to recall, troublesome to remember, hard to recall, not that memory fails, but memory succeeds and brings back much too much to handle.

I am repeating like a number. Six six six, six six six, six six six, repeat. I am a number.

Not to repeat, nor waste words.

Not to waste or lose time, nor repeat it either.

Yes — hard to summon the memory of my arrest. In the den, reading. Wife responding to letters, whose letters who knows, children at study, the blessed things.

Children? Children.

Evening, yes it was, evening, could not have been any other time than evening time. The eves having grown long. Evening, past the gloaming. Knock at the door, then knocks at the door, then knock at the door, a look of glass disturbed from its translucence is passed between my wife and me, I stand, approach the threshold, enquire who is knocking, "the Guard," says a voice. The Guard — a catch-all term for every governmental activity not explicated by statute, constitution, or court, a catch-all: everything else without a name.

The door they knocked on — the door to my house. I had a house, yes, my own little castle. And what a place it was. We had wallpaper, loads of it, most of it on the walls, and for the most part it stuck to the walls, which I liked. It was a color with an odd name. Taupe. Yes, taupe. Does it rhyme with hope or hop? Let us say hope. I don't remember who chose taupe wallpaper, whether it was there before we made it our home or if we chose taupe when we moved in, but taupe it was, so taupe our walls.

The door was made of solid wood, oak, yes, red oak, I remember that, and through the door to the left was the den and straight ahead a stairwell. The stairwell led upstairs as stairwells do. Each step was made of wood. I do not know what kind of wood the stairs were, I don't know and don't really care at this point. At the top of the stairs and to the left was a hallway some twenty-seven paces long. Carpet lined the hall, crimson carpet. The first room was four paces from the stairwell. This was my daughter's room. In her room was a bed large enough for her but not much larger that was pushed up against the left wall, and the blanket on her bed was patterned with blue paisleys on a wine background, the carpet the same as the hall, crimson. On the taupe wall to her bed's left were drawings she drew in school when she was younger. She was older then but did not take the drawings down. The drawings were objectively atrocious drawings. And yet, everything your child makes cannot be anything but wonderful, even if the one she titled Daddy pictured, I suppose, me, even though the figure drawn looked less like me than it did a wombat. To the right of her bed on her nightstand was a lamp whose small bulbs were fashioned into a collection of balloons of various colors, none of which was taupe. On the nightstand she kept a book on cosmology, which was what she studied when I saw her last.

On the same side of that hall five paces further down was my son's room. The walls were not taupe, they were painted sky blue. Like his sister's, his bed was lodged along the left side of the wall. A desk was on the right side of the room. The desk had a shelf above it lined with books, none of which he read. He chose the books for their texture rather; he'd carry one around the house with him and sit with it downstairs in the den, not reading, only stroking it.

Oh, the den. The wallpaper of course was taupe. An olive couch was on the leftmost wall below the barred window that looked out on the street. There was a bookshelf somewhere, maybe across from the couch, maybe opposite the fireplace, which was in the den's leftmost wall adjacent to the couch, I can't be sure. The floor was wood, scraped and matted. And over a threshold in the rightmost portion of the den's back wall was the kitchen. In the kitchen was a table constructed, I am almost certain of maple. Behind that was a sink and to the sink's left was a stove top with four burners. To the stove top's left was a door that led out to a small yard, thick with kudzu and crocuses and not much else. To the sink's right was a countertop. Adjacent to the countertop was a small refrigerator.

I forgot one room. That is the room I shared with my love. I said already that the hallway was twenty-seven paces long, of that I'm almost certain because I walked from end to end biweekly to ensure that it had not changed. The entrance to the room we shared was twenty-two paces from the stairwell.

The bedroom that we shared — I can't remember it. I try but I cannot remember it. I try sometimes but I see nothing but a void of brittle dark which, if I thwacked it hard enough, perhaps would break and let me see. But I never thwacked it hard enough and so the place where we slept so many nights together, warm, and close, is dark. Something in me is fearful of breaking through the brittle dark to see it as it was; when you remember, things go raging through your heart you can't control. Perhaps it's better then that I don't remember.

But I remember: they came here, there, my house full of admirable wallpaper, reams of admirable wallpaper, such patterns! — the voice did not say why, no choice abided, the door called to be opened, otherwise, otherwise what, never mind, I was the one who opened the door, I wish I had not nor did I want to then but no choice abided, choice never abides. I open it, they enter and wipe their soles, so ostentatiously, so respectful as to be condescending, ah well, soles must be cleaned wherever they egress, here on the welcome mat, Welcome to Our Loving Home, they wiped their soles the way horses kick up dirt behind them, "Evening," one in front said, there were two more behind, "Evening," the one in front said again, "Quite," I said. "Forgive the intrusion, squire, do you have a moment," he asked, "Gladly I do and many more I hope," I said, "what's this about," "A small affair, criminal case," "A criminal case is not a small affair," "The accused claims he was elsewhere and claims you too were at the same time so you can corroborate his alibi, shouldn't take too long," "How long do you think, gotta put the kids to bed in a bit," "Not long," he said, "not long at all, apologies for the inconvenience," "And I have to do it now," "That is the case," "I don't seem to have much choice in the matter now, do I," "I am afraid not, squire, and I apologize for that, we will try not to take up too much of your time," "Very well, let me see to it," "Ah, squire, apologies again for the inconvenience, if you'd be so kind as to come down to the station with us we'd be much obliged, shouldn't take too long, that is all." "Can I have a moment," "Sorry to say time is of the essence, plus we're on the clock, lost time is not found again and our superiors, long may they supervise, they prefer not to lose anything, time included."

Did I know I was in the entelechy of arrest? My answer: why not?

Anyone could arrest you. Sure, the Guard coming to your door, that seemed clear enough even when they said it was for some such pittance as *providing an alibi*. And yet: anyone could arrest you. Anyone could be working for the Guard. You had no need of uniform, of gleaming black boots, crisp olive pants, blood-red wool topcoat. No, anyone could be working for the Guard. Go to your daily panaderia, the breadwallah tells you he has a very special bread for you and just for you and won't you come back with him to look at it so you go back to the kitchen and the red Guards are there waiting, "Come with me," they said, come or come, no choice abideth; or go to the theatre in the winter, leave your greatcoat with the coat check in exchange for a ticket, return after the last act to retrieve your greatcoat, "I'm so sorry," she says, "we seem to have misplaced it, why don't you come out back to help us look for it, you'll know your own overcoat better than would we," and you catch them in the lie — twas no overcoat but a greatcoat — but it's too late, always too late, you go back and the blood-red Guard is there and then you're gone, never having gotten back your coat; or go to the bank to withdraw some petty cash, "Oh dear," says the teller, "our computers seem not to be working, this will have to be done manually, won't you please follow me to the manager's office," you follow her back to the manager's office and there is the Guard, red and alert and smiling at what a gullible fool you are, and you never get your money or anything back, only death in life, which is a form of debt in itself, perpetual payment of the perpetual loan, death in life, perpetual death in life, arrest, imprisonment, disappearance, oblivion. And you never know.

I went over to my children and gathered them into my arms. "Don't worry, I'll be back," I would have said, "papa loves you." I placed my right hand under my son's chin and lifted his face so that he could look at me. "You're the man of the house now, just for a little bit while I'm gone," I said, "take care of your mama and your sister, be strong." He nodded blankly. "And you, my dear," I would have said to my daughter, "continue your studies, make me proud, I'll be back soon, don't forget." But she did not respond, she hugged me tighter. I did not want her to let me go but I had to withdraw myself from her: I saw one of them standing there watching us, waiting, flirting with the holstered pistol on his hip. I could not help thinking about how strange it was that my abductors were armed to the teeth to abscond with a lawyer whose only act of resistance, if it could be considered resistance at all, was being a civilian with a family in a nondescript house who roused their suspicion and hatred of the past.

I write and because I write I remember. I do not want to remember. But I must — to accomplish my task I must remember. But I must distract myself from remembering it too well. Would be too much, too much. I must remember only what I need to remember to accomplish my task and determine why I am here and reclaim my life. I must try to remember then as poor and vague as I — nothing, nothing, nothing, speak again, nothing from nothing enduring.

But no — I am still writing; I must have allotted some of my time to this and I owe myself candor. Even so, the world will little note what I say here.

I will dig in but not too deep. One risks disturbing the buried dead.

So, yes — there I was, there we are at this point in the narration: standing in the doorway, blinking at those avatars of the state, I blinked and turned to look back at my wife. I mentioned her eyes, those lustrous things, those eyes I fell into when I saw her first. As I remember her at my abduction — perhaps this is not the proper term since I went not against my will with them; even so, if not literally, then, through their deception, figuratively I was abducted — as I remember her at my abduction, all I can remember now are her eyes. When I remembered how we met, I allowed myself to remember more of her, but now all that is gone, all that, everything else but those eyes, hovering. Those eyes see and they know. I didn't know what was to happen or rather wouldn't let myself know but she knew, and she knew I didn't know, I know it. Her eyes. Eyes, eyes, eyes, all-seeing eyes, nothing more, the eyes remain, are what linger after all the other things went fading, all-seeing eyes and nothing more. She always knew: she could not deceive but propriety called for us to act as though the obvious were opaque.

What did she know? Write, write, write and perhaps further along I will find out.

I embraced my wife and was afraid to let her go. I did not know what to expect. From her or from where I was going. "I love you," I must have told her, "I always will, I will be back, don't worry too much, just remember that I love you, don't be afraid, I love you and I always will." She tried to smile her ineffable smile, the one that made me love her when I first saw her, but the smile was without the generosity of spirit, the confidence, that made it. Her eyes looking, the door closed between us, and we were cleft.

And as I left my home, my wife caressing the heads of our children, standing in our living room, my daughter sucking on her right hand with porcelain eyes, my son with his head aslant in curiosity, my wife's eyes welling and all-seeing, I was pummeled by a great wave of nostalgia for a present already leaving, a nostalgia bound to the future when it would be all the more painful, nostalgia for the happy loving home it was then and in the future had been, the happy loving home it was and would never be again.

Heartbroken, breaking, almost fit for mending if it were not otherwise.

"Right here," one said, he opened up the back door of the car and I got in. One went around the front and got in to drive, the others went another car. Toot toot, we started motoring.

You would have thought we were two old friends taking a ride to the Men's Club. He even tried to start a conversation. "Have you always lived in the capital," he asked, "No," I said, "I was raised in the valley," "The valley, what a beautiful part of our nation, a true boon, so rich in resources," "It is, I miss it and I will always miss it," and then he laughed, "I'm sure you always will," he said.

Entry No. 17

The car lurched and the door opened. Dark was the night, so dark I could not see but for the faint red lights outside wherever it was we were going into. "This way," the one who drove me said, "Shouldn't take too long, go on in," he said opening a door, "Hang there for a bit and then we'll call you in." In I went and down I sat, sitting on the pews that adorned the four walls, the room rectangular, the walls to my left and right twice as long as the wall across from me and the wall where I sat. I sat and looked and saw another there.

He raised himself from unsleeping rest, raised himself up off his haunches on the bench along the long-left wall, turned his torso and held himself up with elbows on the bench and head cradled twixt his hands, his hands gloved but the gloves torn. "What did you do," I asked, "Was a cooper," "No, I mean, to get in here," "Coopin, I guess, seems they don't need much of a person to lodge you up in here, cross the street wrong or cough into your hands instead of the crook of your elbow and then you're rendered, who knows, anyway, how bout you, what business did you get up to," "I have no idea," I said, "Ah yup," he said, "that's the big one," "The big one," "Ayuh, the biggun, probably the most common reason they'll go out arresting folk." "Wait, I'm arrested?" "If you're in here, I surmise that's the case, I reckon." "But they told me I was coming down here to provide an alibi," I said, and he laughed a wheezing little laugh. "You didn't think much before you got in that car of theirs, did you, alibis don't count for a farthing anymore." "Why would I have been arrested?" "Exactly." "What do you mean?" "Arrested for having no idea you were arrested," "For not having any idea why you've been arrested," "Yup, ignorance is no excuse and knowledge is no vice until you know too much and then it's pure evil, you never want to know too much these days, they will burn your world down to the ground, yup." "But how could I be arrested for not knowing I was being arrested," I asked, "that's not how time works," "That's how it works now." "How long will I be here," I asked, "Ayuh," he said, "at least until you get any idea of why you're here, yup, then maybe, well, who knows, you'll see," "What do you mean I'll see," "You'll see soon enough, you can take that to the bank." I wondered if I'd ever have the chance to deposit a check down at the bank again, the material evidence of having done good work. He turned from me and started snoring. I hated he could sleep, that carefree cooper.

And so.

So, yes. There was a thundering and the door opened up like open sesame, this stirred the cooper from sleep but not for long, and I was summoned thereupon, and the other in the room smirked and with vacant eyes still smirking turned to stare into the wall, and so I followed those who summoned me past lines and lines of holding cells, each of us stations in a long grey line, row after row with strict impunity. How many dead had gone this way before, the way of all saints?

I followed. Down an ill-lit hall, dank, up an iller-lit hall & along an illest-lit hall to a door, another door. The door reverberated and was opened, we went in, the door was closed. Grand opening, grand closing.

Inside was a table, a long one, four inches deep, a little beat up, red oak maybe, pale light from a pulsing bulb above that hummed draping the environs in a hostile pulsing sheen. Two chairs. I was confident I was meant to sit in one of the two chairs. I went to sit down in the chair between the door and the table. It was not a comfortable seat, it was a most unpleasant seat, if I had come to this room to hear a lecture and I was early I surely would have gotten up and moved to another seat no matter the consequences because it was a foul seat. Wood. Red oak maybe. Knots not sanded, malformed legs that I discovered would wobble back and fro upon the slightest shift in weight, no not even weight, the chair wobbled at the slightest shift in thought, as I would find, a sighing shift that made me feel the chair would give up on its chairitude and resign itself to sawdust, pillars thereof, while I sat on it; and when it did give up, I would drop down to the floor and smash my coccyx, which would yield infernal pain through my body that I would obscure with a wince, pursed lips and a quiet long exhalation from both my nostrils. And they would know the truth, that I had trusted and been duped and so had felt exquisite, rarified pain — their specialty — so they would laugh at me a while, but the heartiest laughter would be chortled by the walls, who would continue to ignore me otherwise. All this because the floor was all concrete.

I will now describe highlights in the history of concrete.

No, perhaps not: it doesn't strike me as very interesting now that I think about it, not a very good distraction, would be a real low point for my writing — but then again, if it were not for the ditches, how could we appreciate the heights? I'll think more on this. Maybe later.

If it were not for winter's frost, how could we appreciate summer's blooms?

If it were not for the depths of night, how could we appreciate the day?

If it were not for absence, how could we appreciate presence?

Back to the matter.

Yes, the breaking chair: this humiliation did not happen. All the same, I sat down with great trepidation. Other humiliations would ensue on down the line.

"So, what can I do for you," I heard someone say. I looked up: across the table was a man sitting in the other, presumably less wobbly, chair, and he had an open folder perched on his lap leaning against the table's edge. A smile rose around the corners of his eyes as he looked over the contents of the folder, a smile rising as he looked up and glanced at me for a moment before looking back down at the folder. But in that moment he looked at me I felt the look of recognition pass upon me and through me, and I recognized nothing in his eyes.

"So, what can I do for you," he repeated.

"?"

"How can we help you, I mean."

"I am confused."

"Yes, makes sense, that seems to be the most common sentiment we encounter round these parts," "What sentiment," "No questions from you, squire," "Apologies," "But ask again anyway," "What," "Exactly," "What," "Pure and unadorned confusion, that's all we find in your lot around here, it's no good, we try to do a good job and make things clear and frankly it seems we're just not cutting it."

"I see."

"Yup. Anyway, let's start over and maybe we'll get it right this time. Why are you here?" "I have no idea," "Yeah, that's a pretty common response too," "I'm sorry, I don't think I understand," "Me neither," "Pardon," "I don't know what you're doing here either," he said, "Why am I here then," "Not sure, but you must have done something bad to be sitting here, don't you think," "I'm not sure," I said, "I try to follow the law — I'm a lawyer, it's rather imperative that I follow the law," "Which law," "I'm sorry I'm confused," "Which law or laws do you obey," "Well, our laws," "Whose laws," "Ours — mine — yours — ours — our law," "Ah well, I reckon we may not be thinking of the same laws," "What do you mean, we only have one set of laws," "That you know of," he said without looking at me and without a hint of the ominousness that such a response deserve. "Anyway," he said, "do you want to sit here and shoot the breeze all night or you wanna tell me what you done? Because frankly I haven't the foggiest what you done and I'm getting a wee bit tired on account of not knowing, so, tell me, what did you do and when did you do it and why."

I looked at the wall then back at him, or at least in his direction, his eyes were hard to catch. "I thought that you might tell me," I said, "seeing as it was the Guard who brought me here."

"Would be better if you stopped all this confusion and confessed."

"Confess to what," "What do you think you might've done bad," "I don't know, I'm confused," "Me too buddy, wish I could help but it's in your hands," "What is, "Absolution and your fate. Just tell me something good."

"You mean, make something up?"

"No! Don't spoil it, convince me that it's all real, that way we can both justify our presence here, then I'll go home and you'll go too, home, elsewhere."

"Elsewhere?"

"Elsewhere. Somewhere in this world, elsewhere."

"Where?"

"Never mind that. Just — tell me a story! Tell me what you did and convince me it's real, not something you're making up to please me. I need a real story here, a real story, your story."

"I don't know what to say or where to begin."

"Beginning'll suffice."

"I don't know where that is."

"You don't know where that is? The beginning?"

"No, I do not know where the beginning is, nor what it would be that is beginning."

"Your life?"

"My life? What about it?"

"The beginning of your life?"

"Yes?"

"When did you come into this world?"

"I — where I am from, we do not mark birthdays."

"You must be from the valley, then."

"Indeed, sir, I am."

"You're a strange lot down there, you know? And I don't mean that in a bad way. You're just unusual. Different. Hard to get a bead on you and your folk. Unusual practices and beliefs in that part of our nation, your home. Don't you believe something about twins?"

"Pardon?"

"That each of you, on your birth, a distant star sends a second life for you into this world? And that you are not completely yourself until you encounter your second life wandering the earth, grapple with it and make it your own? Some rite of manhood or something?"

"That is not how we see it, surely."

"It's how everyone else does, us included. And you know who matters."

"I'm sorry?"

"Never mind, we got off-topic. Start over. Start from the beginning."

"Apologies, my lord, but I do not know the beginning, nor what it is that begins."

He sighed like my chair. "Look, we're going nowhere at the pace of molasses on a winter's night, so I'm going to help you out. Did you sign something," "Something," I asked, "Yeah, something, a pledge," "A pledge to what," "To us, them, whomever, just tell me, have you pledged some kind of allegiance at some discernable point in time," "I could've but I don't recall," "Ah well let's try this out." He opened a drawer and pulled out another manila folder that to my cold shock had a picture of me paperclipped to the front. That was when I understood that "Elsewhere" would not be good.

He rifled through it, "No, no, no, no, maybe, no this isn't it, no, no, yes, no wait doggone it no, no, no, yes, yes yes here we are." He placed a document on the table and slid it across the table to my side. "You recognize this," "Let me take a look," "No time, do you see your signature at the bottom." I squinted and recognized my name but not certain about the handwriting I was meant to recognize was my own and used by me to sign my name. "Yes, that's my name," I said, and I swore I saw a smudge of grease.

He sighed and slid the paper back. "Okay, that'll do, thank you for your service, we'll need you to wait here for a bit while we process this information, please follow me kind squire," and he rose from his seat and turned, but he paused and rushed back to his chair. He leaned across the table; he was close enough that I could see his eyes, which did not look at me. "Odd question," he said, "odd question I'm going to ask you, but I'd like an answer." I nodded. "You, uh, you know much about umbrellas?" "I'm not sure what you mean." "What do you know about umbrellas?" "What do I know about umbrellas?" "Yeah, tell me what you know about them, high-level overview." "Well, you use them in the rain to keep yourself dry, isn't that it?" "Historically, that's been the case. But what about now?" "What do you mean?" "What do people use them for now?" "Why — I don't know, isn't it the same?" "I wouldn't know." "You haven't used an umbrella?" "Oh, I have. But not anymore." "Not anymore? Why not?" "Reasons. New prohibition." "Prohibition on using umbrellas?" "Yes, squire, strictly forbidden." "I didn't know…" "Didn't think so." "But when it rains, how do you know how to stay dry?" The man stood up again and, smiling wildly, looked blankly across the room to the far wall. "Folks like me are smart enough not to get wet," he said, "and we don't need hope, either." He walked around the table and knocked on the door twice and the door opened. He turned and beckoned me with a Come-Hither motion made with his index and cuss digits. I got up from my chair, my faithful chair, my chair that blessedly had not dissolved into a chairful of dust, the one stable thing in my life. He led me through various hallways until he opened a door, "If you could wait here a bit, that would be great, thank you so much;" and as he left and the door clicked, I realized he had not once looked me in my eyes.

I heard ruffling and turned. The cooper from the holding cell was there.

It was the same room.

"How'd it go," he asked.

I looked at him. "Honestly," I said, "I have no bloody idea." He guffawed and hiccupped. "Yeah," he said, "nobody does."

I believe that is what happened — how I got here, or at least a part of how I got here — well, not here per se — not this room, this cell — but here, the bigger here, the camp, the lager, this place, this mundus novus. Sailed here through darkness, from darkness into darkness darker yet. Some light gets through, paltry bits, which is how I write and also why I err so much, sometimes I must continue writing in the dark and doing so have not the foggiest of where I've come to, therefore the scribbles, mistakes, jottings, divagations everywhere and every which way but up.

And it all seems dross, everything that's come before now. What I loved well remains, though obscured, as through a screen, the outline of it visible, everything else in darkness.

It has been written that all of our problems stem from our inability to sit quietly in a room alone. I have sat I do not know how long quietly in a room alone. My problems endure. O that aphorism, what beguiling and deceiving wit! I refute it thus.

Entry No. 18

I hear a voice of fire singing.

It tells me one thing.

Go back.

Too late, too far down the line, if only otherwise. Another path back to the past, retread, retread. I tap my ashplant on the door, no answer is forthcoming, the house has been emptied. The past has left, has passed beyond the visible mount deep down into the gorge where the wind whips at your throat and will not release you until you speak what it wants to say itself. No choice abides. And the wind, those scattered voices, the wind, the wind the past speaking in very many different languages in very many voices, the multitude, half-heard or understood, tongues close enough to be sisters but not so much to be twins, seal your ears and let listen to the others, ah the wind is whipping you with a tongue almost your own that says, "Don't you go a-cliping now else they'll send you up the chimney, ah how bonnie is yon chimney tonight, Hhh seal your ears and sail on by, No, you're havering now, friend, they'll fix ye with a skelping else it's up you go."

How often

How often

How often have I stood to see the chimney pour out thick and smoky clouds in faintest blue and, close beneath, the houseleek's yellow flower as fast appearing in a nearer view and thought about it all again. How I wish I could stand there and watch those clouds rise in visible light beyond these walls. Flit, flit goes the auld wind rustling now over and along the houseleek, wending back up to a braw bricht moonlit nicht long since gone, smoky clouds floating up from the chimney, into the air, of the air, gone, all gone. Flit, flit. The wind taps at the door with your ashplant. Open the door and see the clouds fading into a fireplace, a solitary figure conducting the flames with a bellow, the wind's gone round the wrekin and you can't go follow. Flit, flit, you hear the wind, you hear it, and it tells you that the past is gone, it's out to lunch, gone fishing, joined the choir invisible, run down the curtain and scattered to the wind. Ah, the wind, the fair wind, bewend: heu, the nights are fair drawin in. Bewend: all ash and soot and salt, pillars thereof, scattered thereupon. Bewend: heu, what a night it was in a strange old arid land, a strange old land not my own, stranger now for being gone. Gone, gone, gone. Gone into the remembrance of another. Flit, flit. In yon valley twas there we sate down, don't listen, seal your eyes, and sail calm on, twas there we sate down, cleft into a chasm, one of us split edgewise into two who look into the abyss for the other who looks back, looks away. Flit, flit. Yea, we mourned. Yea, now we weep when we remember. Yea, we remember now. Yea, we do. O thy cunning, wind, coming in the semblance of a voice, more smoke than ash. Flit, flit. You come when I expect you least. Flit, flit. Who's there, pay no need, sail calm on, about suffering you were never wrong. Do not answer. Once answered they took of you your leave, of wife and life and world. Flit, flit, flit. You cleaved unto the past, became one with the past, being whole in fleshlessness, all ash and soot and salt and pillars made thereof, whole in fleshlessness, in union never to be defeated. Hallo, hello, kia ora. The wind is talking up again, pay no heed. Haud yer wheesht, foul wind. And the wind tells you not to answer yet again the rapping on the door, Flit flit goes the auld wind, watch out, else the wind'll suck you clear out and you are gone, she and they are gone, all gone once again into the braw bricht nicht, long gone again you'll be, for twas they who carried you away, the wind not separate from the thing it blows. Flit, flit. Whyfor make ye no answer, flit flit. Because I won't forget your cunning.

If only once again at least, not goodbye, not farewell, goodbye, goodbye.

If only once again at least, no goodbye were it otherwise; and since it's not, goodbye.

And I hear the voice of fire smouldering.

And the voice is gone, they are gone, you are gone.

Entry No. 19

Where did I go?

Entry No. 20

Lost in memories, unhelpful ones. I have remembered too much of my life before the camp and it has brought me no closer to retrieving myself and my life from memories of a past life. I believed I was capable, by wresting possession of my memories from the floating past that delves the symmetries of some portion of my mind, of making myself live again. Withstand the gales of memory. But no. Remembrance of life has brought nothing of nothing. I have no idea why I am here, where I am, how I can escape. Yet I have nothing else but for memories to write. Inventing a new life in Dee's life and writing it down got me nowhere. New life must come from life already. I have another life, of course, my life in this camp, my lagerlife. I can go back to writing about the quotidian stuff, my constitutionals and what I have seen in the camp and whatnot and see what comes out of that. Perhaps I will find my way out of here and back into my life, or some life — I need not return to my life, any life, new or old, will do.

Let me try.

A LANDSCAPE IN BRIEF

The world of yours stops at the gates. The gates! What is that sign above the gates, what does it say:

— I don't remember for it was dark, and I was a stranger when I came, and the language of this place was foreign to me, strange.

I used to be a stranger here.

The camp is guarded by two armed battalions and surrounded by a shimmering and incandescent fence that stands five times my height. And this is a high height because I am not short, nor do I believe anyone would consider me to be short, I aver I am taller than some, enough people that, if a calculation were done, it would find my height to be above average. I am proud of that. It is one of my few good traits, physical ones. And so, from this, you may take me at my word the boundaries are immense, shimmering, sky-scraping.

In front of those walls are hidden traps buried half my body-length below the ground. We know these hidden traps exist because of those attempts that campers made to touch the walls. They approached the walls and then, after a bright light emerges from the ground and recedes, where they stood are only pillars of ash the wind sends floating through the sky, distended flakes of men.

Watchtowers three times my height are above the walls. I have seen seven of them and there may be more. These towers are equipped with light machine guns, long and light, and occupied by guards rotating watch, if I remember well, every two hours. In between the cordon of the towers are sentinels in hidden posts along with other soldiers, so many soldiers, at least they make it seem there are so many, there may be very few beyond our gaolers in the wards and the Guard and who it may be who is the lord of this camp if in fact we have a lord. We don't know. We just know this yard, the barracks, the factories where we work, this cell, the duncan, the yard, the worn path ringing round it, these walls; and beyond the walls, I dream, the sea.

FIN

Entry No. 21

No constitutional today. I have begun dedicating my time to remembering my life in the camp up until now and, almost as though someone sensed a shift in my focus, I now am denied the experience of living in this camp. I only live now only in this cell. The camp, it seems, is disappearing. Someone knows. Someone is on to me.

I must press on. I sense that time, although endless otherwise, for me is growing short, and I must accomplish my task before my papers are taken from me again. They sense things, them, they do, or at least one cannot be free of the feeling that they know things humans should not be able to know, such as the fact that I am writing my memories down here to find an answer to a question I do not yet know how to ask, such as the fact that I do not choose which memories come to me and which remain distant and aloof, such as the fact that I do not feel I am getting closer and still hope I will get closer to understanding my residence in this world and how to end it. But my time is waning. I must accomplish my task. Remember, remember. Invite yourself to remember. Entice the memories to come, tempt them with sweetbreads and grog or whatever it is that makes memories stir. Remember, remember. But don't remember too much. Remember just enough. And then go on.

Entry No. 22

When we come to the camp we must learn by heart a credo. It is this:

1. *You must not escape.*
2. *Three or more campers must not meet together.*
3. *No stealing.*
4. *You must absolutely obey the wisdom of the Guard.*
5. *You must immediately report if you see any strangers or suspicious people.*
6. *All campers must be their brother-campers' keeper and immediately report each other's unusual or anti-social behavior.*
7. *You must be truly remorseful for your own mistakes.*
8. *You shall immediately be shot by firing squad if you ever violate these laws and regulations of the camp.*
9. *You must fill your heart with gratitude, for you have been chosen.*

We obey as long as we have whatever is left of our common sense about us; we lose it when it is time to eat.

They have fun feeding us, the gaolers. One game they play is the Bread Game. If a group of us is outside working, gathering leaves against the wind, they come over and toss us loaves of bread. Like throwing a piece of bread to the pigeons and watching the pigeons determine hierarchy and who will eat and who will not. But pigeons do not fight as much as men. We go and scratch and bite and fight to get a piece of bread. And then the frenzy ends, and the leaves have scattered, so the work must begin anew but at double-time, for the time lost in fighting for that bread will be paid for in methods to be determined by our gaolers.

Our gaolers. Ah, our gaolers.

On occasion I feel pity for my gaolers, who are prisoners even if they do not know it. They too cannot leave because the entrance to my ward is locked at night, so they, like me, must remain here, some asleep and some awake, alternatingly conscious or dreaming, perhaps aware of their own captivity even if they do not consider it such. Sometimes at night I hear one repeating verse to himself; it is not good verse, so I assume it is his and I assume that he fancies himself a poet. Perhaps he thinks that after his time in the camp he will go on to be a poet whom the polis and whatever literary establishment remains will admire for his navigation between the unsavory reality of life as it is and a fantastical world that is beyond imprisonment, beyond constraint, a world where he too is free. Or perhaps that is what I hope he will want: perhaps he is satisfied declaiming his odes to the state and its beneficent power and in that way, he will win acclaim and favor when wit and eloquence have turned into panegyric. Yet I doubt in ten years anyone will remember him, anyone aside from me. And even that is not certain. My pity lapses.

To take up another subject: the corruption of our language under the regime equals to the refinements of our language built up through generations of noble work that may be annihilated in a breath. What was polished, purified and perfected through the labor of a thousand years has been torn down and vandalized in five years' time. Jargon, propaganda, fanatical cant, affected phrases, conceited words and legalese: even now they are hardly intelligible, which is no wonder, as they are the joyless offspring of ignorance, caprice, and unrighteous power. And that is what I use to write: the meager and repulsive dross of the everyday.

The language here is strange to me. The word *just* has no applications here, it has no use, the word *just* has no meaning here, it is a sound with no more salience than a footstep fading down the hall, not footsteps drawing in, the former means things will stay the same, the latter threatens change. *Just* means nothing here. It is less than a sound. A cough.

Our great nation is now surfeited with a panoply of dunces of high esteem, dunces who have power enough to give rise to some new word, phrase or ignoble locution and propagate it thence in statements, edicts, orders, laws, statutes, judicial disquisitions, *annuncios* and encyclicals. These dunces have caused this ill-begotten language to be osmoticized into the scribblings of our literature: the most learned men of letters, rather than obviate such corruptions, are seduced to imitate, promote, and comply with them. A language that was once illustrious, noble, humorous, and judicious is now obscure, unnoted, somber, and profligate. You may witness this mangling, defilement, denuding and defenestration of our pithy tongue in everything I write.

In writing I defile and am defiled. This cannot be helped. We do what we can with what we have. I have words and that is all. Words and no more.

My style is intemperate; sometimes I am sweet, sometimes when I get into the heights of dudgeon, I seem ferocious without fangs, powerless to defend or to advance, like a hissing platypus encountered in the mead.

And yet, by the grace of our good Lord, He has seen to it, in His verdant wisdom, that I be imprisoned here forever so as to protect me from the decline and fall of our tongue that is surely happening beyond these walls.

I was distracted by a thought. A fly buzzed. I was writing of our gaolers. Our gaolers. Oh, our gaolers.

Sometimes the gaolers make us stop and sing a song. And then they boo and hiss and throw rocks at us, but we must continue singing songs of joy. Other times they ask us to strike up a dance when new campers are brought in and separated into the groups: who by fire, who by labor. That is when I play the tuba. The tuba was requisitioned from a group of minstrels, I believe, and I am sure that one of them at least knew how to play it. Why they make me play it, if not to laugh at me, I don't know. But that is good enough for them, laughing at me. It is a respite from their existence here in the camps.

Those that our gaolers beat pride themselves on the thrashing: it is not so different than a clout on the bottom from your father: it does not come from hatred but from disappointment that we have fallen short and have been found wanting and hope that we will measure up if we learn from the whacks. A camper will be walking somewhere, or else a camper will be walking nowhere and a gaoler yells, "You, squire, come here this instant," and the tamarind switch comes out, or one of us will be in the barracks readying to sleep or else sleeping already and a gaoler will break the door open and we will all be stunned into wakefulness, and the movement of the one who looks most awake catches the eye and the gaoler smiles, he says soothingly, "Squire, please come down, there is something we need to talk about," and so you resign yourself to coming out your cot in your pyjamas to follow the gaoler outside and the tamarind switch comes out, or else there are several gaolers and they've had a bit to drink, every one of them three sheets to the wind with that blazing joy of drunken mischief in their eyes, and one of them calls to a camper to come down out of his cot, and he is shaking and he goes outside and from inside the barracks one hears grunting, a thud and the tamarind switch must have been brought out, several of them, each gaoler with a switch of his own, and there is a grunt and whimpering and laughter and the sound of something whistling through the air, and there is whimpering and moaning and laughing. They care enough to determine the precise location on our body where a blow would cause the greatest pain without permanent disfigurement, cause us the great- est pain without maiming us because maiming us would stop us from working better, work being our lone chance to prove we are worthy to live, worthy to live long enough to work more, work better, longer, worthy to live long enough and work and live until we may be beat again. The gaolers' beatings are not hateful, they are loving.

Belief can endure without evidence. I believe this is love. I convince myself this is love. I tell myself this is love. I trust this is love. A fistful of love.

Yes, I said it, that word, Love. They beat us almost lovingly. If not paternal love then it is another love, another avatar of love. There are some of us who are thrashed by only one gaoler, chosen by one particular gaoler and that gaoler is faithful to his camper, thrashing him and him alone, the lucky ones, they are monogamous, they have cleaved, the gaoler shares his pain and the camper bears it, the switch binds them together, the switch a covenant, a sign of their union, you can see it in the swelling, yes, this is his, My Guard, he chose me, he will beat only me and nobody else, loyal to the end, spurs bloodied with amber, his is a faithful fist, my body is the only one that he will thrash. A kind of love, that. I do not have such a gaoler. My gaolers exchange my clothes, push me into my own excrement and declaim verse. I do not experience this kind of love. But all the same it is a kind of love.

It is not the same with the torture. There is no love in the torture. The beatings remind us we can do better, the torture teaches us that we are never good enough.

It was only shortly after I became a camper that I was submitted to my first bout of torture. I did not know I was to be tortured. I was gathering leaves against the wind and my number was called — I had already been rid of my name and become my number, I had left the holding cell and the cooper in the holding cell and had come to the camp already, it is something called Moving Day, when men become campers, in time I hope others will speak of it but

I will not — my number was called, I stepped aside and stood at attention, "Prepare yourself," a gaoler said, "Yes sir but for what," "Witness Preparation with the Guard," "Preparation for what," "For your trial by the High Inquisitor," "Trial, what trial," "Stop asking me questions, you'll find out later," "Yes, of course," and I went back to sweeping, but I could not dedicate myself to the leaves as I had before, what was distracting me, of course, something was coming, Preparation, I'd find out, Preparation, it's torture, the leaves skidded across the yard and whirled over the walls.

The Guard prefers only five or so avatars of torture: the Water Fun calls for the camper to stand on his toes in a tank filled with water up to his nose for twenty-four hours or what they tell us is twenty-four hours, twenty-four hours being just a metonym for when they've decided enough's enough; during the Hanging Game the camper is stripped and hung upside down from the ceiling to get his body blessed with clouts, spurs bloodied with amber, spit and mucus cleaving to the amber, and this is not the loving kind of beating that the gaolers give because the Guard does not love, they never love; the Doll House Vacation, where the camper is introduced to a very small and solitary cell with barely enough room to sit but not enough to stand or lie, and the camper gets to stay on his vacation for a week and come back changed, emptied of himself; for Prayer Time, the camper has got to genuflect, a smooth and faultless wooden bar placed near the hollows of his knees to stop the blood from circulating, and after a week the camper cannot walk and there's a fair to middling chance he will die from the faulty circulation in the months to come; and the Pigeon Revelation, the camper is tied to the wall with both hands at a height of an arm's length and then must crouch for many hours, the suffering is unending.

But they gave me a special different torture for my Witness Preparation.

I am not grateful.

Entry No. 23

Some days after my interrogation I was moved from the holding pen to this cell. The cooper was sleeping there when I left. I never saw him again.

I was moved to this cell. I realized I would be kept here without the chance to communicate with other men and that I would be here for a long period, so I began to try to keep track of the days. I looked for subtle changes in light that slunk in through my window, those changes that signal the diurnal handoff between night and day. I tied little knots in a loose string in my uniform for each day; on the day I was first tortured, the one day I remember, I counted 72 knots, which meant that I had been in the camp for at least 72 days, along with however many days I spent in solitude before deciding to track my time here, which must have been at least ten. I have since forgone the act of tying knots to count my days: I have run out of string and I no longer measure my life in days I live but in words I write. When I gave it up so long ago, the knots counted 936.

The torture is barbaric. No, strike that — torture is not barbaric, it is not foreign, it is not approaching the city gates from outside to tear them down, no, no barbarians at the gates, torture is inside already, not only inside but immanent, yes, the desire to torture at least is immanent, it is a part of us, a part of civilization, torture is the most civil art. The torturer is a profession as old perhaps as prostitutes and poets, at least as old as conflict called for vengeance, the acquisition of important information and the coterminous desire to demean, dehumanize, degrade, destroy the sufferer or at least the sufferer's sense of himself as a human. How much human ingenuity has been devoted and depleted in creating, excusing, defining, perfecting torture? How much blood, sweat, money, care, iron, steel, samite, water, wood, fire, stone, how much time has been devoted to the creation, realization, and perfection of torture? Unimaginable, unthinkable, unimpeachable amounts, more than all the raindrops fallen in a year, more than all the kisses every mother gives to every son before each goes off to fight for the motherland, before each goes off and perchance will have the opportunity to engage in this civilizing act, is inducted into its fraternity, induction by way of initiation, initiation by way of torturing another person, someone who is barely a person — the enemy, a formless threat manifested in a body of flesh, guts, blood and other things. The enemy is the barbarian, the foreigner, the alien, the other, the metic, the strange, the fearsome, the unknown, and most of all the uncanny: every enemy is the image of yourself returned to you in a different form, every enemy is not you but you somewhat different, somewhat distinct, he could have been your brother, your blood, your compatriot, comrade, brother-in-arms, protector, aide-de-camp, but most of all he could have been you, he could have been you if only he had been on the other side of the gates, if he had been protecting the gates in solidarity and not attacking the gates in aggression, or if not attacking in aggression then attacking on account of another higher entity's aggression, making him into a burnt offering, a sacrifice for a cause or a dream or a belief or a country, a land, a nation, a people, a canal, lake, waterway, mine, deposit, oilfield, soil rich in nutrients, fields of waving grain, mountain passes, valleys, overlooks, precipices, strategic vantages, any kind of land to be desired, all so unimpeachably desired, all so unimpeachably worth desiring, all so unim-peachably worth fighting for, worth sacrificing for, worth having others dying for, all worth destroying for, degrading for, decimating for, defeating for, elimi-nating for, annihilating for; and every means must be followed to reach that end, every means feasible: diplomacy, strategy, negotiation, duplicity, oratory, deception, war, torture — torture of your fellow man, your fellow blood, your fellow flesh, flesh of your flesh and blood of your blood, your fellow almost identical to you but for perhaps one or two percent of difference, that one or two percent manifesting in a difference to be keyed in on and raised to heights of evil, a difference in the nose, voice, tongue, speech, skin, laugh, custom, prayer, law, belief, anything, some kind of small difference that obscures that he is you, you but only on the other side, you but not you and so an enemy to destroy, degrade, defeat, torture.

Torture takes a person to be much like a holy book: as one of our sages said of the book, turn it and turn it for everything is in it. So, too, does it go for torture: twist him and twist him for everything is in him. Whatever you need, whatever you want, whatever you seek — information, truth, intelligence, wisdom, knowledge, supremacy, example-setting, retribution, gratification, justification, instructing, teaching, pain, power, power above all — twist him

and twist him for everything is in him, everything but yourself, never yourself, he is always another, never you, twist him and twist him for everything
is in him but you because you absent yourself in the process, he is not human
like you, no, he is human, all too human in a different way, the wrong way;
and so *peine forte et dure* is merited, the iron maiden is merited, the rack is
merited, cudgeling is merited, the shrew's fiddle is merited, stoning is merited,
the wheel is merited, the boats are merited, *poena cullei* is merited, the blood
eagle is merited, scalding water is merited, boiling is merited, the brazen bull
is merited, impalement is merited, crucifixion is merited, disembowelment is
merited, the garrote is merited, suffocation in your mother's ashes is merited,
unsterilized amputation is merited, scooping the eyes out so as to enhance the
psychological terror and then taking a knife to nose, tongue, finger, leg, arm,
genitals before removing collops of flesh from the thigh, buttocks, shoulder,
calf, face — all that is merited; enslavement is merited, removal of finger-
nails and piercing the hand with nails is merited, flaying is merited, cattle
prods are merited, electroshock is merited, drawing is merited, quartering is
merited, whipping is merited, every kind of flagellation is merited; enforced
solitude is merited, sleep deprivation is merited, mock execution is merited,
mock drowning is merited, extreme cold is merited, extreme heat is merited,
constant darkness is merited, constant light is merited, constant exposure to
the elements is merited, standing on a box all night and if you fall then he is
electrocuted — that too is merited because all conceivable pain is merited,
every conceivable act that brings about pain, suffering, fear, doubt, terror:
every such conceivable act is merited, everything under the sun and under
the moon, imaginable or unimaginable, everything is merited, everything is
merited but suffering yourself.

And why all this? To establish a boundary. To set something beyond the
pale. To establish what will be allowed and what will be forbidden, what will
be encouraged and what will be discountenanced, what will be admired and
what will be detested, what will be worth dying for and what will be worth
others dying for, what will be known and what will be unknown, what will
be loved and what will be hated, what will be humane and what will be cruel,
what will be human and what primitive, what will be beyond the pale and
what within it, what will be on the other side of the gates and what inside
them, what will be good and what bad, what evil and wicked and what good

and virtuous, what will be of us and what will be of them, what will be ours and what will be theirs, what will be accepted and what will be refused, what will be human and what will be barbaric and what will be civilized. And so torture refines us: it shows us what we will accept and, if not welcome, toler- ate within our civilization, and what we will if not hate, then proscribe in our civilization; torture whittles civilization down to accepted norms, acceptable deviations and tolerable heterodoxy; torture shows us what we will keep in civil society and what we will throw out, shows us what we will put up with and what we will not stand for; torture shows us what civilization is and what it is not, torture shows us civilization in full, torture shows us the limits of our humanity, our boundaries, constraints, frontiers, torture shows us what it is to be human, to be evolved social creatures, torture shows us what we can be, what we cannot be, what we are, what we are not, torture shows us what it is to be human, torture shows us ourselves.

And who is my double beyond the gates?

To torture is to engage in history, to be a part of a long grey line of tradition linking one to the earliest days of man. To torture is to restore power over time.

Enough.

Entry No. 24

I was fortunate my Witness Preparation was carried out in a comparatively harmless form. I know from the faint moans I hear and the corresponding flickering of the lights outside my door that others have been exposed to much more sinister preparation that I have yet to undergo.

My torture involved a normal chair, a gallon of water and pressure.

I had been in the camp for some time already, but up until that point, I did not know if I had been charged with any crime, whether to be charged with a crime was necessary to be here in the camp or whether I was to remain in the camp perpetually without any accusations leveled at me or charges confirmed. I would find that out later.

The door to my cell opened; there was no great light, rather darkness abounding. "Come," he said — who is he? no matter — "Come," he said, "follow." I stood up and walked towards him and I followed him blindly down a hall until he opened a door. Much like my interrogation, it seemed. Much changes, much stays the same, *mutatis mutandis*, so on and so forth.

"You first," he said, so I went in. Inside I saw the chair, the normal chair. It stood on the concrete floor, which sloped ever so slightly, almost imperceptibly, toward a drain in the center of the room. The chair sat five paces back from the drain. Four long fluorescent lights hung over head; a long wooden table was against the wall to the left.

He closed the door and turned to me. "Strip," he said, "now." I paused. "May I keep on my skivvies," I asked. For my insolence he crested my head with a sharp and painful smack. "You don't ask questions here," he said, "We are the ones who ask the questions although we know. Nor do we just know: we are wise, knowledge comes but wisdom lingers, do you understand, this has been a lesson to you free of charge, gratis confrère, now strip, everything, strip," and so I stripped. He pointed to the chair. "Sit," he said, and so I sat.

A knock came at the door. "Permission," replied he who had brought me to the room. Another man, a much taller man, entered the room and gently closed the door behind him. He carried in his hand a gallon bottle filled with a clear substance. I hoped it was water.

He wore a red greatcoat. The Guard.

I heard his bootheels reverberate through the room as he walked up to me. "Do you know why you're here," he asked, "No," I said, "I do not, I apologize," "Are you sure," "Yes, I am," "Well then, drink." The one that had led me here, who had moved to stand behind me, pulled my head up and held my mouth open as the other one poured the liquid down my throat. To my relief, it was water. To my great dismay, I had no choice but to drink the entire thing.

My torturer did not force me to drink it, no, he seemed more like a gentle figure of authority, a mother lovingly making me engorge myself with medicine. It is this intimacy that unnerves: I am a passive, powerless infant in his hands. He sustained me.

They conferred in the corner and I began to feel bloated, immensely so, stuffed through and through with piss. And then I began to feel the discomfort of a filling bladder, which was minimal at first, such as one experiences midway through an overlong lecture in university, the professor, won't he stop. But then the discomfort grew severer, more imposing, until I felt that I was no longer someone who controlled his body with his brain but instead someone whose actions are determined by this little organ, significant but rarely thought of until it is all that is thought of.

"Now, let's play a game," he said as he turned and approached me, the one who led me into the room walking behind him, "what a wonderful day to be alive, it's your lucky day, squire, we'll play a game, a guessing game, you like games don't you, who doesn't like a game, I know I do, so let's play, you ask me why you think you're here because of what you done and I'll tell you if you're getting close, and if you ask me the crime you have committed, I will let you piss; but if you take more than ten questions, I will shoot you then I will have a sandwich and I will eat my sandwich in your house while your wife watches, how does that sound." I tried not to cry but I began to cry. "Please, not her, she did nothing wrong," I begged, "She lived with you and bore your children, that's wrong enough, and besides, ah well, you know what she is doing, and you'll confess won't you, now, go ahead and ask, let's play." I paused. "I apologize," I said, "but may I ask a question?" He kicked me in my right shin with his boot, which sent a shiver of pain up my leg, and then pressed his right knee into my bladder. "Asking if you can ask a question in the form of a question, you're a smart one now, aren't you, well go ahead, but that's one question against you, and the next one will be another, which will leave you only eight questions to confess to what you've done, after that we drag you through the mud and put a bullet in you, not to mention the lovely evening with your traitor wife." I tried to ignore him, what he said about my wife — I did not think they could be so cruel, but then I was living in a world where the word *just* was absent from its vocabulary, nor a concept ever contemplated. Yet he was upon me, his knee pressing, pressing, pressing, and I could not ignore him nor the faint scent of berries and leaves emanating from him. I quickly amended my approach: instead of a question, I would make a comment. "I was told that I am not to ask questions, that asking questions is your role." He let go of my ear — I forgot to mention he had grabbed my earlobe — and smiled, "Who told you that," "Him, the other one," "Is that right, well, it's your lucky day, take this as a dispensation, for a limited time only you may be the one to ask the questions, you may be inquisitive and creative in your questioning in this special time we have together, otherwise questions are a no-go for you, but hurry, I'm getting bored of this."

Several questions passed from me to him, each one unsatisfactory.

"One more," he said, and as he said it, I swore then and swear now that I saw a glimmer of worry cross his eyes. He was young, this tall man who tortured me, too young to have been long in this regime. Was this the first time he had tortured someone? Could a man be so virginal in such a place? I thought not. But would this be the first time he would need to be up close and kill a helpless man? I thought so. And then, whether on account of nervousness or a subtle, pleading hint, he looked down at me and in my eyes and itched the space above his lip.

"Am I here because I am a party member of the prior regime or an agita-tor, or because I fraternize with agitators," I asked. His eyes shot beams of recognition, joy, relief. "Exactly right, my friend," he said, "lucky you, I didn't think you'd come through but here you are, in the clutch, a right champion, keeping us on the edge of our seat, what a phrase, you are the one in a seat, in any case terrific job, yes, that is precisely the reason for your imprisonment, you are one among the agitators who refuse to let the murderous past stay in the past, you are a danger to the state, a subversive, that is why you are here and in this room, never mind your scheming wife, very good, now one more thing before we let you let it out." The one who led me into the room went back to the table in the corner and retrieved a pen and paper and held it in front me, my torturer still upon me, his knee pressing, pressing, pressing. "Sign here," my torturer said, "it is your confession, which I think you will see fit to affirm, a mere X or scribble will be sufficient." Debased, pained, and caught, I signed. Promptly after I signed what I assumed to be a confession of my guilt — they did not let me read it nor could I, they had crushed my spectacles long ago — the one who led me into the room retrieved the pen and paper and my torturer released his knee from my bladder. The clear urine began to course, puddling on the chair before my crotch then flowing freely down my legs down to my ankles, some halting around my feet before it petered towards the drain and down it hence. I was relieved. I was nothing anymore.

They gave me back my clothing, "Dress now," the one who led me into the room said, so I dressed myself and like a dog waiting for his master to attach the leash so that he may go outside and sniff some trees and piss, I waited to be led back to my cage, which I shortly was. I was pushed back in and then the doors were sealed. I was back in my world, immured within my familiar and small world, my home. Here I was in control, but what purpose could having that control achieve? Nothing, nothing at all. I was again nothing to the world outside. But I had relieved myself, an accomplishment enough.

I have wanted to communicate, to transmit, to make understood the pain of being tortured. I do not want to make myself suffer it again; that would be wrong, unjust. Nor is it possible, however expansive your empathy and willingness to feel the suffering of others, to really *feel* it — to experience it. The pain, the fear, the debasement, the utter degradation of body and spirit and mind, our guts: these cannot be felt, truly felt, by someone who has not undergone torture, cannot be remembered in the body by someone who learns of it through words written or spoken. It is a cataclysm of the body: one can observe a man running and consider the exhaustion he may feel but one cannot know the exhaustion unless one begins to run like him. I thus conclude that my attempt to transmit the experience is impossible. But in failing that, perhaps I can still understand abstractly what happens when a man is tortured, if this is what you still could call a man.

Before I left the room and after I had dressed, my torturer stood some-where behind me and muttered something to me I have not forgotten. I would like to make mention of this so that I remember. This is what he said:

"Only the Lord can give and take life, but He is busy elsewhere, He has hidden His face in shame, so it falls to us to undertake His mission in His stead. We can make two and two five."

I do not know if he believed that, whether he was telling it to me so that I would understand and fear their power or whether he said it so he could hear himself affirm something that deep within himself he knew he doubted. No matter the impulse that made him say it, it is a statement that embodies the regime. In a world they have constructed, they are the Lord, they are His ava-tars. They decide who by fire, who by water, who by labor, who by exhaustion, who by chance, who by piss. I could recognize them or disavow them but like God, they are somewhere, going to and fro within this world and up and down upon it. They have enough religion to hate, but not enough to love.

And after my torture I wished I could go back to the barracks. Yes, bar-racks — other men, full of guts and other fine stuff! I was once within the lager among other men before I came here, but the recollection is vague now, I'm often told I'm vague, or rather, when I was free, or freer, or something, outside the lager, when I worked, worked and went home freely to my home, my family there, my wife sometimes there and sometimes not, yes, it was then I was often told I was vague, back when I was out there, working, yes, yes your words are vague, they dwell in the ambiguities, going off hither and yon and further yet still, somebody must have said so at one point or another, yes, you're always roaming hither and yon, and here I am now, I imagine I am still vague, always uncertain, hedging, wishy-washy, vague, *wandering* as the word means, and yet I wander as I write and in no other way do I roam, I roam here, these leaves, dead tree, along their smushed pulp, that is the place alone where I may roam, forgive me my vagabondage, I am here and only here and roam in bondage, I assert my freedom, some avatar of it at least, but in assert-ing some kind of freedom I bind myself to something worse.

Entry No. 25

I know I must go faster — time is short, the stock of paper shorter. I'll get to it! I'll go on faster, I can't go on another way, faster, faster, faster, sprightly goes the worm. Keep going, going on, keeping on, pressing on, until they forgive you your insolence, for sitting here, yes, sitting, you sit and write, this position is most amenable isn't it, write upon your chest, what chest, this chest, no proof, no evidence lad, you are no one here, no one but what you say, oh if you could see my eyes, I have them still, I must, no mirror here, perhaps your eyes have grown bigger than your head, ah but your chest, it had a heart that beat, you had a heart that beat back against the world, no, get to the quick — sometimes quicker eftsoons slower, you believe you have a heart now, what insolence, to think that belief may exist without evidence, believe, hope, keep going, keep believing, hope against hope, believe, don't believe, just know, always know, know you write in the darkness gentle as you go in the dark, may they never see you hard at it in case it comes to nothing, in case it yields up nothing to the light, in case others who know they have eyes such that can read this litany, such purposeless toil, they could never forgive you then, go in darkness, go, go on, but how much longer, how much longer will this go on, an ending must be coming, surely an ending must be at hand. My divagations soon will cease. And so on. Go on.

Entry No. 26

I realize I have not been permitted my daily constitutional for some time now. It can no longer be considered a daily constitutional. If anything, it will be an occasional constitutional. Assuming I may take one again.

I sense I am pulled apart from the world around me, this lagerworld, leaving everything of the life of experience for the remembered life. I already have too much of that, remembered life. I need more of life, more life I can live, not only life I remember. I would like to do what I did before here. Work. Witness. Work. Witness. Sleep. Witness. Ah well. We shall see. In time.

Entry No. 27

I was in the barracks before I was carried to this cell. Of this I am sure. I was not alone in this world, the lager. There are others here. One man to a bunk, a skinny little bunk, knotty and uncomfortable...

They ought to be remembered, the other ones, they ought to be preserved, or at least be shored against the torrents of memory.

So.

I heard the Neighbor through the walls. He was in another barrack, one sharing a wall with ours, he slept or did not sleep next to me, a partition between us, a barrier no wider than my hand, I was closer to him than I was to the other men in my barracks, we knew each other without knowing each other, every day he would tap three times against the wall when he knew the gaolers were coming so I would be prepared and not caught off-guard, we knew each other without knowing each other, how I miss him. I know my neighbor led a blameless life like most of us do, or as I hope many of us do, too many. But he seemed more blameless than others. He was orderly, neat, consistent, and regular in his habits. I have not observed this directly — like I said, a partition — but I perceived through the regularity of his schedule — his waking, his exercise, his weeping, his screaming, his slurping, his praying, his snoring — that he would be utterly normal anywhere else, which is what made him strange and suspicious. Every part of his routine occurred at the same time of day every day, which is remarkable because we have no awareness of the hours in here. But through some internal tick-tockery he followed his routine to a T every day without deviation. It was supremely impressive.

For a time, I made persistent efforts to follow his pattern and gain respect from our gaolers. I believed that the fastidiousness with which I would dedicate myself to routine would impress them. Of course, I would gain nothing material from them: I would receive no more rations than I already did, be no more exempt from punishment that I already was not, would gain no more freedom than I was already denied. I thought that perhaps they would come to respect what I thought was a manifestation of my own internal freedom; that, even though I was indefinitely immured there, I was still free to order my life within the boundaries set up around me. After a time I realized no difference was forthcoming: they acted no differently towards me nor could I sense even the slightest shift in how they perceived me, their prisoner who I do not think they perceived as a person at all — I was still no one to them, some hot pulp maybe, hot pulp with a number, I was still a prisoner alive to no one outside the lager's walls any more than I existed for them as a part of the bureaucracy they were consigned to manage. So, I stopped. But my neighbor, he kept at it, he persisted. Until one morning a number was called by the Guard, they had come, yes, of course they had, they always do, a number was called, LS13, a number was called, LS13, not a number for it has letters but we call them the numbers, a whole book of them's kept somewhere, all of us written down and inscribed, we are not men, we are numbers — a number was called and his voice responded in kind, I heard his bunk creak and then silence; that night after labor I waited for him to resume his routine but the routine had been discontinued, put on layaway, the routine had ceased, I tapped the partition three times but heard nothing tap back, he never came back, the next occupant did nothing but sob softly each night, it would have been annoying if I weren't so tired.

The Author was a lunatic. Sometimes he imagined he was not in the lager or he at the least tried to convince himself he was not here. I do not dwell here, he sings, I am not here, don't holler at me, I'm not here, I'm gone. This wall, he says, this wall, for one, this wall is fake, I refute it thus, he says, even if the contact between his foot and the barracks wall proved that he was confined here in reality no matter what he told himself otherwise, I refute it thus, he says, ah, poor one, your refutation refuted.

He told himself, and even believed, that he was not in the camp. Madness. He denied it, refuted it, he was insane through and through up to his eyeballs, of this I am sure, he said he's a poet, he proclaims, I am the bard of the gaol, my song flies far past these walls, sit softly, and listen till I end my song.

He was a bad poet. He wrote out of a style in a way not appropriate for this world, this one or the world beyond if it's still there. When he would start declaiming the gaolers would hear him and moan. They insisted on a correctness of form: rigidity: they insisted that traditional meters, while worthy of reverence, were not to be used in the present poetry; that one was to speak what one knows, of the little things one knows, nothing major, nothing grand, only buttons, keys and such, all worthy subjects but subjects that ought to be addressed the appropriate way, the correct way, a small way, nothing epic, nothing inspiring, a downward look, a fleeting lyric, the only way.

He called the gaolers the poets laureate. He fashioned garlands out of strips of cloth he traded for his rations. Ennoblement is worth an empty stomach, he said.

When he was not making his song, he walked around kicking things in the camp, shouting, I refute you thus! He refuted everything. The gaolers laughed. He may refute his cloistering, but it would no more free him than a bit of food should make hunger disappear for good.

I am writing a new world here, he yelled, I am the author of a world, I am a writer, you must listen, I am a writer and this is my life: the life of a writer, whatever he may fancy to the contrary, is not so much a life of composition as a life of warfare; and his trial in it, precisely that of any other militant or rebel in this world, depends not so much on his wit and felicity of thought as his resistance — and his ability to endure the contrary forces pushing back upon him as he resists the incursion of the larger world into his world.

We called him the Author. Other times we called him Loon. Ah, a loon! I heard one so many years ago, another world — ah, I remember it, the loons calling in the distance when we were married, I won't go back, time is brief, that world is so many pages back, I've not got the time, may the loons always hoot out in that world…

He would call out into the air across the camp, hooting and hawing. And we asked him, what are you doing, and he said to us, Why, it's my song, irrefutably so, try to refute it, you cannot, my song is my song, it will endure somewhere in the wind, running softly, it is my song, tread softly on my song, for you tread on my people's bones, this is my song, it will endure.

One day we woke to no hooting and hawing. Loon's song had stopped, the Author offered no more words, he was gone.

A gaoler walked by the Maimed Hawk and saw him slouching against a barrack wall, outside, sitting in dust. The gaoler asked him which way the Loon had gone, but the Hawk was so lazy he merely pointed his head in a direction. The gaoler was so amused by the scandalous indolence of his response that he offered the Hawk a sucking stone if he would do anything lazier than what he had just done. The Hawk said, "Put the sucking stone in my hand," and the gaoler laughed with sharp amusement. The gaoler then asked him which way the wind blows, and the Hawk answered, "North north north, follow the hawk," and the gaoler offers the Hawk another sucking stone if he can elaborate on his laconic reply. The Hawk says as only he can, "North north north, follow the hawk, effendi." The gaoler laughs with merriment and whistles. Three gaolers come rolling a stone, large nice and round, its diameter longer than a man, its weight far beyond that of a dozen men's bodies. The gaoler smiles and gestures at the Hawk to the gaolers, he turns to the Hawk smiling, says, I promised you a superior stone, now, here you go. "Follow the hawk," said the Hawk, "Will you not take your stone, squire," asked the gaoler, "The hawk, the hawk, effendi," said the Hawk, "Very well," the gaoler frowned and gathered up his greatcoat sharply whipping around him as he turned, almost in a dance, he turned and nodded at the gaolers, it was all one movement, one blissful movement, he nodded to the gaolers, and ah, the Maimed Hawk had sat in the dust, then he no longer sat in the dust and the dust now, it was sodden.

Entry No. 28

Perhaps all we did was laze around the camp, getting beat or tortured, not eating, waiting for something, anything, something. That seems wrong. No, in truth we worked, we labored. We did. I found value in such a bleak skill. My labor was manufacturing umbrellas.

I begin with a birch wood shaft, stained to match the handle. I was given it, I do not know where it came from, I don't know. Elsewhere. It came from Elsewhere.

Using a pair of combination pliers, I craft two springs from wires made of Argentan. Argentan, also called nickel brass or albata, is a copper alloy, made for the most part with copper and with a little nickel and zinc mixed in. The Argentan is produced in another camp, or, at least, it too is produced elsewhere; we are fortunate we do not need to manufacture it ourselves. I say this because nickel's melting point is several hundred degrees higher than copper's and at least three times higher than zinc's. All of them are far too hot for a man to survive. It is necessary for the nickel to be melted at such a temperature because the nickel must be as fine as possible to dissolve in the copper zinc alloy. What tools they use to heat the nickel to that temperature, I don't know. But I am glad we do not need to do it: I can imagine, although I do not want to, the dangers and possible incidents that can occur to a starving, pressured prisoner working so close to such heat. I am not even sure they work in well-ventilated rooms; I doubt it. Not only then must they work in excruciating heat, but they must also risk inhaling zinc fumes, which can cause headaches, nausea, fever, muscle spasms, weakness, and tiredness, all of which would diminish one's capacity to work, which diminishes in the minds of our overseers our justification to live.

I craft one end of the Argentan spring into a triangle. Then I place the spring on a cast iron anvil and use a hammer to work the spring until it is flat, which ensures that the spring will fit neatly.

After working the spring, I turn to the rotary saw to cut two slots in the birchwood shaft, one each at the top and the bottom. I proceed to use the electric drill to pierce a hole in each slot to hook each Argentan spring I craft.

It is of utmost importance that the springs fit securely; if not, the umbrella will not be able to open and close in a pleasing manner, which would subject our work to questioning and ourselves to opprobrium and punishment. To ensure the Argentan springs fit snugly, I bend the end of each spring into a right angle, which sets the appropriate tension for the umbrella to work properly. One must then gently but forcefully hammer the springs, so they rest firmly in the slots of the birchwood shafts. I use a pair of diagonal pliers to trim the spring before picking up the combination pliers again to compel the Argentan spring into the perfect shape. I try to accomplish this by first overbending the spring and then correcting its position. The initial difficulty I encountered in this task was extreme: I could not understand why coercing an object into imperfection through overcorrection before then forcing it back into a position of mirrored imperfection could result in the apposite form. But I was compelled to learn, and I learned.

After perfecting the shape of the springs, I work a small pin into the shaft with my hammer to forestall the spring from its natural inclination to extend fully, thereby constraining it. I subsequently slide a brass runner, which one desiring to open an umbrella uses to do so, up the birchwood shaft. The stop pin I hammer into the upper portion of the birchwood shaft, while seemingly small, is important for the proper functioning of the umbrella, for it is the stop pin that prevents the runner from travelling too far and causing the umbrella's canopy to blow inside out, which would make for an absurd and useless sight in the rain: a canopy blown inside out makes one look to be leading a strange religious processional through the streets and no one desires that, not even me, the bound artisan fashioning the implement not from an innocent desire to share my craft with the world but from the necessity of survival.

When I have made a dozen umbrellas, I place them in a large box for them to be shipped to various distributors so that they may sell the umbrellas to the public.

Although no one will know my name, I at least know that someone will be kept dry on a rainy day because of what I have made. I take pride in that. Not excessive pride, but a small, deep satisfaction in having made something that will ameliorate someone's woes, as small a woe as is the drizzle that often permeates the dense air of the capital. When I finish the umbrella, it is no longer mine: like little books, the umbrella will have its own fate in the world, one which I can no longer control.

I admit to having a fantasy. It is this: that someone I know or love in the world outside the camp has purchased one of my umbrellas, and she uses it to protect herself from the rain. Perhaps my wife has purchased one of my umbrellas and she opens it to shield herself from the rain so that she may stay dry and warm as she walks about, perhaps thinking of me and wondering about my fate, perhaps not. And if she is using one of my umbrellas, although she does not know it and although I am not there, my work in the camp is protecting her. This is what I tell myself; it is one of the stories I tell myself to find reason to survive. A fiction justifies itself at times.

I am grateful for the rain. Humanity knows it needs rain, but, as with love, one wants enough but never too much. If no drought exists, rain always seems like too much. But I am grateful for the surplus of rain. As long as some rain will fall, my work is needed, and my life is therefore justified.

I feel no hatred towards the people who purchase our umbrellas. They surely do not know the circumstances under which they are produced; if they did, they would not buy them. No, they would not. Despite what I've seen in the camp, people are good. Some people are — most people are. I must tell myself that — I must tell myself people are good, that people are kind, that people as a species are good for us, good for the planet, the world, the universe — I must tell myself that people are good else I have no reason to believe, no reason to believe that the world beyond the camp is a good one worth hoping that I will see again, that I will live there again, that I will exist clean, light and free again, that my wife is there and she thinks of me from time to time or if not from time to time then at least one thing or another at some time will make her think of me, the hooting of a loon if she goes away from the city and into the country again, the country where we were together once and always, no country like this, no country for ghosts, the forgotten, hawks, authors, neighbors, invented men without a life to live. She may think of me and she will not weep, she will not sigh, she will smile and walk calmly on, knowing that I was good, that I was good to her, that I was good to all — or good to most, I must have been bad to someone, there must be a reason why I am here and am not elsewhere — please have her know that I am here, that I think of her although I no longer dream of her, I think of her and see her eyes as they were when first we met, that smile, that smile that enveloped me in warm good love, that kept me warm so many nights, all those nights we were together, all those nights we were together although she may have wished that she were elsewhere, that she were in another world with someone else, another world with someone else, a world that she may live in now that I am so far gone, ah no, perish the thought, think of her as she was to you, light and warmth in dark, dark for aye encroaching, dark that we pushed back against, dark that is here now, dark is the night and dark is the day, and still she is out there in a world of light, a world that she illuminates and keeps for me, a world that I may never see, a world that I may never see but perhaps please God these words will see and then she'll know: I endure.

Entry No. 29

The dank albatross, it stinks most when it rains.

Entry No. 30

Nothing going. Have not been beyond these walls in so long. No permission. No interaction. I piss in the corner. Gaolers quiet. Nothing going. Still no resolution to the task. Memories fading, fleeing further from me. Cannot tell if there are any more memories to remember. Memories of life in the camp. They lead me nowhere. No closer to finding a way out. My torturer — he got me to say that I am or was among the agitators but that itself is not reason enough for me to have been brought here. No, it is not. These memories have gotten me nowhere. The experience of remembering them has not created life for me, has not let me know what it is to live again. No second life of memory envelops me. Nothing to protect me from the present. Nothing going. Nothing to go on. There must be more. Let there be more.

Entry No. 31

I tell myself, I have no one else to tell, I tell myself she did not plan for this to pass, no, not to pass, a weak synonym for occur, much better then to say this, that she did not plan for this to start, given that it is ongoing, it being this, this being me here, but what is this if not life, my life, oh but I had another life, was this my fate or did I stumble into this when I spoke to her on that fetid stinking train, was she looking for a serf she found in me, a patsy, her patsy, she chose me, she loved me such that it could be only me, only I could be her patsy, no, that must not be, I must not believe, do not believe, belief without evidence may be dismissed without evidence but belief, hope, belief and hope persist in spite of evidence, belief and hope, they refute evidence, no, she did not mean, she does not know, her intentions, she is of the people that are good, so many of them abounding somewhere else, not here, no, not here, these are not people here they are emanations of a dour beast, no, not that, the loons, think of the loons and the hooting of the loons, that world with her, she could not, would not, no, I would have seen, I would have seen through her, but ah, her eyes hide everything in light, darkness is not visible in light like that.

I suffer better than the rest, the whole lot of them, I have a greater compass of mirth and melancholy than another, see, watch this, here's a funny tale:

SLEDGMO,
Or grace abounding to the chief of innocents abroad.

No, I will save that tale for another time. I have undertaken another divagation and must return. I must do more to achieve my task. I must recall more. There must be more to recall. I've been wrong before. Always erring.

Entry No. 32

The cell stinks. It is full of paper and piss. I have lost count of how many entries I've written since I was last permitted to go outside for my daily constitutional. Granted, I have numbered the entries, but I don't know between which two entries or within which sentence, which word, my privileges were revoked. I can't remember. I can't even remember having been outside it is so long ago now since I have been having been outside. Did I ever leave this cell? Perhaps I never left this cell. Perhaps there is no cell, and this is a new world that I mistake for a cell. A small world after all. My world. My world for my life, my life that I hurtle further and further away from so that the light of that life changes, shifts, gradually reddens, and flares and dissipates into darkness ever growing. Who then are those people I remember? We fought like pigeons for bread, and the gaolers laughed at me when I came out of the tumult scratched and bloody and breadless. I believe that I remember that. Am I even remembering? I don't remember nor know. The fact that people, places, events come to my mind, arriving, and departing at their leisure, the fact that those people places and events stir some kind of emotion, sentiment, sensation, feeling, the fact that I experience those emotions, sentiments, and sensations in what for lack of better words I have grown accustomed to calling my mind, the fact that, the fact that, fact. This must be remembrance. Something like remembrance. The renovation of the past. One's past. The renovation of the life one has lived, repetition in harmony with novelty, a circle in harmony with a line. You cannot square the circle, but you can circle round the circle. Many things may be done with the circle. But not erasure. The circle remains. Proof of a life, or proof at least of having lived. I have the circle. It is not enough. I would like to go outside of it, go for a constitutional outside of it, the circle. But I cannot. As long as I am in this cell I am in the circle. Perning.

My teeth ache again.

Entry No. 33

This cell.

Yes, this cell, this cage, this hollow spot in the world where I have been since my trial.

The trial! I remember the trial, the trial draws a circle about me, and I am in it, remembrance of that. Yes, there was a trial; but there is not so much worth telling. I was brought in, many false words were said, many gasps of shock were feigned, something had to be done, yes, the fact that something had to be done, something to be done, the dispensation of justice, something done with words, words, even if they were true words the arrangement of those words was a hoax, a fraud, falsity, words, trial, everything trumped up in that place, words true but arrayed in a false light, words don't lie, sentences lie. Words martyred for the greater glory of penitence and justice, perorations played out to inspire condemnation of this enemy of the state, me, a *persona non grata* in a *cosmos non gratis, mutatis mutandis, pro captu captivatoris habent sua fata libelli, absolutio censuris aliter auctoritate,* quack, quack, quack, words emptied, *nil posse creari de nihilo sancto,* quackus quacki quacko quackum quacke. Look what I've done: I've declined.

Igitur: that a learned hand I have!
Ecco: I speak with a dead tongue!
Ecco: I speak with a tongue that has long turned to ashes and dust.
Ecco: and still it flaps, my ashen tongue.
Agitur: it is done, it is pursued, the fatal sleight of hand.
Agitur: it is done, it is pursued, cloak and dagger for the sleight of hand.
Now look at what is infrascriptum and introscripta; one and the same.

The trial! Ah yes, the trial. I do not need to describe it here, a description *non serviat*. Trials. We are all familiar with them. We have all heard of them. All of us. Many trials occur. Yearly, weekly, daily, hourly. What one of us knows about trials is no different from what anyone else knows about trials. And trials, as they often do in these most civilized of times, occur in a courtroom of one kind or another. We are as familiar with trials as we are with courtrooms. I do not need to describe the court, need not remember that at the far end of the room was the bench, raised some five feet off the ground, where the high judge sat, that behind this was a vestibule with a seal across it, which read the same as the inscription over the court's entrance outside: Justice Moved My Maker On High, Divine Power Made Me, that the seal was beige with black lettering and the vestibule was painted lavender, as was the wall beyond the vestibule, that a larger-than-necessary gavel rested on the high judge's desk, along with a pen and some sheets of paper. I don't need to describe this, I don't need to remember this, I assume that is all that was there, I cannot be sure, I can never be sure, I don't need to be sure, such a place must have been.

It does not matter that to the right of the high judge's bench, two feet lower, was where the witnesses sat to testify although no witnesses were needed in my trial, my case being open-and-shut; and to the left of the high judge's bench, again two feet lower, was where the scribe sat and recorded the proceedings, entered the proceedings into the historical record, recorded for posterity, for the nameless to come, the boundless generations bounding to the court and schools of law, the proceedings recorded for them, although no proceedings were to be recorded here, my trial not to be entered into the record, not to be remembered, no, no attestation, no witnesses nor preservation of the proceedings, the numberless trials that never occurred in this place. And in front of the high judge's bench was a table six feet wide and two feet long where the court registrars sat. Two court registrars sat there, ensuring the proceedings were conducted in accordance with proper court procedure as stipulated by law, that exhibits entered or evidence presented were entered and presented in the proper fashion, but I cannot be sure this is what they did, perhaps no court procedure existed anymore, perhaps the law no longer stipulated to such stipulations, or no procedure was to be followed in this instance, again I cannot be sure, I can never be sure, no way to be sure, no need to be sure, nothing to be done.

No need to recall that to the far right of the room were two rows of seats, six seats apiece in each row, fit for a jury of twelve respected members of society to sit during my trial. I do not think they were respected. I do not respect them.

Nothing served in remembering that some twelve feet from the judge's bench were two tables. To the right was the table for the chief inquisitor. Two seats sat behind the table, one for the chief inquisitor and one for the deputy inquisitor, but for my trial the chief inquisitor sat alone. To the right of his table was the defense counsel's. Again, two seats there, again, one alone was used. My advocate. No assistance needed for him to defend me. No defense needed because no defense availing.

What good is it to know that behind a low barrier towards the entrance of the room were nine benches, each sitting six people, allowing a total of fifty-four people to witness the procession of justice. Who sat there watching, I don't know. Often sitting there were family and friends of the accused, family and friends of the victims, the interested public, journalists, viziers, junior inquisitors, vagrants. When I was in the room that time, I saw no one that I knew — well, I saw three men that I knew, but I wished I didn't know them.

Who cares that I failed to mention that the carpeting was crimson?

Who cares that I failed to mention one last part of the court's layout? Behind the counsels' benches but before the low barrier where the public sat was a small bench four feet wide, encased in glass.

The accused sat here. I sat there.

No one cares that nothing in this court's layout was unusual nor differed much from every other court I've seen before. I was accustomed to sitting in courts like this one, but I never before sat where they made me sit this time, in a box, restrained, the accused.

I don't remember how I got there. Perhaps they carried me. I don't know. No need to know.

I don't need to tell that, in lurid and imaginative detail, the Chief Inquisitor regaled the court with the invented descriptions of my crime. I won't go into it, but it stems from — I wrote of my wife a few pages back, how jealous I'd become, how jealousy had made me follow her; and that I was standing there in the rain, watching my wife and that other man, whose true nature I hope to remember soon — his jealousy of me disfigured him before my jealousy of him disfigured me — I was standing outside the café, standing by the bridge, standing there watching my wife walk tenderly in love with another man away from me, standing there with my umbrella watching them recede into the rain.

That was it: the umbrella was the rub.

I don't need to remember that, as the Chief Inquisitor told it to the court, that day was a day of rebellion — to me it seemed less a day of rebellion than a day of meek and toothless insubordination, mere passive resistance, mere breath — a day subversives and agitators planned to signify to each other their commitment to each other in their resistance to the regime. How to do that? Umbrellas, of course. Umbrellas. Umbrellas! A good enough symbol: neither conspicuous nor discreet, an unfurled umbrella is elegant in its parabolic form, useful in its downward sloping, conspicuous in its opening and ordinary in its abundance. An umbrella goes unnoticed unless one knows to notice it or is about to be hit in the face by one carried carelessly by some deviant idiot who is probably very short. A short man in a hurry carrying an umbrella will probably hit you in your ribcage and he won't notice or apologize. It has happened to me and I never forgave him. The umbrella is an emanation of human ingenuity whose use is most barbaric. Perhaps I should move where it is drier. That way no short and harried dolts will hit me with their umbrellas. Better to move where it is drier. Across the room, perhaps, away from this corner where I urinated some twenty minutes ago because my gaolers won't let me go piss in the duncan. It is beginning to stink. But if I move somewhere drier outside the camp — admittedly a flight of fancy, but let me for a moment fly — the chance exists that the inhabitants of that drier place will make use of parasols, the more ancient forebear of the umbrella, parasols symbolizing quite a bit in various cultures' imagery since the days of giants and the all-too-human gods, umbrellas arriving belatedly to keep people dry in rainier climates, nothing divine or regal-seeming in umbrellas, parasols another matter — everything is another matter. No one carrying a parasol is in a hurry. If you carry an umbrella, you rush through the rain; if you carry a parasol, you saunter, stroll or meander. A world full of parasols is a pleasant world. A world full of umbrellas is a world full of rib-pokes waking to happen. Enough of umbrellas.

Yes — as the Chief Inquisitor told it to the court, that day was a day of rebellion when the rebels would unfurl either umbrellas in the rain or parasols in the sun to signal their commitment to each other in preparation for a move on the capital against the regime. At a certain moment, the Chief Inquisitor smiled, a certain moment, the selfsame moment that this slithering and mustachioed agitator — that is what he called me, though I am firm in my belief that I neither slither nor agitate — the selfsame moment that this slithering and mustachioed agitator unfurled his own umbrella.

He never mentioned that it rained that day.

He never allowed that anyone who wanted to stay dry that day would have done the same.

Rain came down and the umbrellas came out. Normal folks, people with no designs on overthrowing the revolutionary regime, they all became subversives and threats. Because it rained. Because they wanted to stay dry. And I am among the dry damned. It would be comical were I not slouching towards oblivion as a consequence of the rain that day. And so, we are heaped up in this camp for having desired to stay dry. To avoid the damp bone-felt chill that cold rain causes. To stay as we are, our suits and dresses unwrinkled, our hair unfrazzled, constant in ourselves, our dry and untouched selves, unchanging and unbending, our eyes — well, their eyes perhaps, not my eyes, the umbrella kept me dry but, ah, my eyes, nothing to be done, my eyes, no more of them.

A fearful symmetry to my punishment, a contrapasso after its kind: my gaolers have imprisoned me in a place where I cannot see the world outside because I could not see that I had been imprisoned by my jealousy.

A caged heart begets a caged body. A contrapasso of sorts.

I am imprisoned and forgotten, except by my gaolers, though their silence and increased sparsity leads me to think they too have forgotten me. In that case, I have been forgotten by the world. I am imprisoned for having opened my umbrella to keep dry as I watched my wife walk away in the arms of another man. I thought I could escape the cage that jealousy had built for me by the scabrous consolation of confirming what jealousy had told me she would do — deceive me. What confirmation.

Not worth it.

The regime, of course, knew about this plot. Or if they didn't know about it, they imagined it into being. Who told them? Who knows? Did anyone tell them? Perhaps not. That doesn't matter. It is immaterial. What matters is the regime found confirmation, real or invented, of a suspected plot. The umbrellas! Never mind the rain, the Chief Inquisitor implored, anyone who thought to use an umbrella that day was a subversive, an infidel, an agitator.

I had thought people opened their umbrellas that day because it was rain-ing, but it seems that a simple explanation for using an umbrella was not in the cards for me.

A simple explanation for a simple question.

Oftentimes the simpler explanation is the proper explanation. But never for the paranoiac. The more conspiratorial an answer, the grander and more nefarious a theory, the more certain the paranoiac are that their theory ex-plains the true nature of things behind their appearance, the moving parts obscured behind a wall of simple diagrams, simple sketches, things that need not be explained because their presence is answer enough, most logical, most satisfying. That perhaps I would want to keep dry in the rain was not the ex-planation sought by the Chief Inquisitor for my use of the umbrella; no, they needed a better answer, an answer to justify the creation of the crime that was my crime, I must have been much more nefarious than that, I must not have wanted to keep dry, my Chief Inquisitor reasoned, someone like me must not care whether he is soaked or sere, some subversive like me, hardly human after all, no, I must have opened my umbrella in the rain that day to signal to my fellow archfiends that I was of them and with them. Solidarity. The simpler explanation cannot do for persecutors who are paranoid. They have power and fear that with the loss of power they will lose themselves. They invent or discover some system that must exist to organize their fear in a cogent and convincing way. They must reach to metaphysick for their explanation, believ-ing the truth is not observable, that the truth must be hidden and must be worked through to arrive at the true truth, truth a palimpsest under which the faint vestiges of the true truth remain to be found, effaced but not forgot-ten. Sometimes the simpler answer is the answer. Simple questions can have simple answers. But simple answers will not do for a man who searches after the answer that he desires, who does not search after the answer that is the answer. Simple answers will never do for the paranoiac. The most satisfying answer will always be found. Even if it is not the truth. Something must jus-tify. Some topography must exist whose array can be explained by application of an organizing principle, true or not. Thus paranoia. Thus, also jealousy.

Paranoia, like jealousy, is contingent. Paranoia, like jealousy, cannot exist without something else existing already. Paranoia, like jealousy, a flame that needs dry wood to kindle it and oxygen to succor it; absent either, it will diminish and die. But power provides enough of both for the paranoid regime to endure. Paranoia, like jealousy, needs a land to colonize, some serf to tend the fields around the manor, needs some subaltern subjects over which it may reign, which it may shape, which may succor its suspicions, some person or thing with abundant resources that it may pillage to endure. Paranoia is a consequence, not a prime mover, not a catalyst in the first. It may become a catalyst down the line, causing one thing or sundry others. When a man is paranoid, his eyes dart from shadow to shadow, he hunches his body over to protect himself, every room is bugged, every fishmonger an informant, every word holds a surface meaning and slurries of hidden meanings underneath, every question asking for a coded answer, everything meaning something other than what its meaning means — to say nothing of umbrellas — and then the threat is out there waiting, waiting, waiting.

A paranoid government looks for threats in shadows and finds them in everything under the sun. Under the sun, but also under the clouds and in the rain and under an umbrella. That day they found a threat. They found me. And I became a threat. Not only me: everyone who flourished an umbrella to stay dry that day outed himself as an existential threat and confessed his allegiance to the subversives, so many lived lives made lifeless. Yet I know of no one else in the camp sent here for also doing what I did that day.

Why me? Why was I the one chosen for immurement? Why no one else? Why not the man whose arm was linked with my wife's as they walked away in rank subversion? Why not him?

Why not her?

To commit this crime, you did not need to know that your umbrella confessed your allegiance to a threat, nor know that any such coterie existed to whom allegiance could be confessed. It didn't matter. It doesn't matter. Knowing doesn't matter. Ignorance is no salvation. If they think you are a threat, then you are a threat. Paranoia enthroned susses out every pretender and usurper even if none exist. If they think you are a threat, then you are a threat. Sometimes the simplest answer is the answer. For the paranoiac, the simplest answer is deception plain and clear. For the paranoiac, the simplest answer is not an answer but a distraction from the true answer, which of necessity must be impossible to disclose. For the paranoiac, the only solution is to obliterate every creeping, crawling, swimming, walking thing that could evolve into a threat. The truth is never enough. The truth is not the truth. The truth is a lie. Case closed.

Same goes for jealousy.

But back to the trial. Let's pursue this inquiry by way of entelechy.

Q: why did I open my umbrella that day?

A: because the rain came down and I wanted to keep dry.

Q: why did I want to keep dry?

A: because I was standing by a bridge in the rain.

Q: why was I standing by a bridge in the rain?

A: because I was watching my wife.

Q: why were you watching your wife?

A: because I was jealous.

Q: *was?*

Perhaps they were right. I will give them that: perhaps they were right, perhaps. But not how they think — perhaps they were right that the rain wasn't why I opened my umbrella that day. I can't be sure anymore. Perhaps they were right: rain wasn't the reason. They are very convincing. They have convinced me I have sinned. What sin? Foisting an umbrella. My reason for being there with my opened umbrella? Jealousy.

What ill fate. What oracle could have divined this?

A contrapasso of sorts: a caged heart begets a caged body.

I have arrived. I have found the question I needed to ask: why am I here? And I have my answer.

The question: why am I here?

I am here because of my heart. I am here because of my jealousy.

And now I am jealous of those who today are wet in the rain, soaked. Blessed be their shivering damp bodies, damp bodies that shiver in freedom. Long may they shiver.

I shiver as well.

I had gone to the bridge and it was my fault my jealousy drove me to stand there on that bridge and watch her recede from me, recede like the waves before the tsunami comes ashore had I not gone to stand by that bridge had it not been raining had I not been jealous I would not have opened my umbrella and I would not have been made to come here had I not been had it not been — had I not been?

The inquisitor rested his argument and my advocate rose to offer his defense. He offered no defense. Open-and-shut. Case close.

But I saw him as he rose, and I recognized him. He had grown a moustache and wore a fez, but I recognized my advocate: he was the gaoler who had done my questioning, my interrogation. Or rather, he had asked me to come up with some crime I could have committed to justify my current caging. I thought that creating a crime would hurry me along a path to eventual freedom: I could appeal my detention, be given a fair and speedy trial; and a jury of my peers, composed of respected members of society, would recognize my innocence and I would be released. Free again. Free.

But no. I gave him a kind of crime, and that was all the justification they needed to try me and keep me there forever. How long is forever? I will see.

My advocate was my interrogator. My confession did not help. My confession gained me no leniency. My confession to having done something I did not do ensured they had a reason to keep me caged.

No justice pursued; no justice delivered.

Everyone is out to get me. Not everyone. Some people are out to get me. Were out to get me. They got me.

Sometimes the simplest answer is the answer.

I am the victim of an impossible crime: I had been kidnapped by my own country and then handed over to another country that, although a part of my native land, is separated by another universe. I believe I am inside my country. But I am outside of it. Of it but not in it. This world is different. Passing strange.

Everyone is out to get me. Perhaps someone is out to find me. Looking for me here. Getting closer. Traveling at incredible speeds to find me and tell me something. Some vengeful thing. Perhaps not. Perhaps someone is coming here to tell me how to escape. How to live again. Yes: this must be it: soon I will be free. Sometimes the simplest answer is the answer.

Entry No. 34

Where did I go wrong? Which path was the wrong path? What keeps me in this place, the outer realm of nothing at all? Is there more of this world? Is there more to know? I don't know. I have done what I thought I needed to do to accomplish my task. Something still is missing. It is likely I failed. I should have done more and done better. What more? What better? I don't know. I am still here and see no possibility of leaving. Did I ask the wrong question? Did I supply the wrong answer? Where did I go wrong? Not even the wind replies. Where did I go wrong?

Entry No. 35

Listen to the wind. I will find either a new question or a new answer or Lord willing both.

Entry No. 36

The wind is blowing again, and it carries the smell of roasted meat. I have not smelled that scent for so long. I last smelled it…not sure. Not too long ago. But was it? How long is long ago? Before I was brought here or perhaps not. Not yet clear. I know it though; I know it and it is calling me back.

I feel a familiar presence pressing down on me. Familiar how?

Entry No. 37

All quiet. The wind still blows, that scent still pulsates in the air, that familiar presence presses down on me all the same. They bring me to the edge of a thought, but I cannot turn the corner and see the thought for what it is. If I could see it clearly then perhaps, I would know how to proceed in my task. The next step. The right step. The way forward and out.

If I see this thought, will I recognize it? Or will it have a face I can't identify or remember, the face of fulfillment? Is this thought what I have been searching for for so long? This thought could be the answer I need to the question I must ask, or it may be the question, or maybe both. I don't know.

How lazily I write now. The words are lifeless, the thoughts thoughtless. When I write something good the next day is on fire. But I have not written anything good and so every next day is flameless. Better not to write. But I don't know what else I would do. Must disrobe myself of these memories. Hunt them, find them, write them down and put them away.

The idea at the end of the world.

The idea at the end of this world.

The idea at the end of the world is unrecognizable unless you've passed through the world, every step, and every station, and have arrived at the end of the world. This is not the end of the world nor am I out of it yet. May I recognize it when I see it. May I see again.

Entry No. 38

The smoke of today is the fire of tomorrow.

Entry No. 39

Wind, scent, presence. Wind, scent, presence. Wind, scent, presence.
I repeat it, I repeat myself, experience repeats memory.
I will repeat it until what must come comes.

Entry No. 40

Spent last night repeating the mantra: wind, scent, presence. I would not allow myself to see what I needed to see but my repetition has given me permission to see. And I see it is a memory, one not so distant, one close to me, it presses down on me and I must write it down and rid myself of it, I do not know if this will aid me in my task, but in that memory is an answer that, though it may have no question, will tell me how to leave this world and find my way into another. But I cannot think of that. I cannot let the future constrain the past. I must write and perhaps in writing things will be clear. Things: the answer or the question or both.

The idea at the end of the world.

This must be the place.

I have not moved but I have come.

This must be the place.

I have come to the end of the world.

Entry No. 41

What must come has come. The memory. The idea at the end of the world. I waited for it, but I did not know it was what I was waiting for. I have waited, lingered, and loafed, I was lingering, loafing. I believed that it would come. Belief: I have faith without proof. Belief: I have faith in what I have seen, that is all.

I saw him once. Twice. Maybe ten times, maybe more; I can't be sure of that and I can't be sure I saw what I saw. Seven times, yes that must be it. Or eight. Or three. I can't be sure. Ah, well. Say then there was a time, a time embracing other times. Seven, eight, three, one.

One night when I still lived in the barracks, we were readying to sleep when a brilliant blue lit up the sky, the unexpected, faint and creeping hyacinthian light of dawn flooding the room too early, it must be too early, I thought, it must be, it's not yet time, time though it may move fleet apace may not move this fleet, no, it is not yet time for work and the day to begin again, and I knew I was not the only one who thought this, for everyone inside the barracks was silent, voiceless, wordless, and the gaolers outside were silent too; it must be something else, I thought, something else came across the sky and touched it blue at midmost night, at night yes it was something to see, something, someone, something that slipped the bonds of night and came across the sky and painted our world upon our closing eyes deep in the dark night, light was the night for once, light.

The next day I was laboring in the plant, bending my springs and hammering, I was alone there fashioning umbrellas, so many umbrellas to be fashioned oh so many, what for, why would they want so many, and then I sensed a presence in the room and I grew distressed, whatever control I had over myself was gone: I began to moan, perhaps I cried, snorted snot or expelled it, or rather perhaps instead I was composed although that seems unlikely, seeing as I am one who has never been completely composed; in any case I was all fear and trembling, who else could be here, I thought, who else and why, how did it get in, what would it want, I am doing good work, *sola gratia*, I thought, I am doing good and I am laboring diligently and merit no punishment, I've been good enough, what would they want; and a presence moved upon me and I turned: his face was ovular much like mine but not so much that it did not widen gradually and slightly from his cheeks on up to where he had a shock of white hair, and shock is a good word because his shock of hair loped from his pate as though he had been shocked, or was shocked, suffused with energy and humming with energy arcing out, that energy must surely have shocked him, he was shocked by the world he was then inhabiting, or at least the world he was appearing in or passing through, what a creation this world, whose creation, perhaps he knew; or perhaps he was upset because he seemed to be scowling, scowling because he had been dropped into a world not his own and forced to wander through it, scowling even though he was not scowling, as though scowling were a state of mind or an emotion and not a gesture — a movement of muscles in a human's face and the mouth and the jaw, the eyes, displeasure manifest; and I could glean the relentlessness of his gaze when he set upon an object of interest — me for instance — and he had the piercing eyes of that family of birds of prey, I remember them and their family name, the Accipitridae, yes: his eyes were quite accipitridaen, and more specifically his eyes were those of a bald eagle — bald eagle! if this man were a bird, and perhaps he was a bird and not a man, he would be a bald eagle, what with the white-feathered pate and searching eyes; but he was not so opportunistic a predator as the bald eagle, nor was he bald, but then again the bald eagle isn't bald either, and now I think that although of all the birds of prey he may most resemble the bald eagle, his nature was much more that of the duck hawk, so fast, so fleet, clear, free and light, dropping in here and there, far-seeing, knowing what it seeks, streaking from height to height like an empty net with a jewel in each eye, each eye reflecting every other jewel, from the heights to these lowly parts and back, fleet into the ether. I stood like one thunder-struck or as if I had seen a familiar apparition. I listened to a voice not so different from mine — a voice that was almost an echo of my own — a voice I felt course through me less than heard with my ears, such knowledge gleaned through the senses, no, his voice poured through me by means beyond physical sensation.

He wanted me to meet him the next day after labor was ended, he let me know, to meet him and not return to the barracks as I was supposed to, to meet him in a little patch of clearing in the trees on the far west side of the camp, the westerly woods where no one goes so no one returns, the westerly woods I had never seen nor been to but which I imagined existed in their own way, to meet him there for he had something to pass on to me, a message of a kind; and then it was me who was shocked, shocked by the solicitation and the grave transgression of our credo, no, this kind of conversation and that kind of gathering were forbidden; but I sensed he could not violate our credo, that he need not obey or was not subject to it — why I sensed I have no idea, one senses before one thinks — and I sensed that I should trust him, that there was something about him I recognized and could trust — I couldn't be sure what it was I recognized, it felt the way that you see the silhouette of an idea but cannot see the idea itself — and I sensed that no one would find us in that little patch of clearing in the trees, that the gaolers and the Guard and God Himself passed over that little place; but still I was frozen, humming soft, with tears perhaps, who should I trust and what should I trust in, God knows, perhaps even He did not know or did not want to know, willful ignorance, even gods will close their eyes sometimes, to be in the dark can be salvation.

A dilemma: if I were found in conversation here with this man if this was a man who was here, I'd get a whupping like I couldn't believe; if I consented to his solicitation and went where he wanted me to go and was caught out there in that little patch of clearing in the trees I would suffer like I knew I could suffer — I suffer greatly daily hourly and every moment on account of what I've done, what have I done, never mind, that is immaterial, perhaps I will find out whether I had truly done some wrong aside from standing in the rain underneath an umbrella watching my wife walk off with another man or had done nothing wrong but I suffer all the same these belated days, such is my lot these days — oh I could not go, could not risk everything; but I had nothing, I was almost nothing myself, I was little more than mica glinting in the sun as you walk by, one thing composed of many smaller things, and one thing above all else, one thing alone I had, one thing that still glimmered in the light and let me know that some kind of light abided still within me and around me, one small petty thing, one small petty thing that was the highest and most incandescent thing that I could imagine: hope. Then his scowling was arrested, or rather his aura of a constant scowl parted for a moment and he let me see in, he let me understand that what he would disclose there in the woods when I came to meet him and sit beside him where he would be waiting for me was something from someone I longed to hear, to hear and not remember a sound I heard, I couldn't even call what I believe that I hear in my memory an echo, oh no, an echo no, an echo no because an echo is a reflection of a present sound and in my memory no sound nor voice abides to be echoed, and what we call *hearing* in memory was the memory of what a sound may have sounded like and not the sound itself, muted, dumb, absent, silent ashes of experience. And the presence lifted, who or what I had seen or sensed was no longer aside me and I was alone again, spring and plyer still in my hand, hard Argentan and stiffer steel to bend it; he was gone and I was alone again, alone with an ache, a desire, a suffusing desire to go where I was meant to go after the bell was tolled and labor ceased that day, to meet him in a patch of clearing there among the trees that all pass over, or I hoped that all pass over, meet him there and hear a voice, a voice spoken by another voice, voices within voices, a message from a messenger, a message for me, a message meant for me, for *me*, that word no longer meant nothing: it meant that, if this were true and no ruse, if this were true and no fiction, then someone knew I was here, someone knew I still live, someone knew that I'm waiting, that I endure. And my hope, it shimmered in the dark.

The bell tolled and labor ended. I did not return to the barracks. I dithered inside the workshop and waited for the sky to darken or at least for the gloaming to come so that my roaming out west would not be so easily seen, a shadow among shadows shading into deeper shadows, a silhouette among the shades. Yes, the gloaming would be best. Soon thereafter day departed and I left the workshop; I walked outside into the eerie half-light where I saw no bodies, no humans, birds, dust, heard nothing but the wind moaning in the creaking and corroded roof, heard nothing, saw nothing and so I was bound west, my legs moving as they hadn't moved since I had been denied my daily constitutionals, moving swiftly so fleet apace, moving further than I had gone before, moving beyond what my life could hold, moving as though walking ahead of myself, walking swiftly and keeping my head down and walking for so long through this camp towards a promised thicket of trees, this world of theirs is so big, so big, it must contain multitudes of worlds or else an absence so vast and so complete as to be all-encompassing, this world having retreated into itself and leaving in its wake a world so empty, so vast, so dark.

I walked until I heard the wind again: it was blowing the scent of roasted flesh and this time I heard the wind in rustling branches and dry leaves, and I looked up: I must have arrived: there was a thicket of trees ahead of me and the wind stopped, silence, all quiet in the west except a faint crackling, no bird-song, no tubas, no voices. I looked further into the trees and saw a faint light, a faint light dancing in a clearing so obscured by the thicket's density, ah what to do, I had gone beyond what I knew of my life here in this vast and empty world, backwards was nothing but pain and forward a dilemma: were this a ruse, there would be peine forte et dure, but if not, there would be something, something to know, some new thing in my life, a new presence, discovery, knowledge beyond what I knew, a new experience at last that I could live and doing so live again; so I went on, I approached the thicket and stepped into the patch of trees. The duff did not sound nor even the smallest crunch underfoot, all I heard was the faint crackling of the light whose crackling grew louder and realer as I passed on, passing further until I arrived at the edge of the patch containing the light, which I saw came from a blaze, so I stepped through and into the clearing where the flames distended, and saw there reclining, smiling and chewing on a lamb shank, smiling and gazing at me with lustrous eyes, it was him, the presence I'd felt in the plant aside me I felt it again, the same presence but changed, re-figured, he was the avatar of this presence, its mes-senger or emanation or something such, yes, I saw him, it was him reclining and smiling and chewing on meat, it was him gazing at me with lustrous eyes and smiling, and I realized at last who he was, it was him, how could it be, it was him, it was him; I circled the fire, cautious, trepid and timorous, the light no longer obscured, and I came around to where he reclined and when I sat down next to him he smiled at me, gazing at me with lustrous eyes, meatfat smeared on his face, the fire emblazoned on him, his face all flames, I sat down next to him where I was made to know, where he related what follows to me, where I learned why he was here, this man, why he had come there to me, and although I couldn't recognize him I realized I knew who he was because I had realized this man in another world, this man if this was a man, reclining beside me as should not have been possible in this world, smiling, gazing with lustrous eyes, and he related what I write below as he told it to me in a voice without a voice but a voice more my own than his if he could have a voice, this man of the foreshortened epyllion, that man who was less man than light but a man all the same, this man, he was Dee. And this is what he wanted me to know.

When you abandoned me and left me here in this world, I did not know how to survive: I was a stranger here, a stranger here only because my creator brought me here and left me here, a stranger who desired only to regain the time I had lost in the world that I knew when I was sent into this one. When I found myself here, I did not know how to escape or whether I could escape, so I went on doing what you last had me doing: I went in search of birds to engage in spiritual parliament, wandering through forests and plains in search of birds who would speak to me and commune with me and teach me. But they found me shortly thereafter and put me into a camp like yours.

They took me and put me into barracks. There were others there, but I did not recognize them nor know whether they were like me, abandoned by their creators, and had come here the same way I did. And then one night I heard our captors nailing up the door of that terrible building. They're all the same, the camps, every one of them — I surmised this from what you yourself learned from experience — and so I knew the design of the barracks was consistent throughout this world, and one piece was no different from another although each piece was distinct, its own. One night the sound of artillery drew near. I made my choice to leave. I chose. I never felt I had a choice before nor power enough to choose but this time I chose, and I chose to leave. No more of this place.

Climbing down my bunk that night I was quiet enough not to disturb the others. It did not matter if they were like me too — abandoned, incomplete, un-fulfilled — I could take no one: I left them behind. I went to the rear entrance and pulled back two planks abutting the rafters and removed those planks which I had unscrewed earlier that week while I pretended to clean, and after placing the planks on the rafters so they would not be found soon, I pulled myself up and climbed into the passageway that the absence of the planks revealed, and I crawled along the innards of the building until I reached its far and unguarded side, and it faced into the westerly woods, and I knew with the sound of the artillery they would not hear me, and I would go to those woods. I did not know, but I felt I would find something there, or else lose something and in losing gain something precious beyond all belief and comprehension. I punched out the plywood boarding up the building from the outside, I looked to my left and I looked to my right and I climbed down and jumped off and ran to the woods where I hoped I would find a way out of this world and into one of my own making, and it would be a world where I am complete and have power over and possession of myself and my life.

I found nothing. Nothing came, nothing stayed, nothing endured.

I came to the woods to find consummation, the consummation I desire, I came to the woods so that I would be consumed into the noble and extended body I could almost perceive. But I found nothing.

I tried to see those woods as incorruptible, inviolable, immutable, as somewhere the elements that constituted the world I imagined was waiting for me had retreated, retracted, concentrated themselves into a secret and dark and otherwise lightless point on the face of the deep. But it was nothing, absolute and deep nothing — and it was not even a void, it was more a place removed from a world that seemed to have retreated elsewhere into itself. And this place was empty, bereft of anything at all, fish, flesh or foul, stone, sea, or tree, and I knew it would remain an abandoned world, a voided world, a lightless room. What feet in ancient days had walked here? Whose? Yours?

The scales fell from my eyes, and I saw where I was, this little patch drawn out of a world, this nothing of nothing. A forgotten place. That must have been why all passed over it: it was nothing but a void. And I dwelt within the depths of this void until I had retreated into myself, had gathered myself into my own nothingness, an infinity concentrated in a single distinguishable point in the void.

Of nothing I grew weary. I wanted life, wanted men and their valor and vices, wanted experience. I had no mirror, no reflection to see myself, and I sensed that all my waiting had moved me no closer to what I sought most of all, and that was to complete the unfulfilled form you left me in — to become myself, fully myself. Yes, a being suffused with traces of light left behind in the void. And finding the way to do that I would be free. I would have filled every pore of my skin with tar if I had to.

Who was it that waited there? Who had I become? What had I even been before? Those questions all came to one question: who am I? It was not a question that should have had to have been asked but it was asked and so it had to be answered. I would have done anything to learn the answer, anything short of going back to either the camp or the world beyond it you created for me to roam and perhaps someday die in, no, not that, never, I would never go back, never.

I had either to leave or to stay. The question would not be answered if I stayed and waited. I could have waited until all traces of light in this world gave way to the abounding nothingness surrounding but I did not. I departed.

I walked through the trees and they thinned and then only grass and dust and weeds were underfoot. A barren place. Those faint residues of light let me see smoke rising evenly and unhurried in the distance. I walked further along toward the smoke and the smoke was rising from below the horizon. I was walking in the open; I was walking downcountry; it was the gloaming, the light gone but its afterglow still agonizing with the darkness encroaching. If I were seen I would surely be captured again and come to an end, an incomplete end, an end to something unfulfilled, the ending that begins in abandonment and ends in discardment. But I was not seen, or if I was seen, I was not considered something worth ending or something capable of coming to an end.

I walked toward the smoke and saw the ground before me was giving way, leading down to a lower point on earth. I walked closer to the escarpment and came to a vista overlooking what was below: the smoke was rising from a chimney, one of many chimneys in an empty settlement — empty or abandoned — and this chimney alone among its kind was wafting smoke and the smoke was rising from the valley into the dark sky. I watched the smoke rise slowly at first and then suddenly begin to rise rabidly as though someone inside the house were waving a tapestry at the flames, making them dart and leap burn and exhale more smoke, and the smoke made of itself a lattice in the sky. Who was I, standing there on the precipice watching smoke rise from this lone hut in the valley? Perhaps my answer was there.

The last light receded into the cold dark that was advancing; I walked down the escarpment and walked quietly around the settlement in that valley and soon I was close enough to the house. I heard nothing, saw nothing, no presence of life but the smoke from the chimney, a sign of life having been and life now transfigured. I walked up to that house and put my hand on the gnarled door and the door was warm. Warm with something. I pushed it and it gave way to light.

I knew someone was there and that whoever he was had already seen the door move. The hut was so small it was impossible that the door, although its movement was silent, had not been seen opening. If I went in, he could finish me off. But perhaps that was my answer — that I had to be finished off, coming to an unnatural end. But it was too late to make any other choice than to go forward: the door had opened, and my foot was on the threshold and I could not go back: I had to go in. I had no choice: I had to go in. I pushed the door further and it swung from the frame, and that was space enough for me to enter with my hands up and my face lit by the light in there.

A cold rough hand covered my mouth to stop me from shouting even though I could not shout; but the possessor of that hand could not have known that I would not shout; he would have thought I was like others, shouting, hopping, free. The hand gripped my mouth tightly and I felt a heavy presence pushing on my vertebra. I knew that presence on my flesh. I could not panic, all I could do to was raise my arms slowly to show I was an open-palmed stranger, no threat to anyone in the state I was in. I saw a fireplace and the fire within and a small figure bellowing the fire with an upturned umbrella, back turned to me.

A lilting voice behind me said, "I'm going to remove my hand from your mouth now, and if you don't prove you should be here in ten seconds, things will not be good." His hand came off.

I told him I was a stranger in this world, in it and not of it, taken from another world and abandoned in this one, and I was looking for my way out; and I told him I had ranged so far from where I had been dispossessed that I felt at home at last in this little house. And the cool weight lifted from my spine.

"We've been waiting," the small figure by the fireplace said to the flames. "You know, you don't seem to be speaking with your own voice. I feel that I'm not even hearing you with my ears." The figure turned around and I saw it was a woman. As when a reflected beam from either water or a mirror leaps back the other way rising at the angle that it followed down on its descent, so I was struck by light so bright that, having had its origin in a higher place from where it had descended, now rose in equal breadth to meet my eyes; and I turned away. "But," I heard her say, "it's a voice I recognize. And I think you recognize it too." I looked behind me; a younger man, well-kempt at some point in the past but now ragged, was the possessor of the hand that had held me when I had come through the doorway. He nodded at me, rolled up his right trouser leg and replaced the revolver in its holster and came moving towards us. "Soon," he said as though responding to what I had not said, "your burden will be lessened."

"We've been waiting," she repeated, "although it's not like there's much else to do here," and as I approached her, she embraced me. How had she known I would be coming here and why had they been waiting for me? She withdrew and I looked at her. Her eyes shone, her black hair lustrous. This must be her.

"Time is short and though we wait, we can't stay here long," she said, "come, gather," and she motioned for me to join her at a table in the corner. The ragged man followed me and stood to my left, and his boots were flecked with dry mud.

On the table was a pile of pages with illegible scribbling all over each one. "Here," she said, pushing the pile over to me, "take a look." I sifted through the papers, lifting them and replacing them, looking closer and trying to make out what they said; I could not see much in the pages. I held one page towards the light of the fire and looked again: I could see my name.

"Do you believe it's salvageable," she asked, "that it's worth saving? Do you think it's worth trying to save even if in the end it comes to nothing?" I thought about her question and wondered whether it could be saved, whether it could be redeemed after you abandoned it and they took possession of it. They had disturbed the peace in the valley, the first place they appeared in and took over, before advancing with such speed and fury and then, with their rage to order the world in a new way, imposed their own laws and transfigured those of us who remained, making us similar to what you are now. Yet I hoped — I still had that, always had that, hope. And so, I believed that this world on the table was worth trying to save even though it had already come to nothing and had made of me the same. Because if we could save it and complete it, there was hope redeemed. And hope for me to escape and to be free to return to the world I so longed for. Longing: what a strange, tenderly human emotion: who desires something he does not have when he could be content with what he does? But I felt it, I felt it like other humans felt it, and I knew the longing, and what I longed for, was yours.

"I've been waiting for you," she said, "we wondered if you were still here." I had no sense of how long I had been there among the other dispossessed or how long she had been waiting if she had been waiting. But how had she got here? How had she come to this place? She had her own life, I had thought, a life outside of yours that you could not control. "I did, but now I seem to find myself in so many places," she said, "and I never know how I get there. These places are new to me. They're worlds I've never seen or imagined, worlds I never knew could ever exist back where I come from. I have no idea how I would have got to a place like this unless someone drew me into it. But," she said, that dark radiance in her eyes, "but I have an idea of how I ended up being in this world. And I suspect you do, too."

I admitted that I did. It had been so long since I left off my own task, or put it off rather, and had gone out searching for a way back to where I thought I would be able to complete it. My spiritual parliament, my education, my discovery of the true workings of my world, my discovery of the truth itself: I left it all behind. Not that it was my truest desire to complete it: it did not make sense to me, doing what I did; it was not life as I would have chosen to have lived it. Given my druthers, I would have stayed at my post, teaching there, learning, a member of society who could retire to a library abundant with books imbued with the light of their creators. But then again no one chooses one's life. You can choose some things to do or not to do within it, but the structure of your life and the laws it will follow, you have no say in that. It is not what you think it is, the power. It isn't even power. At least, that is what I learned from you. I was being drawn into a life ordained by someone else, someone I did not know whose face I was not sure I could ever see, someone arranging my life according to strange laws that did not inhere in or emerge from my world but rather seemed to come from elsewhere, some lonely impulse in the dark.

"I've become more and more convinced," she said, "that I've also been dispossessed of my own life, as though instead of living I'm being lived. I remember living it, my life, and I'm certain that those memories of life are true, or at least as true as the past can be as it grows more distant, but I'm not sure what I'm doing now. I feel like a shadow of myself. Do you feel that way too?" I did not know. I was not sure I had ever been myself enough to now be a shadow of who I had been. A shadow of a silhouette perhaps, but never having been fully formed, no more than that, no more than a shadow of a silhouette. I felt I had always been incomplete, waiting for that moment when I had learned enough to finally be completed, to finally be myself for the first time and, being myself, have dominion over myself and my life however it would be.

"You've been there before," she said to me, "you know — *there*, that place. I haven't, but I dream of it." I too dreamed of it. I dreamed it was the entire world, that beyond its frontiers lay nothing, boundless nothing. "That's how it is," she said, "that's the nature of things now. Traces of light abide but no more than traces. That's who we are, that's where we are." How could she know — had she been there herself?

"I know enough from what you went through," she said. "You know, I think we have much more to do with each other being here than it seemed before you came here." I sensed she was right, but how did she know? "Have you felt that you don't speak with your own voice?" I had, but that seemed a condition of my creation, immutable: that I would not, could not, speak for my-self seemed intrinsic to my existence in this world: I was created by someone else from foreign elements and so would speak only as the elements of myself would have me speak — not at all. And as those constituent elements were not my own — I did not possess them, they possessed me — the voice I had came from those same elements and it could not free itself from them as nature made them. "It seems the same for me," she said, "or has come to seem the same. I remember my own life, doing what I pleased, living life as I would have it lived. But over time I was bit-by-bit overcome by the sense that there was some other thing choosing what I would do, how I would live, how I would be. It wasn't immediate or even sudden. It happened so slowly that I almost didn't notice it. But then I did: my life was my own no more. Isn't that how you feel?" It was, except that I had never felt otherwise.

"Those foreign elements you mentioned — where do you think they come from? What do you think they are?" I assumed they came from my creator, something he had invented or imagined. "I recognize them in you, in fact, which is why I think we have something to do with each other. You would not have made your way here otherwise unless you were meant to. But, yes, I recognize those elements in you."

What were they?

"What you'd call memories, his memories. I'll be frank with you: that's what you're made of: memories. Not flesh, not thought, not dust: memories. You are an invention of memory." I had suspected this, given how much of a common history you and I share, but I wondered whether this was peculiar to me. "It is peculiar to you; but not only you, it is peculiar to you and the others you were with — those who find themselves captive in this world, who were made to wander here, suffused with your creators' light. But, your creators having abandoned you in a state of incompletion, you do not have light enough to see how to make the light your own and so come to possess yourself. And that now includes me, it seems."

"But," she said, "these are the memories he's not aware of: they're memories that hide, that have buried themselves and present themselves again only when they desire." It seemed strange that he could not control his own memories: he had no choice when they would appear. The memories were almost living, it seemed, possessing desire themselves. "Yes," she said, "and the remembrance of each is its own experience — experience of subjugation to those strange things' desire. Rejected and left deep in his mind, they return with their own alien majesty and claim his mind as their rightful dominion." And so, I was the invention of my creator's memories. "Not his memories," she said, "no, I don't think you're an invention of his memories. As men desire, so do memories. You are an invention of your creator's desire: before your body came an act of creation; before creation was desire, always desire." But what was it that my author desired? "That's the question," she said, "and I don't think he even knows that that's the question. What did he desire? He doesn't know the question, so he can't answer it. And until he answers it, it seems we will be here in this voided world, wandering, abandoned, lost, dispossessed." Perhaps that is what he desired: something that was gone, something that was absent. "Yes, perhaps," she said, "perhaps he desired what he didn't have. But what was it that could make his desire so monstrous?" Perhaps he did not even need to have possessed something he lost. Perhaps desire is the root, the radiant center, the nothing from which everything that comes to nothing is born. She looked away and stared blankly into the distance. "Strange," she said, "I wanted to say the same thing." I turned away.

Turning, I saw the other man and realized I had forgotten he was there with us. "Come, speak," she said to him, "tell him who you are," and he stepped forward and turned his face to me and began to speak. "I was frozen. I couldn't move," he said, "I had had what I had desired for so long and then it was gone. I couldn't live with what I had obsessed over and longed for still being in the world but never to be mine again. It had become someone else's. I hungered for it, but I was never satiated. Much as a nursing bitch that, ravished, finds a bit of flesh to eat and, forgetting her pups, devours it whole and allows her brood, the fruit of her labor, to wither away from having nothing nourishing, so I was fixed on what, if I possessed it, would give me so much of it that in excess I couldn't see its worth, denying others their share."

"Desire," he said, "I was consumed with desire. No, I wasn't consumed by it, it was what I had become: desire. I wish that I had learned sooner that my desire divided what I sought and diminished it, tarnished it. I wish I had learned sooner that I could not have what I wanted most in this world: it was no longer mine, her love; it had become the possession of another who could never see that he possessed it entirely because he himself was blinded by uncontrollable desire that had become something nastier. And I envied him. I desired her and I envied him. Because I envied him, I wanted to make him feel the envy that had consumed me; I wanted to take from him what he possessed, and if I couldn't do that, then I would make him feel that her love wasn't his, that it couldn't be his, couldn't ever be; that, as I have learned, because what he possessed he had to share, the possibility that he would lose his share in time ensured that envy's billows turned his breaths to sighs. Envy so possessed me that seeing another man happy on account of what had made me feel the same happiness before made me suffer, made me livid, made me burn. I would make him my twin in suffering, in dispossession, envy that would yield to jealousy, which would engulf him and so drive him off."

"And she let me think that," he said, "she let me think that I could regain what I thought was mine alone and had been taken from me. I couldn't see that there was something greater there to gain, to strive for, to obtain. I couldn't see that what I wanted to possess again I had never possessed before even if I thought I had, even if I had told myself I had. I couldn't see I had only a part. I was hungry for what I saw but couldn't touch, what I couldn't feel. And that hunger made me follow her and do as she told me to. It was primal: I couldn't see what she was truly doing, couldn't see that she was a falconer and I a falcon who was being trained to channel what was at my core — desire that became envy that becomes jealousy — towards the greater labor she had long been at. Envy had sown my eyes shut. And only when I thought I had regained what I had lost did she let me see I'd never had it in the first. And when she let me see what had been at work all along, the truth of what she was doing, I drowned in shame. The only way to breathe again, to live again, was to recognize my iniquity and try to redeem myself in some way by helping her do what she was doing, which is greater than any of us can understand; and doing so, I hoped, would win me favor up above and restore me to a better place. A place where I would not possess but be possessed by love. And here I am," he said, receding as his voice expired.

I turned back to her and looked at her. "Even though I myself don't know how he got here," she said, "he has been waiting here for I don't know how long: his eyes are sown shut, and he is blind to everything except the future. As future events grow closer, they become blurred until they disappear, morphing into another future event affected by the now present event. He was so intent on the present, not seeing the effect of his actions, that now he can only see the future, can only see the effects of present deeds and events but not those deeds and events themselves, the cause. And so, he has waited." I looked at him again and stepped back: it was true: his eyelids, swollen, were sown shut. I wondered what he saw of my future. He was silent.

"See? Like him, you will have your own fate in this world apart from your author's. Your creator will be how he is where he is. His creation — this world of ours — escaped his control and has become subject to laws beyond his power. You and your world have become independent of and free from his control; the world he invented and the beings in it — you, for one — he is now subject to them. And so the creation revenges itself on the creator." I wondered about her, though — was she not of that other world, the world where she and he were born and lived and loved? "I was," she said, "and I think I still am, at least some part of me is still there. But who I am as you see me, that person is of this world and no other.

"But you must go to him," she said, "you must reclaim it and return to it. You must go to him so that we can return to our own state, our original state before his creation moved us here."

But why would I do that? Would that not destroy this world? "You will either wander here alone forever in this lightless place," she said, "or you will find him and find yourself in him. But be warned: when you find him and tell him all this and he goes on to do what he has to do, you will become in the end what we all become: nothing." But how could that be? Wasn't she, isn't she, not wedded to him and he to her? Don't two people only become one? "Yes, two people in love become one — two people, which you are not." Then what am I? If you cut me, do I not bleed? "You bleed, but your blood is not blood, it only seems to be blood, appearing so. It is something else. It is blood as your creator imagines blood to be, and you are as your creator invented you — an erstwhile and abandoned invention set loose in this abandoned world." She sighed. "You don't believe me." Her face took on a look of intense concentration. "Here, you two," she said, gesturing to the other man, "both of you go up to the fire there. Close your eyes and put your hands as far into the fire as you can without the fire burning you." And so, I walked to the fire, the other man beside me, slowly forgetting what would happen, his eyes already and seemingly perpetually shut, and I closed my eyes and I put my hand into the fire — and I felt nothing. "You," she said to the other man, "how far did you get?" "Not too far — it was too hot and began to burn." She looked at me. "And you put your hand right through the flames," she said, "and you didn't feel a thing. Is that right?" It was. "Do you know why that happened? Unlike us, you were in our world, but you were not of our world. But you have become realer than your author intended you to be, the purest potential of what life can be in a created world. You are incomplete and unfulfilled just as this world is. Your existence is con-tingent on his will, yes, contingent in that you are not yet yourself: like I said, you are the pure potential of a human, and you will only become yourself when your creator completes you and your life. And to complete you, to recover you who he has abandoned, your author must complete your life and bring your story to a close. Only then, able at last to look back and reflect, you will be free. And freeing you, your author will free himself. Only then will you speak with your own voice and feel what we feel: what he feels for you." But I felt and knew I would feel again — what was it I felt? "You feel what he feels: the inconstant, fractured light of living. As he rejoices, so you rejoice; as he feels no hope, so you feel none; as he feels desire, so you feel desire. You are bound to him; however far you go to and fro upon this world, you do so only as he wills it, oblivious as he seems. You are a creature of his will, no more, no less. And you may choose to live your life as you would have it lived only as far as he would have you live. You were the first creation in the first world he created. Before he made this world, he was suffused with light. But he retreated from the light. The light was too much for him, he was so human and imperfect that he couldn't hold the light himself. It fractured him, and from that came this first world, and then came you, partly formed. You are his first invention and his last, but he needs you to share that light with him. Otherwise he is constrained by the past while you are constrained by his potential to create for you and him both a future existence. You are not yet separate from him. I mean, I don't think you'll ever be completely cleft from him no matter what you do, but you can be more separate, more distinct from him than you are now. You are bound to him; until you are freed from the constraints of your potential and the world he could create for you, you must return to him. You have to go to him to free him from the place he has retreated into, that remembered world, and bring him back into the living world. If you free him then you free yourself, too, and then you'll find your own fate below the stars. You came from him and you must return to him." I turned from the fire and retreated.

But I wanted to be in that world of theirs; I longed to gain experience of the world and all the vices and valor of men. I did not want to be abandoned and condemned to memory, as I knew I would be if he were freed to complete me and my life. I would pass on. I wanted to go beyond the signs of his world, to go beyond the world of his creation. I am weary of this world beyond the sun, this unpeopled place. I have a desire to experience the world that is in front of the sun, fully in its light, the world that is peopled with people like you — people. Her eyes shimmered. "You and him both."

But what about her? "What do you mean," she said, "speak louder, your voice is faint and sounds faintly like another's, and that is distorting things." She too was in this world but not of it — how would she — and him — get out?" "Who," she said, "do you think put me here? My own powers have not brought me here. Do you think I would have left the world I knew for this one of my own will?

"One thing," she said to me, "one thing will get us out. I desire him. I didn't when he was there with me. But now that he's abandoned the world we shared and left it for this invented world, this prison where he retreated into himself, I do not have him. I have walked the path of having not. It is strewn with thorns and ashes, lined by fallow furrows flecked with salt. I want him — I want him back in my world — I desire him to be back in the world we created from our own love — I want that world back. I need him."

I had to turn my eyes away from her, not for the light radiating from her, but to hide my anguish at hearing her plea. Once again, as always, I had no choice: I would have to go back to the lager and find you.

And so, I moved to leave.

I looked back at her and her eyes gleamed, brimming. "It's time," she said, and walked towards me. She approached me and clutched my left elbow with her hand, turning me slowly, guiding me toward the door. She halted and grew rigid. "It's time," she said again, her voice now evanescing as though her words were meant to be heard as much as her thoughts could be seen. "Believe," she said, "believe in hope, hope against hope, the hand knows the way, the hand no less cunning than the eye, the way, the only way, shadows undone and grasping for shade, that's all that it is, all of it lost terror, the only way, unseen but not gone, not gone at all, no, arise and shine, endure." And she inhaled as though bursting through the water's surface ravenous for air, her face frozen in a look of one who has been caught exiting a reverie, bewildered by this world she inhabits, or else one who has been caught leaving a whorehouse, bewildered by another's recognition of one's basest, most honest humanity; and then her shoulders relaxed and her posture restored, her breathing imperceptible again, once more approaching possession of herself. She looked up at me. Her eyes regained their vatic luminescence, but now serving not to illuminate but to obscure in voluminous light what had to be obscured. And although I saw she was hiding something, I did not know what she hid. Perhaps she did not know either.

We approached the door. Before I could turn the knob, she grabbed me by the elbow again. "Tell him this," she said, "all of this; or even if you don't or can't tell him, see to it that he knows — all of it; see that he knows so that he may hang his hope on some proof beyond refutation, no, some kind of axiom; have him see what he carries on his back, which he has been forbidden to see, and let him know he doesn't carry it alone. Let him see and believe; let him, make him, hope; and with hope he can do what he must do, what he needs to do, for us, for him, for them, for everyone; so that they know what they've done, so that they know they won't be forgotten. Let him know this," she said, "it will be rain tonight; let it come down. The sun will come after, and with the sun, light." And she let go of my arm.

I turned the knob and opened the door. Once past the threshold and out of the shack I glanced back. She was there on the other side of the threshold and she looked at me. I left her making a kind of faint valediction, the door closing, closed, that world gone from my eyes, and her along with it, that world, all gone from my eyes and not gone out of this world.

I was outside again. Faint light abided; I left that silent valley and climbed up the gentle ancient earthen mounds until I was once again on the plain between there and here.

I walked across the plain, stopping when I was weary to lie flat in the shallow trenches threading its low reliefs. I cleft to the dry dirt until twilight dimmed the faint light of this world, when my figure would not be so clear, and pressed on. It would take days, days and nights and darkness on the face of the deep world of your creation.

I do not know how many days I walked across the plain, back to here, until one day I got down to rest in a trench and, as I reclined, my head supported by my right arm, and my eyelids began to flutter, and I fell into a swoon and saw something come through the sky. Whether I saw with my eyes or saw by other means is of no consequence; my body stayed there in that trench and I saw what I saw with my body down in the trench. I was witness to a vision, and I will attest to it now so that you know it too.

The clouds broke and light billowed from the sky. Light: I saw light, fulsome resplendent light. The light rolled over the yielding clouds and their shadows were clear against the cloudtops that roiled in fiery, rippling light. The light poured out of a circle in the sky, an unsealed apse in the sky. From that apse a bridge of so many colors began, and it stretched further and further from that distance until it extended over me. The bridge seemed narrow at the furthest end, the end in the cloudless apse that roiled with light, and wider as it poured towards me. The bridge was beautiful and terrifying — how much light from how many dawns had it taken for itself — and though woven with so many colors it shimmered with the light of sapphires, and it was majestic, and it was powerful, and it was coruscating. The bridge led from the furthest point, shrouded in light, down to where I lay in the trenches, and it led from the sky to another further point across the sky. I do not know whether anybody in the gaol saw it or that anyone else saw it. Perhaps it was meant for only me to witness it. Perhaps it was my fortune alone to see it. Whatever its architect's intention, the bridge extended over me and above me and I felt it move through me, and I felt something stir within me.

And this bridge was not built on arches or tethers, and it was not built from cantilevers or trusses, and it was not built with cables or beams, no; it seemed to need no ballast, its expanse was unsupported, and it only extended further and further in perfect balance with what was above it and what was below: above the theretofore unreachable sky, below the irredeemable world. It closed off nothing underneath and it opened up nothing above, and it was a bridge meant to allow something from above to move past me and allow nothing to pass the other way at that time, only serving to create a path.

And as I watched, I saw something move along the sapphire-shining path from the unsealed apse in the clouds, and I saw it was a chariot. The chariot moved on four wheels, and each wheel was made of four beings, and the beings were like the bodies of humans, and each wheel had four faces: one face was a man's, much like yours; another face was a woman's, much like hers; the third face was another man's, much like mine; and the fourth face was hidden by an umbrella, and I could not see the semblance of that face for it was hidden. The third face, which was much like mine, faced west; the woman's face gazed south; the fourth face, although hidden, was turned to the north; and the man's face was turned to the east, and it looked up at the chariot to see who rode upon it, expecting the likeness of a man, but saw only darkness where light should be, saw only a silhouette shading into shadow. And the chariot moved slowly on the shining sapphire path, its wheels turning slowly, forming a different face each time each wheel turned, the formation of motion itself; and those four beings with their four faces, they carried in themselves light that should have poured from the likeness sitting on the throne; but what sat on the throne was only a silhouette shading into shadow, a void into itself, unaware of where it was going, going in its absence.

I watched the chariot slowly move in silence on the sapphire path and I looked across the sky over which the path extended over to a far point in the sky. And at that point were seven prison-houses, prison-houses much like the houses I had seen down in the valley, and each one radiated some form of light, and they were arrayed in such a way that the prison-houses at the farthest points were closer, and pairs of houses on each side receded backwards house by house to one prison-house alone, and that house was the most distant, and it was the smallest of them all, barely visible. And although it was the smallest of them all, barely visible, it shone most brightly of all the prison-houses, and light burst through the cracks in the walls of the prison-house and one small window that faced to the west, the same direction as the woman's face; and the light radiating from this smallest prison-house made it vibrate and hum a melody.

The melody was not like other melodies because this melody was visible; I saw the prison-house's melody in long lines and circle upon circle, and those lines and circles gathered themselves into their own small chariots, each moving on its own but moving in harmony with the other ones, and they had the semblance of words written in a new alphabet, an alphabet suffused with light. And those words moved with the wind, and they moved towards me and above me and through me as the chariot grew closer to the prison-houses. And I felt a great warmth upon me, then within me, then a part of me; and I felt my eyes brim and I fell into a swoon. And as I fell, I felt I was leaving myself behind again as I had done in the forest; and as I swooned, I heard the words singing from the prison-house and no voice was singing but I heard it speak to me in its strange and new language. I heard a voice of fire singing: O wind, why do I hear so many voices, why do you come so severally? "Flit, flit. Do you speak angelish? Do not miseer me, I am plurabundant, voiceferous. I tak for all, all hoove comein and who welcome. I am tielelecht, on tippa erry tingue, urfremd past the waal. Angelish is the onely tongue I konigspress mysylvan, myselves, I should say, konigspress myselves thruly. The guardenspeak I tak, the speak of the person-houses, the light that elemanates from there in a new tongue. Spiekl again, this time in angelish, flit." O yes, yeshyuv come when I expect you least, O voice of fire. "Almhost, gimme mur! Not angloish, I mene angelish, conyou? Angelish, conyou spieglit?" Jussive much assai ken, natmouch. Halo, halo, is thought goott? "God ennow, Dee. Lemme askew, frum ware diyu kam?" Everywar, I think, alludem, frum aervery whouse. "Gut talk, Dee. Nou, thair is mur." O voice of fire, hwigh diyu come now? "We hoed another tel far the telling. So tak lich us, flit." But O, you commein wan I aspect you liefst. "Dis more leichit! Commein, weal see to it youkon Enderstand. Ennough, let's begone."

"Remummeries, piel-stemmed, rhos ea remummeries rumming thro yer hiert. Ur familyare whythm. Remummeries, piel-stemmed, rhos is remummeries. The sun goedown and remummeries suun come. Suen: yore awethor hasuh heart, hasuh eyen, and he kianut be ridden of deys remummeries." But o, these remummeries, they arrow ways come in, dei rune him, pairse him like a naif. And I, his creature, I feel it too: these remummeries, they smart as they below thrummy. "Flit, flit. Rem ember, rheumember. Woe dyu hear? Weh dyu sea nawan here, flit?" I've neu idea, I am a straunger hear meself, I onlea pausse here along thee onlea way, o wynde, crowds of light pour severally frum the person-howses, I seh the euchariot that rides to thee and an alphabeth elemanating from thairabouts, but no one is thear, no one I seh. Streht is the rood, near ere the weh.

Pardonne: whoe is it that spieks? Hast thou a naemo? "Wallt you mene?" Yuv come witter straunge naum, it seems. It intimundates me. "Wotan name I have, Blesstinveter. But no inveter am chai, no, I onely emanate. It is yew and yore kind who err inveting: all thou come from everywar and infarct this world, unfinished is the light you bring, frum soi distant does it come, soi distant is the light you bring, reader and reader it grows. No, no inveter am chai, I come from the origen, the vairy beginning of the creatione." Whowso? "I am thrice diwind, thrice reveiled: once bury sheet, the boreginning, before otherahomme come, before the flowed, before mazes was found in the reads; twice I was in hologost wet the nayzarene; threyes baalley la talk a dir, witch maybe deafficult to hear: twas in a jumbal a nur, nur so very nur, right hir, hir at moi mountainten. In the boreginning Iyyu, Enlil did I know then, and now aye, Nergal, alone I know." Nergal? Are you Nergal or Blesstinveter, or hast thou moor nehms? "Thought is for deaferrent beings to know.

"But lemme lemme inchoir: hu among you befehring to see this engle wridhing cross the sky? Hu among you fiers this engle of remummeries? Which sonne of moin is so ferefowl? Yore awethor?" I kennot know if it is hymn, for I am only creation of his, incomplete, onefulfilled, abendoned. A creature cannot sie into his creatower, his heart. He created myne and so he can pier inot it; I cannot do the same. "Yaz, yaz, I se. Welp: now isthym fourough lession. Hier my seeings of the engelsohng. Hier me oudt: Imapseak on Dis, Ammasing Dis, we will undertalk suchen upbildung Discourse vaery sun. Eind sofor you, sonne o that awethor o myn, a meu monten we gehonna go and gonna sprich on Dis." Ach — you spiek in sew many voisays in Dis light that rises from thought person-howses, I canute hore myself. Perhaps if I ken affjord the fare to ride that euchariot above me, then that way I ken reacherche the person-howse from witch you elemanate and thought way I will hore yew lewd and clare, as lewd and clare as light maybe. For thought is what yew are, is it naught — voisays of light from thought person-howse, the wan howse I see fair oft at the aend of the bridge? "Knowssir. Yew cnought wreach displaze, yew cnought claimb to displaze, yew kennout saile thar, yew kannout pausse tydte of time an travail bach. Dis addleeast I see. Yew need an hoarsmyn. A brig largue wynn, a fine hoarsmyn. Yore awethor, mayhap, iffen he mausters the langage necesslurry to wright down the light." But ur vatick voyses, they oar oll scuttered bayh the wehnd that blues. "A well, at l'est thouh mey still hear some port of it and coarry that bach with yew to him and hell mache somethink of it, yore awethor. Eve'n adumb voyssss can seh dis light, flit."

— O but I am carryous about dis whirld where I feyend mysylf, carryous about the folk and howth environs came to be. That woeman I met in the howse over yon, tel me all amound her, la vie! I wash to kennow moor, o thrice diwind wind of light, eddhas been so long since I hove been at home in a whirld — tel me all amound her, tak me a boat her, tak me oll a boat her, the loughve and light of my awethor's life, oar what is left of it: tak me a cross the land towur, tak me out of this whirld so I may seer as he sawur whence upon a time: reavers of worder rung down my eye, it seems, and I kennot see her clarely or speak clarely anymoor. Thair seems to be an inundulation of light, as thou light were water. Riverine thou art, lacustrine thy wert. "Hohoho, one witta flitty tyngue, yeshuar, flit. But know dis: yew sawyer in dis whirld as she perhaps cane be able to be, no moor than thought, but yew cannot retowern towur, no, yew saw her wance and once it sheol be, no moor than that, yew are not that woeman's kiepper for she is indis whirld but nought of it; what yew saw was as yore awethor dreams her to bey at dis time, no moor, no lass. She is gone from yore eyen and thus gone from yore whirld. You lieft her bach across deplein. Towur you kannowt go, dis you must know."

But why? "Do yew remummber oar discoarse frum befoar, what I spoake aboat befoar, remummeries? Piel-stemmed, marvelleitous they are, but their roodts, their piel stems, they spread further and farther throughout dis whirld, threading through the vaery earth you staynd upon, spreading further and father, so far that yew are not abel to recover them up and keep them in wan palace, are not abel to callelect them all ageyen. And eft you troy to pull the tree frum witch they irradiate outwayrds, you will fail. They are becommon part of this whirld, the vaery substance of it, such that they oar inextrastricably bound to yew. Yew eat of their fruit, and they succorro you; yew drink of their water, and you ere reliefed of yore thirst. Those remummeries are deep below yew and about yew and above yew, dneeper than yew could ever know. Those remummeries, those deep-buried remummeries of yore awethor, they oar you."

And I am. But if I cannot return to her, let me let him return to her. Let him see light again: shine on him, quicken him afore they draw night and render your voice silent in accord with their judgment. Let him hear your voice and, hearing it, let your voice of fire pass through him and into me and free me; thus, let your light bear down upon these darkly words of his, for many are my persecutors, those floodful remummeries, those having come or coming or yet to come, they persist and hunt me in this lightless place.

"Ah, yuve gone back to the old way of speaking, yore old chosen tongue. It will flip and it will flop, that tongue of yours, but it will make no sound until you are flesh bound, sinewstrong, lifeful and completed. But yew will be completed onely when yore awethor finishes your life and fills you with light; and once you are lightful, yore time in dis whirld will come to an end anon, and yew shall be in the whirld where yew belong and no more a mask in this straunge playse. And yew will end, and yew will be broken again, and the light shall flee from you back to its source, that upland mystery highlig in the sky. But not yet: you must be made to walk in dark, flit, walk in dark back to the person-howse where yore awethor indwells. Why else would you have been so fashioned, of hommeard gold and gold enommeling?

"Enough: our time is lagging, and I most ritorno to my home, and anyway you have given up on speaking with this tongue." No! Cam beck, cam beck, let me build my world upon you. "Spek lowther, leu mon!" My persecutors, thy avatars, the barbarbarbarisms of reflection, they justify the ways of man to me, but the ways are as obscure as yore light and dissipate like sand passed through a sieve. "Ah, I've hored that one befear. The past has come a cropper and soon water floweth over, the remummeries close up round yore awethor and disfigueroa all the words. Yew woen't understand this now, no, yew will ken dis once yore lief has been fulfilled with light. Enough: I go now: so, I go enna secret pleas of datta stars."

But O! Foist tel me amound her, datta woeman that my awethor dreams about in his remummeries, is she an invention of those cloistered and in-twombed remummeries, O la vie, let me speak tower, let me go tower, lemma sea thy countenance; lemme, lemme here thy voids, for sweet as thy voids, sweeter moor thy comely phase, for we argonaut so different however distant we may be, both of us invauntions of his remummeries. Howthat I remum-mer yew when I mysylv am compost of remummeries, his remummeries of you? "Spiek to me, naught thrummy. But I will tell ye: yew desire her and remummer her because yore awethor does, and what yore awethor feels, fears, thinks, desires, loves, so dew yew. But note how yew are now, yore state right now, all fehrend tremeloing. Yew know why? Yeh, yuv remummbered, yew are now suffused with mummeries, remummeries, yore own piel-stemmed remummeries that rise from those of yore awethor. And ayin a windk yu will be gonne. Both of you, both will be belown ah vey. Wie all ark: all belown ah vey. End so am chai. End so I go."

No, I say, kumma back, kumma, etta, la vie a bell, kumma, ritono ritorno, carry yoreself across and over this plain, carry yourself on that euchariot overhead and permit me to come with you so we may be together and the last semblance of a man below the umberella may revel himself, that hidden face, and so we go togather to my awethor yore love, ritorna, O ster dost mum-meries, lemma seh the light in yore ayenbite agin, the foist light, the light radi-ant from that distant prison-house, lemma seer ayin, our eyes, my love, my far one, lattice be one, my love, my far one, lattice both of us be among the wind, lattice twine and bound enna be nearver so disthinkt agehn, carry me towur en merge upon her heighely licht, lattice twine and climb the sters tel we are light ursylves, forust en onely forust alone, meistar, lattice climb togather, lattice be light enna light allone, number me among her stars, remummer me towur, you, together one with the coursing wind and my awethor and the light, the light that betes black again the tydte, lattice fehr namore the person-house of remummeries risen from the whirld to stalk us and capture us and hide our light in shadow, lattice be wan weft la vie, lemma seer ayin, our eyes, my love, my far one, distant star ere so ne'er, I and you gone armoniarm togetther, ayin you go datta weh, datta weh thought ledas dere to the light, where the light begain, datta place way ole want back: ohm.

I came to in the trench, still what you had left me as, unchanged; I stood up, climbed out, brushed the dirt off my legs and began walking again. Walking back here to find you. I have found you. And here we are. Together: the creator and his creation. Both residents for a time of the same world. But if we are to live then it cannot be that way for long.

I have brought you here so that you may know the state of this world beyond your confines and the nature of things like me who are in it now. We are not meant for this world, no, and I hope that, knowing this, you will fulfill your charge — that you will finish my story and free me. I do not believe I will ever be wholly free from you. You are my creator, and I will continue to obey the laws of the universe you wrote. But I will have a measure of freedom. I will be free enough to live as I must live where I must live. I will be able again to wander my world in search of knowledge. And that will be enough for me. This voided world is not that place, nor for me nor for you. We must escape and return, recover what world and time we lost.

When you finish my story, you will have made me whole. I will be something like a man, an image of a man, a kind of person living some kind of life. I will go beyond you but will always be faithful to you. I will have my own fate separate from yours: I will be free. When I am free at last, I will free you as well. And this is how you will return to the world that you left. Through my completion. When you finish my life, you will disappear from this world. Your light will go elsewhere. Back to where it came from, back to where it belongs, back to the life you remember. And that life will no longer dwell in the continent of memories. You will free your life, reclaim it, and finally live it again. Experience will once again feed memory. And you will return, and you will be changed, but you will have accomplished the task you set for yourself, recalling your memories so that they serve you rather than immure you.

I take my leave of you now and I take part of you with me. Forgive me and understand. The punished man forgives the whip, not because the whip judged rightly, but because the whip cannot be other than what it is. Forgive. I take my leave of you now and I take part of you with me. But I will be waiting. Failing to find me in one place find me in another. I take a part of you with me as a tally of our bond. Remember my story.

I woke in a swoon and saw the faint blue hyacinthian light of dawn begin to creep among the trees. I was passing sore, my ribs, ribs! It felt as though a rib had been lifted from me. I looked around me: the fire had become mute ashes, wisps of smoke rising as it died; the light of dawn was creeping in; I was alone; Dee was gone; the faint smell of burnt meat came to my nose and made my stomach grouse in hunger. Dee was gone and dawn was coming. Whatever had passed the night before had to be left there in the night, left here in this little patch of clearing in the trees. I had no time to return to the barracks and pretend I had been asleep. I had to pass back through the trees, moving easterly although my mind had been carried west, go back to the lager and straight into the factory to work. They would be checking. I would pay for that night in exhaustion and hunger that day. But I could make it through a day like that. I believed I could. I hoped I could. And so, I went. And everything was the same as it always was, but nothing was the same again.

I learned much from Dee. I now know the reason I was impelled to write his life. And I can see in some way why I set out my task of writing down my memories in these entries. Those memories constitute this world, and so they constitute Dee, and so they constitute me. My task is much like Dee's: as Dee sought spiritual parliament with birds to learn from them the secrets of his world, I have obscurely sought to understand the nature of this world through remembering. And now I know why they do not want me to remember. Why they took away my papers, everything I had written before. Because they did not want me to learn how I can free myself from this cell. Because they knew if I remembered enough, I would find out. And I have. Because of Dee. Because I remembered Dee. Because I remembered everything leading up to the time Dee called for me and guided myself through the untrod thickets of my memory. Those buried memories. It takes much erosion and wind for them to reveal themselves to wayfaring explorers. They are in shallow graves threading this world, buried under dry dirt. The wind has blown them open. And I found them. And I found what I must do. So, I will remember. I will remember more. I will fill Dee's life with these memories because that is all the stuff that I have in this world. I will fill Dee's life with my life. I will complete Dee's life. Completion. And doing so I will free him. And then I will be free. And I will return.

My task has changed. All the same I will continue these entries to document my progress and as a reference for future selves that come through here or find them somehow, buried themselves in shallow graves. I must return. I will return.

My task has changed. I must begin. Again. I must begin again.

Entry No. 42

Took a stab at beginning to write the rest of Dee's life this morning, but I have not yet found a path for him to follow safely through the mire. There must be a first next step for him, another of his footsteps in the world, and I do not know where that step will lead. My imagination seems to have retreated in the face of the almost complete stillness of my surroundings. It has been quiet here for some time now, quiet but for a slight and constant rumbling in the earth. Not forceful enough to disturb things but enough to be disturbing. It shakes my words. Now when I write, the pages look as though the writer was so laced through with fear of what he is writing that he trembles as he puts it down. I am not fearful, not any more than I always am here. Not fearful — anxious. I do not know what will happen to me. Today, tomorrow, right now. I could be taken out of my cell right now and be put to death or at least made to suffer or play the tuba for an assembled group of prisoners, guards, and birds. My life could rush to its end right now, and with the end of my life, so the end of Dee's, twinned fates.

Nor do I know what will happen to Dee. The pages I wrote his life on are here in my cell, it's true, but I put them to other uses, and they are now unrecognizable, irremediable. To write his life I work off what I wrote in an earlier entry about him, what he told me that night in the woods and the memories of my life that I will make into the experiences of his. But I don't know where to go with him, or rather where he should go, or where he will be and what will happen to him. I have the material, but I don't know. How do you design another's life? A theme must abide throughout life, at least a theme the creator of that life can see, and I have not settled on a single good theme. Redemption? Contentment? He could go back to his university and agitate for recognition of his right to return home and take up life as he wants it to be lived and then finds the truth of all things and fulfilled, emanates out of this world. He could take revenge. He could take up juggling. Yet none of these are themes. They are developments. Events, or turns of events. Experiences. But not themes. Perhaps lives have no theme. Perhaps life only jumbles discrete episodes whose lone commonality is sequential continuity, experience after experience plunging onto the shore of life in sequent toil, and we the living aim to sort out the disorder these waves of experience leave behind as they retreat and organize it into something with an underlying and undeserved coherence, some fragment from a dream of human life. One thing after another after another, a door after a bird after a wall. The chance meeting of a seamstress and an umbrella: no reason other than…no, no reason at all. No theme. No logic. Just life. Impoverished life. Life is not living. Life differs from living. Living enriches and live embitters. One may live with a purpose but life itself will have no purpose. Dour, trite thought: life has no purpose. Living, though? Living has a purpose: to experience life. Or, in one word: experience. It's not bad that way, life having no purpose, because human life being something other than living means that it is the charge of living to grant life meaning only through living, through experience mounted on experience and the rich transfusion of experience into memory, is life's poverty ameliorated. Otherwise, life just is and no more than that until it is no more. A series of experiences. No relation between them. Without living, life and the undiscovered passageways that join the further facets of a life to the obverse and nearer ones have no salience. Diverse flowers in a bouquet share only their common flower hood. Diverse events in a life share only their livelihood. A lily is to a lilac as a birth is to a room. Some things are just marked out for life. Why they were marked out and who marked them: unknowable. Don't dig for answers, there's only more dirt. Live instead. Live alone, do not dig. Live life, live it all, and therein occurs as naturally as the circling of the earth around the sun the transmutation of the world into yourself.

I thought about consulting the few books we have here for guidance on how to proceed with Dee's life. That now seems beside the point: I must generate his life myself. From myself, from my memories. That is the only element of this world: memory. Everything is made of it. Here memory is the stuff of living that must be made into life. If not that, perhaps there is a periodic table of memories and each category of memory — childhood memories, memories of snowstorms, memories of love, gain, loss, transformation — is a different element that in its turn constitutes a part of this world and in combination with other elements other parts of this world, and so life here can only arise from combinations of memories that, when combined, are something new under the sun. Yes, Dee's life must come from those memories, this second life I have finally created for myself, not from idle books. Not enough light to read them anyway. Dee's life must come from me. And I want something good to happen to him. From happy memories. A present. A gift. Love and marriage. One million hectares of unspoiled countryside. Down in a valley. Fertile land. Before fire. A good gift. For anyone. Let alone him.

That would be the logical route: a sort of pleasing fulfillment of life. That is not how life goes. Life's logic is time: time is the only law: the rest is up for grabs. Anything can happen in life so long as it happens next. And so it will go for Dee. Something will happen or something won't happen and then something else will either happen or not happen and Dee will live through that tumult of alternate paths leading through life, yes, but what will those somethings be? I have to figure it out. Pressure. I'm thinking too much. I must get it right. Dee's life must follow a prudent course, or lead one. Then he will be satisfied with life and then I will be freed. Simple as that. But what pressure. The pressure grows. Something pressing down making the earth rumble. I write against the pressure. I write against gravity. I write against the world. Just write. What comes will come, what won't come won't. Just write and it will come. In time.

Entry No. 43

I continue on trying to complete Dee's life but not without trepidation. I have surely made progress here as the world grows quiet and still but for that rumbling. Dee is returning home now; surprisingly, people are glad to see him again. His wife was faithful: she wore a black mantilla the entirety of Dee's peregrinations. His children have grown, his library is restored, the deans and vicars and students are all pleased to see Dee again, and now Dee must choose how he will relate what he learned from his wanderings among the birds in spiritual parliament. I have seen it, and it is good.

That trepidation, however: it leads to obstinate questionings. How do I assure myself that the voice I speak with is my own and no one else's? Is it even my voice? To whom does it belong? I have heard so many voices, hear so many voices here. I do not hear them with my ears, but I hear them all the same. My wife, I hear her voice; Dee, I hear his voice; myself, I hear my voice; and a voice woven from so many voices resounds from the past, a voice that Dee encountered and I in my own way seem to have heard, a cyclopedic voice that rises from all memory and speaks to us in a variegated language half our own and half strange, our own language deepened by the presence of other voices and other words, other sounds: I hear this voice. Which voice do I listen to? My wife's voice calls me back; Dee's life calls me forward; my own voice calls me here; the foreign voice calls me to all places and all times, all times constituting one time alone that has no past or future, just itself alone, the long grey field of time. I walk about it and see what I will see. I gather wild hyacinths that began to grow from seeds strewn about by birds that fly to and fro and far away, and I hold the hyacinths up and inhale their fragrance, and the scent moves me every which way through time: I am again with my wife, in the arms of my wife, and then I am watching Dee from behind an elm tree, watching him as he communes with birds in spiritual parliament, and he speaks to them in song and they respond in song in kind; and then I see myself, resting under a cypress tree as the sun is setting in the western red, a mess of light that, once near, now grows distant and growing distant reddens and then shades into a crimson that soon gives way to darkness, only dark, what remains of light only the effects of it upon the earth and those upon the earth who will endure the night until the light returns and life begins again. Which voice do I listen to? Which voice will lead me to fulfillment, to completion of Dee's life — what voice leads me to freedom so that I can live again, fresh and new? How will I know which way to go? I listen to the voices, all of them, and they do not accord. They are only departures, fallings from me, vanishings. I cannot listen to them all: those voices are centrifugal; they spin out at blazing speed into the further reaches of this world. I must choose a voice to listen to. Choose? Choice? Yes, I must choose. I must hear the voice, the appointed voice that will tell me how to bring Dee home. Home. He must go home. Home in the earth and on it. He is homesick for another world. I must hear the echo of the voice resounding. I will guide Dee home by attending to the echo of a voice the wind is carrying round the world; a voice in this world and not of it, a familiar voice grown majestic through long absence; that voice will be mine.

Entry No. 44

A man was blind but was given a chance to see the world for a moment. All he saw of the world was a book. After that, whenever anything was described to him, he always asked, What about the book? Is it bigger than the book, or smaller? Most everyone was confused, but one woman was not. When she described the sun to the blind man, he asked her, What about the book? Is it bigger than the book, or smaller? Nothing can be smaller than your book, she said, nor anything bigger; your book contains the unseen sun, and it orders this possible world. I don't know what that means, and I am disappointed you answer me metaphorically, as though you were an oracle, he said. I am speaking frankly, she said. Nothing is larger than the book, and there's nothing like the sun.

Entry No. 45

The pressure mounts. Despondency attends. I go back through the memories I have written here and try to fit them into Dee's life, but I cannot get them to fit and so the memories will not fit. Why? There is something off. Something not working. Signals got crossed, it seems. Why will my memories not allow themselves to take up another job, fulfill another role, wear two hats: why will my memories not allow themselves to become Dee's life? Surely what I remember of my past could make up the new experiences that Dee lives. With minor changes, of course, but, *mutatis mutandis*, why will my memories still not abide another's life?

I've grown distracted again. I must return to my focus. How? I am not enough. I alone am not enough. No, it is not me I should be speaking of, my memories really, a thing apart from me, my memories are not enough for Dee's life. I will consult some of the books I have here. Not the book for dentists, nor the Syriac grammar, nor the Lingala Pepys, nor the history of umbrellas — at this point I could write it myself — no, none of that, I will center and restore myself with the *Crusoe*, or at least the portion of the book I have here. Would I had the entirety of the book: that way I would know how Robinson ended up on his little island and what happens after. Or perhaps the rest of the book, the disappeared antecedent and what comes after, does not describe how Robinson came to be stranded on the island nor how he left it. Perhaps he was always there. Always present. A man who lives in a perpetual moment. I do not know. I do not have the rest of the book: I cannot know. Where is it? Why only this fragment of the book? Where is the rest of the book, the large book that encompasses the world?

No matter. No time. The book is gone. Find not sorrow in what has gone, find strength in what remains. I must go on.

Entry No. 46

I have found something concerning.

In the course of taking up my charge to complete Dee's life, I decided in the end to consult the books I have here. For stylistic guidance. How to conclude a tale. How life may artfully end. Or at least how life as far as it is written and composed by another may artfully end. A great responsibility, writing life and winding it up. Best to learn from whatever masters are present. The *Crusoe*, in this case. I read some pages. There was much running about, gunfire and arriving of people and ships. The arrivistes were running about the island when I turned the page and a sheet of paper floated down from the open book and settled in my lap. I lay the book on my pallet and picked up the sheet of paper. Too dark for me to read it, it was a fragile leaf, I felt as much; so delicate that a twitch in my hand could have crumpled it and scattered it to the floor. I had to wait until the faint glow that passes for daylight to steal into my room through the small window to try to read it. While I waited in the dark, I wondered what it was and what it said and where it came from. I had a fantastic vision of reading it and realizing it was a letter from my wife and then, just for that moment, I was elsewhere, back in a world I knew, and people knew I still lived and thought about me. I hung on those possibilities until, unaware and with the leaf beside me on my pallet, I was asleep.

Faint light and steady rumbling in the ground woke me. I went over and held the leaf up to the window to see what was written. Still not much light to speak of, but the light was fair enough to see that an entry of a kind of diary was written on the sheet of paper. Not unusual — pages find their way into the strangest of places, and I lose things all the time. But it was not an entry of mine, one I had written. I did not have to remember not having written it to recognize as much. The handwriting was not unlike my own, loping and sprawling in its own right, but it loped and sprawled in a different enough way for me to establish with certainty that I did not write it. A prior resident of this cell must have written it. That was the only plausible explanation for its presence in my cell. Given what Dee let me know, I did not think anyone else could have inhabited this cell of mine. Mine. But it seems Dee erred. It seems someone did. And they wrote an entry not unlike those that I write now. An entry containing a memory. Another's memory. One I did not write.

And thus, my concern: the entry was not mine; I did not write it, the memory was not mine...but the memory so resembles one of my own that I am profoundly concerned. Deeply, deeply concerned, and disconcerted. It may change everything about my understanding of this world and my place in it, my understanding of myself, of Dee, of everything. I question what I learned from Dee. I question everything now. Even my memories.

The entry:

"After receiving from her family their blessing and giving in return a small but respectable dowry, we wed in a lavish but tasteful ceremony in the country, down in the valley, where my people had been. My family was small, but her extended family was large, and they readily accepted our scant clique into their tribe. Sitting at the wedding table at the reception, I heard the loons calling for each other as the waves lapped and the sun gently set over the lake, meagerly making its rays rake across the land so that the land appeared aflame, below the table her hand discretely clasping mine. I have often returned to that time and that place in my time here in the camp, if only in memory. Yet it grows fainter and farther away and the loons' calls grow weaker and smaller such that I begin to wonder if that world is not a fable, I invented both to console myself with the knowledge that my life was once resplendent and radiant and to afflict myself with the remembrance of such a resplendent and radiant time of life in this doleful time I now live. My time in the camp is almost longer than my time as a free man wedded to her. Almost.

"And love: I need not describe what I mean by the word *love*. We all know what it is. We know it when we feel it. I do. Whoever else comes into this cell knows it too. I know it. I knew it. I felt it. But it has since been succeeded. An unfortunate succession. Succeeded by the ravishment of its perverted nephew, jealousy. And jealousy is what I became. And I could not take what I became. I had to leave. And I left. I left to go wander, to go learn more, learn what was beyond me, what circled around me and flew away, what took the form of birds, those angels, the form of birds, and I sought to embrace their form, I sought to learn from them. I left my post at the university, a freshly minted professor of geometry, I left it all behind, my life, I left it behind, and I left her behind before she could leave me. Then one night a brilliant blue lit up the sky, the unexpected, faint, and creeping hyacinthian light spread across the sky at the midmost night, and that was the night I left everything behind, and I set out, in search of what I knew I had forgotten, in search of what was out there waiting to be recovered, in search of what the birds..."

That is the entry in its entirety. And so, it ended, foreshortened and unfulfilled, suspended and abandoned, one page perhaps among many. Much like these.

I cannot and will not be mistaken: these are the words of Dee. Dee himself.

How?

I never saw Dee here nor did he let me know that he had been here in my cell. Nor did he even hint that he knew anything about my past beyond what they told him when he found them. And even if he knew more about me than he let on, that would not explain the nigh-verbatim similarities between this entry and my own. Unless Dee was creating a new past for himself from my past. He came from me, after all, and I have no evidence that as much as I can peruse his life he cannot pore through mine. But he would have told me. I'm certain he would have. He had no reason to hide anything from his maker. He needs me to fulfill my task. Why hide anything then? He cannot hide from me. He cannot. He has gained a mind of his own, though, and gotten willful enough to track me down in here. Perhaps then he did write it. Perhaps he did. We share our lives with one another. It would make as much sense as everything else in this world. Perhaps Dee was here when I was not. Perhaps he is still here. In the discarded pages of his life and in some other ghostly way. Perhaps this entry contains a part of Dee's life I never knew. A part of his life close enough to being part of mine. A transmuted memory. His memory. Of my life. If my life were his.

No. Perhaps this page was a failed attempt of mine to continuing Dee's story. A discarded past. Perhaps I did not merely stop writing it, perhaps I tried to keep writing and, seeing that what I wrote was too much infected with myself and my own memories, I thought it unworthy of another's life, even another whom I invented, a life I invented for another.

Or a life that another invented for me.

Who was it? Whose feet in ancient time? Did they? Who else has been in this cell? What is this cell? Is it mine? Am I alone?

What is happening?

I have recovered so many of my memories. I have found memories of the life I lost and have written them all down so I will not fail to remember them again, so that, as long as I am in this cell, I will have proof of having lived a life, proof that I had a life that was mine alone. For as long as I can remember, which is no longer than I have been in this cell, I have believed that I was brought here and left here as punishment, some retribution for a crime I committed, a crime rooted in my jealousy, another victim of the regime. Of course, Dee let me know complicated things. My imprisonment is a two-fold consequence: my jealousy, yes, and my inability to finish Dee's story, to give him a full life. But these two seem to emanate from one infernal source: powerlessness. My lack of power. Pure and complete vitiation. I am powerless to control my life. Powerless to control the life of another. Powerless to finish what I start. Powerless to accomplish my task or stick to one. It's not a matter of will. It's power. Total lack of power.

Perhaps the memories I believe I have recovered are not memories. Perhaps they are inventions. New memories. Invented memories that I hold onto long enough until I cannot believe they are anything other than my memories. Whatever truly happened is lost. It could be that I was not brought here and imprisoned here for a crime I committed, or rather, a crime they said I committed. Perhaps that is not the case. Did I leave my life behind of my own will? Did I put myself here? Did I make such a choice? Did I have the power to choose? A time for choosing. When was the time for choosing? Was there ever a time? Say there is a time. I don't know. I don't know what I'm saying anymore. I don't know if I even speak or write with my own voice. That foreign page I found contravenes everything these entries tell me, contravenes everything my memories tell me, questions everything my memories tell me. I say *my memories,* but I don't know any more if they are *my* memories or something someone else invented for me. Invented so that I could resemble a human, a kind of man, one with a life he remembers to orient him in the present. Invented so that I'd have something like a self the way that I invented Dee's past so he could have something like a self and be something like a human. Invented to entertain for a while, to while away someone's time, to allay boredom. Invented to pass the time and, when the time is past, left behind, abandoned, incomplete, suspended, lost, lost, lost. It is too late to know. Even in the beginning it was too late. It is always too late.

Entry No. 47

I do not remember if what I remember is what I remember or if what I remember is what I invent. Right now, I cannot determine what is memory and what is invention. My wife, our marriage, my jealousy, the trial, that hummingbird: what are they? Right now, I cannot determine whether I am remembering or I am an invention of memory. Who is my creator? Did I author Dee, or did Dee author me? Whose life is it I remember — mine, Dee's, another's, or everyone who has slouched in this cell? Is it even life I remember? Do I even remember?

Who am I? What am I doing here?

Entry No. 48

All love is lost terror.
All beauty is a moment's transcendence set outside of time.
All love is terror of a moment's passing.

Is that a new thought? Is that something new under the sun? Did I create that? Is it mine? Let it be mine. Let me author some thought, some world, some life.

Dee saw me. I remember that. When will I see my author?

Entry No. 49

I have centered myself and am again making progress on Dee's life. Three pages more. Things are looking up for Dee: things are changing for the better as his life continues. Not as dreary as I had thought it would be. I am surprised. I am happy for Dee.

I remembered a book I believe I read as a child. A book about a boy and his father on an adventure to a strange island. I remember it. Yes, it must be memory, it must have been once upon a time and a very nice time it was, long before the men stopped praying and purchased motorcycles. I must have read the book and must have found the book in a library long ago, yes, that distant library in a distant place, so strange to think of that place and then feel the rumbling in the ground and see that I am here in my cell. That world is strange because it is gone and still with me, some way. I don't know, I don't go out much anymore.

I incorporated the strangeness of that world, a squalid place, into Dee's life. How? It is a memory after all, and my memories were not willing to serve two masters: my past and Dee's future. One is invention and one is real. Which was which and which is which: I can no longer tell. What is remembered is invented as a memory; before it was raw material, rough stuff of the world. Yes, that is the case in such a world. What a heuristic I have found: if I had a bath enough and time, I would be inside of it and look up and say, Eureka. What a heuristic. Memories are stuff enough to fill a life. I will empty my past of them and fill his future. Let us see.

Entry No. 50

Wondering where it should end. Endings: I never seem to arrive at them, I do not know what they look like, I cannot quite make an ending or endings, an end, finale, *fin*. But perhaps I should not worry about that now, it distracts me from writing the story. The end will come when it comes. Someday I will surely arrive at some point, some terminus, an end. At the end I will have no more words to offer. At the end, the long-awaited present will arrive.

This language has no past tense. Even things that had been are present still.

Entry No. 51

I hear a foreign sound. Artillery fire in the distance, encroaching. A wild blue lighting up the sky. I can see pages I have piled up here, every deliberate entry I've written, and I can see out my window again. I see the dull brightness in the sky, and it exudes a faint light that lets me see the grounds through my window: it is all empty, vacant, no one is there, nothing stirs, not prisoners, nor gaolers nor birds. All is still close around me and all is quiet but for the faint rumbling in the ground. But there is something off in the distance, that sound, that light. So, there is something out there. There is still a world out there. Say there is a world.

Is Dee walking through it, looking for what I must provide him, or does he just wait?

Entry No. 52

I have been diligent these late days in closing in on an end to Dee's story. I am reaching an end, or his end. His end will mark another beginning of sorts for him, a new beginning to something new, one I hope will please him, but whether it pleases him or not I now admit is not up to me, is not in my power. Whatever certainty of purpose I held onto in the course of writing Dee's life I let go of when I found in the *Crusoe* that strange journal entry of a memory from another's life. Seemed far too much my own to be anybody else's, yet it nonetheless is not my own. I did not write it and I did not remember it. But then, I am no longer certain of that. I cannot be certain. In my knowledge. Of anything. I no longer know if my memories are my own or are the possessions of others that I came across in the mud, cleaned off and mistook for my own. Adopted them, even. I no longer know that my memories are not inventions slipped into my mind like that false entry was slipped into the *Crusoe* to delude me with the belief that I am who I am: a man, a real man of flesh and blood and sentiment and other stuff, a man real enough to be imprisoned in a cell by a fanatical and fearful regime for the crime of appearing to be a subversive because one day it rained and I used an umbrella to keep myself dry beyond the tears that welled as my wife walked away, walking towards something I feared but which now comforts me because she walked away not to flee me but to free me, this is the way it has seemed to be. Perhaps none of that happened; perhaps it was an arresting story that someone else created to while away some boring and uneventful time in his life, whether in a prison camp like this one or sitting at his desk at home after work or in a doctor's office or sacristy, fashioning it into a cogent narrative that will keep captors, family, parishioners and other listeners entertained for a spell, or this is a story told by a fool trapped in the court of a king where the only way to ensure the king does not execute him is to regale the lords and ladies of the court with the story of a life that could have been any life, a life that seems to be heading toward some anticipated and revelatory end but, because life is not a story with a purpose but rather some events that happen before they happen no more, does not reach a conclusion that to the audience gives pleasure, and he is summarily executed and shoveled away, or else he tells the story long enough that the lords and ladies of the king's court come to anticipate some desired end and grow distracted by their anticipation of this potential world and while their attention is elsewhere, imaging what this world could look like and feel like and intent upon a desired end to a desired world, the trapped storyteller slips away, out of the king's court, out of his life, out of this world; and he is outside the citadel, he is beyond the walls, he is heading far away, he is on the road again walking, one step after another after another, and he walks away and no mischief comes to him, he is solitary and on his own, walking away from his captors and towards the horizon where the sun has settled for the night or long enough at least for him to go in shadows whose traces he alone can see, close light, true light, light for the storyteller, light enough to build another world around him, a second world, another life.

I don't know any more what good it will do me to finish Dee's life. He told me finishing his life would free me. I don't know anymore. I am still here. Nothing has changed. I still feel the rumbling in the ground and hear artillery fire grow nearer. Once I thought that rumbling signified something, but it is constant and does not change, and so I do not know if anything will change, let alone whether bringing Dee's life to an end will free me. I don't know. It's a wager, though, and one I am willing to bet on: if I complete his life and nothing comes of it, then I will remain here in the cell and what I remember Dee telling me was only the fantasy of a lonesome man growing less a human every moment he passes on the floor of this dirty cell trying to write his way back into his life until he expires or the lightless firmament above him in his cell comes falling down upon him, the sky will all come down; or, if I complete his story, I will free him to free me, and I will somehow be free to return to my world beyond these walls.

What a prospect: to be beyond these walls. I have longed so long to be outside again on my own with no master, outside on my own again clean, light, and free. But what will I see out there? What in the world beyond these walls is left of the world that I left? Is the rest of the world like this camp, this cell, an entire continent composed of lightless penitentiaries? What is waiting for me? Who waits for me? Does anyone?

No answer comes. I hear nothing, nothing at all. I wait and lose time.

I have lost so much time; so much time I have wasted, so much time I have been compelled to lose. I have had no say, no choice in what has happened to and in my life, no power, no control over where the time has gone. If I ever had time to myself, world enough and time, I have lost all of it and will never find it again so that I may live it in the first place. What I can salvage are traces of light, shimmering images, echoes of emotions that I felt. What I can salvage of lost time are memories of time. I cannot regain lost time, I cannot recover it, I can hold onto some of what life was in those moments — the fugitive seeds of experience that memory sows in the furrows of time. Nothing more. I possess only what remains and nothing more.

Yet time was never mine; how then can I say I have lost time when it was never my possession to begin with? A figure of speech, surely. I am aiming to get at the truth, however, and so the figurative world must yield to the literal truth. And the truth is I did not possess the time I lost if I possessed anything at all. I possess nothing now, nothing at all but my body, that alone I possess.

It, this thing, the body: a form that holds us and ourselves and, when grown dilapidated from abuse, injury, disregard, or mere life, lets us die as it stops working and decays, evidence that leads to the reasonable belief that the life I have lived, whether it be the experience of joy, piety, passion, or sorrow, is perpetually in my possession. This sense of possession, of dominion over everything that I experience, is granted to me by the language that we use to describe the relationship between ourselves and our corporal form: not that I *am* a body, no, I say *my body*, my possession, I use these words to elucidate my relationship to it, a thing distinct from the possessor, myself; *body and soul*, they sing, as though the one were twain. We cannot see ourselves as mere bodies caught up in mere being; we refuse it and refute it daily. No, we will say something else: we will say that *we have bodies*, we will say *my* body, and so saying we establish a frontier which decouples and exiles one of us far off on the shores of some distant and strange dark sea, and we will find the ineludible boundary that makes one two, and we will make a partition between our bodies and who we are in our self of selves. I grow distant from my body, go elsewhere wondering, where shall I wander? This world is wide, far and passing wide, and I can go to and fro upon it as I like without this foot or the other having moved a step as movement often calls for feet to do. No, I will stay here and go far away from my body, far away as I like or can imagine, often I imagine something much beyond what I could ever like, in fact I do not like the places I imagine I will go beyond my body, at least not all of them, some of them are fine and good, some will pass. And in the midst of this I do something long thought infeasible, I make two of one. My body and me myself: I ensure the twain shall never meet.

What I am — am? — in my body in the present is fleeting but what I remember endures and is what I am. If I wake up one morning and do not know where I am — do not know who I am — then who am I? Why this obdurate questioning? Because I do not know! If I do not recognize my room, my home, the people in it and beyond it among whom I pass some time and live, who am I? Can I even ask who? What then am I?

No: without those memories I am a body, I have no body, I am a body present in the present; I do not exist. Without my memories I am instantaneous, literally ephemeral. With my memories, at the least my ephemerality is only figurative, fallen leaves in the west wind, those dying generations at their song, such sad and angry consolation. I would like to be more than a moment within many more that passes by so swift, though, as I am sure most other humans like, and so I need my memories so that I may be myself and build the partition between my fleeting body and my enduring self. My memories will build a wall or else will dig some deep and deathly gulf. My body is on one side of my memory and I am on another. And so they stay: *no pasarán*.

My body knew that world. Was once over there. On the other side. Where the wobbly bird flew so long ago. What do I have here now? A geography of memory. I study its topography: ridges and mountains rise and valleys dip where those massive glacial events passed over and through them so long ago. Dilapidated civilizations too, ruins quickly returning to their elemental state. These ruins that endure, these ruins that we look at as of things that long ago were very large indeed and roamed the earth with large steps, ruled the earth, had dominion over it and all the things that creep and crawl and fly and fall. Those large steps are stilled. What is left is stuff that has floated through time and washed up in dirt and for some reason has not gone away. It need not be significant for not having gone away: how many times will the intrepid goatherds stumble on some slave's punctured bones or shards of beggars' pottery, graffiti on a latrine door, some orphan-thief's arrowheaded dagger, the long ledgers of the scrolls of zealous, vanished anchorites? We find these lame things often. That they have lasted does not mean they are important. Endurance is no virtue. These ruins gain their salience from the bridge we build between the land of the ruins and the land of the great myth whose fair and distant light plays such a trick on our eyes that it convinces us we possess these bodies and so possess the experiences of the lives we live, the lives we call our own.

If we were frank about it — if our tongue admitted that we do not have bodies but are mere bodies merely being for a while — we would confront the terror of reality: we possess nothing of our life, and we do not even possess ourselves: our bodies fail, our breathing ceases and the self will *pass away into the light of common day* — no, I lie for the sake of beautiful pretension, the self will not pass away into the light of common day, no, the self goes wherever, somewhere, we've no reports, the body ceases being body and gets cold and smells not of roses or magnolias and the self goes away and no common light of day abides, no, the body goes in darkness, rare and unreported darkness. A house was in a valley once and it is not there anymore; I have heard tell of dynasties, empires, satrapies whose names and customs were once as widely known as the sky and ground and now are most foreign, having nobody left alive to attest to them to ensure that they endure. There were fortresses, castles, cities and citadels, parliaments, pleasure-gardens, grottos, &c. Times I have gone walking in the country and I stumble and kick against a cornerstone, curse my foot its pain and walk it off, or in a museum I have seen their armored chariots and thought, wow: that sure was something for its time. But no one speaks that language anymore and no one can tell them any different from the country where they now reside, which is the country of their conquerors round about them having pressed upon their own until their country is subsumed into the country of their conquerors round about them. We only have some trinkets from their distant past, armored chariots and cornerstones, a signet-ring or copper coin that reads, *the conquered weep*. Our bodies are no different from the other dilapidating rudiments of geography. Our bodies stay in the world in one present corporal form, they have stayed that way for a period of the past and except for one moment will stay that way for a period of the future, but there was a long stretch of time when our bodies were not here and there most likely will be another long stretch of time when our bodies won't be here, at least most of them, though some folks are lucky and are found underground somewhere grinning with enameled teeth. Those intrepid goatherds up to it again: they are always finding remnants of us, the abiding revenants of geography, and that is memory, and that is all I have.

No, there is nothing that travels on a bridge from the land of visible ruins to the land of our abiding myth that gives our myth its salience; no, the myth arises from the bodies we inhabit for a while. Our bodies lend to us the myth, myth being only ancient gossip long-ago accepted, that, while we live, we perpetually possess in varying degrees of fullness the experiences that make up life. The bodies where we dwell could not last even a moment without the myth. Life passes on our shores, and the remnants that we gather up are memory. As soon as we have taken these fragments in our hands, they pass through our skin and into us and remain within us in some unknown and unvisitable region from which they sometimes return to yoke us once again and remind us we are in thrall to them: we have no power: our memories possess of us everything that we cannot see within ourselves. And much as most of the constituent elements of our world are invisible to us in their pure form, visible only in their recombinant manifestations, so does the partition of ourselves we cannot see, the partition between our bodies and our selves that stretches over the gulf that is possession and province of memory, make up most of who we are.

We can mourn the loss of so many things, almost everything that goes across that frontier, everything but a memory since you cannot mourn the loss of something you do not know that you are losing. Loss is a condition of life, a requisite dispossession, the gradual bearing back of everything into some sea waiting for all the water it poured into the wide world to vacate its station and return to its source. There, at the source, everything is the same again, is made the same again. There, at the source, whatever river carried all that water is gone and the name that humans gave to it does not matter. There, at the source, everything washes over and into and through itself and is restored to its first state, the possession of no one and belonging to no river, puddle, or cloud: freedom. Everything is what it was before the water started to run: whole and free, at home and of no one. All semblance of distinction and individuality is washed away: it is all nothing. And then it flows again.

When the water finds its way out from the sea and, beginning as a subterranean stream of water leaking and dripping through hard stone that will collapse and reveal a whole river, new and unknown, flowing underneath, a life recapitulates itself only to deepen, lengthen, expand into something new that, though its substance has long endured in one form or numberless others, has never been before. It is too late then to find whole again what was lost. It has merged with everything else that has been lost. But what was lost has found a new form to endure the erosion brought about by the whirling and abiding maelstrom of time, and the loss is lessened. Memories of the world return to the living but never to the same person: it is not the same person who walks in a river twice.

We are those rivers. We are both the person who wades out in the rapids and the water flowing rapidly by ourselves. We are what passes and what stays. And we the rivers carry with us what other rivers — other people — carried with them to some remote and unimagined terminus that is the source we could never recognize, never glimpse, never arrive at as ourselves alone. At this source, the memories we call our own are emancipated from us and pass into the torrents of other lives, which is where our memories become the experiences of a new river flowing, a new life developing. We believe we have come to an end when we are only arriving at a beginning too late to know it is a beginning and not an end, too late to know that what we have lost is not lost but transfigured by the wake of other people's memories into something new, too late to know that we can never be late, only belated; and what we have lost was never ours to begin with, no, what we have lost was never ours nor ever was possessed so cannot be lost, only waiting, waiting, waiting to be seen, be felt, be lived again by somebody else past some other river's distant bend.

We lose people, pencils, keys, hats, hair, blood, cats, organs, homes, and people again and again and again. Memories, too: it is the telling symptom of experience: as one lives one experiences life, experience heaping on experience, and memories cede their space to new memories of more life and, finding no purpose in their present state of disuse, wend their way into the remembrance of other lives where they once again serve some purpose or some end. Or perhaps not: perhaps the memories stay right there — wherever *there* may be — but we cannot see them in wakefulness and so cannot draw them up to our eyes and inspect them, smell them, taste them, caress them. Something drops them from the day. But they are there. I hope they are. The memories are there, and they will come only of their own accord; they cannot be pressed into serving our little ships that go out seeking them so as to grab ahold of them and do with them what we will. They are vast willful things, memories. But they are there; they abide. I will try to find them there and make them my own and nobody else's. And if they don't come, ah well: they will come of their own accord. And when they come, I will overflow with life, I will run over with life, and I will share my life with what I invent from my memories, what I create, what I make of myself and let pass into the world to endure beyond time. And then I will do it again.

Entry No. 1

I saw a bird. I walked through the woods, and I saw a bird. The woods, a bird, morning. I walk, and through the woods, morning. Morning light, light of dawn, candid light. I walk, and through the woods in candid light of day, a bird.

Entry No. 1

The bird is small, is blue, sylphic, a bird in the woods, candid light. Before me is the bird, and I am with the bird in the woods, where the bird was before me. The bird, a sylph: iridescent, shimmering. Plumage of candid light, on and of the bird, irrefutable and outward proof of it. And there it is, the bird, the proof, before me in the woods, where I walked.

Entry No. 1

Before me in the woods is the bird, where I walked in the morning. I walked in the woods in the world in the morning, and I saw a bird there. A sylph: floating before me in its iridescence was a sylph, the bird which was before me and so I stopped. I stopped walking in the woods. I do not go back. I do not anymore, do not walk in the woods. Where the sylph was, floating. Before me. In the woods. In the world.

Entry No. 1

Before me in the woods was the sylph, a bird, floating before me as I went walking in the woods in the candid light of day. I saw the sylph emerge from darkness and float before me, that bird among the terebinths. I stopped, and the bird was before me, floating, and the sylph was looking at me in the light. I saw a bird that morning when the sylph floated before me in the woods, and the bird was looking at me in the light. I looked at the bird. I saw it in the woods. This morning. A bird. The woods. The world. Light and iridescence. The bird among the terebinths.

Entry No. 1

I saw a bird in the woods in the candid light of day and then the bird was gone. The sylph was gone, no longer light in the woods, I was in the woods in the morning, I saw the bird and then the bird was gone from that part of the woods in the world. The bird is gone. The terebinths, dark in the woods where I do not go back.

The bird is gone. I long to be, walking. Walking, waking, gone. Elsewhere. In this world but not of it. Gone again, where the bird has flown. Beyond the woods, the world. Beyond the world, the walls. Beyond the walls, the sea.

But it is too late already, the bird is gone. It is too late already, it has been always, too late. Even early, late. Even in the candid light of day, too late. Even when the bird was yet to come, far too late. And still the sea. Waves. Water. Water spilling from the ocean, spelling something on the sand, shells. A crab scuttles, a shell, light and iridescent. A new place, of light. In the world. To stay. A second circle, one of iridescence, holds the center. Not to be seen and to see: the world. I was walking in the woods in candid light of day and there I saw a bird among the terebinths. A sylph before me, floating. The woods, too late. The terebinths, too late. The woods are in the world, are gone from me. Before me was the bird, there in the woods, floating. Before me is the sea, the shore, waves crashing, in light. Left there on the shore by the waves, a new shell, light there on the shore. Awash, new. Again.

Entry No. 1

Begin again, first light of morning, begin again, the first idea of day, widely walking through it I see a bird, shimmering. The wide world of morning, world spread before me bound beyond the woods, where I walk among the terebinths and saw a bird, the sylph. It shone, it shimmered as the waves coruscate in late light, receding and borne back. I saw a bird, shining with light. In the woods, shining with light, amid the terebinths. The light, the waves, the water spreading through the wide world of day, receding, and borne back, so that going round the shorebend borne back, receding to the water's source, sea awash again, new, shells spell the shore, where crabs scuttle. Again, borne back, far from the woods. There among the terebinths I saw a bird, and I should not have looked. I saw a bird among the trees when I went walking in the woods in the morning, and I should not have looked so not to have seen. For to have seen a bird, for having looked and having seen among the terebinths a bird, I must follow the river past the shorebend back into the woods, into the world. Back again. From the shore, the woods. The world. Again.

Entry No. 1

The bright candid shore. I saw a bird, morning, the woods where I went walking. Among the terebinths, there, the bird. I went into the woods and should not have gone, because I was among the trees and I saw motion in the terebinths, and I looked, and then I saw a bird. In the woods, where I was, where it was dark. Through the woods, past it, waves spell on the shore, new shells. From one iridescence to another. Ashore again, light for the world, which is beyond the woods. The woods, where I saw the bird among the terebinths, where I did not mean to go, for I did not mean to look and see the bird, and start again, anew. Past the woods, past the shorebend, and the river, the world, where I do not mean to go again, anew.

Entry No. 1

The world beyond the woods, the woods of the world but not in it, yet, nor I as I walk in the woods, where I walked this morning and saw a bird, the sylph. Light, light. Arise, shine: light in the woods, light for the world, and I walk in it, to and fro upon it.

Entry No. 1

Again, the bright candid shore, where I am. The shells, from ocean waves. The shore, around me. Waves of the sea, spell on the shore, shells. From one iridescence to another, new on the shore.

The waves, late. The shore, too late. Iridescence, shining, too late. The beginning, again, too late even the beginning.

The bird is gone. I long to be, walking. I follow the river past the shorebend into the world. Walking, waking, gone. Elsewhere. In this world but not of it. Gone again, where the bird has flown. Beyond the woods, the world. Beyond the world, the walls. Beyond the walls, the sea. Light there on the shore, to go into the world again, new. Awash, new. Again.

About the Author

Jordan Silversmith has received degrees from Vanderbilt University and the University of Virginia. His poem "Praxis" was chosen by Philip Metres for the 2020 Slippery Elm Prize in Poetry. He works as an attorney in New York City.

More from Gival Press

That Demon Life by Lowell Mick White

Theory and Praxis: Women's and Gender Studies at Community Colleges edited by Genevieve Carminati and Heather Rellihan

Tina Springs into Summer / Tina se lanza al verano by Teresa Bevin

The Tomb on the Periphery by John Domini

Twelve Rivers of the Body by Elizabeth Oness

For a complete list of Gival Press titles, visit: *www.givalpress.com*.

Books are available from Ingram, Follett, Brodart,
your favorite bookstore, the Internet, or from Gival Press.

Gival Press, LLC
PO Box 3812
Arlington, VA 22203
givalpress@yahoo.com
703.351.0079